陳和揚◎著

就能學會的基礎財金英文

不用一個月就成為財金通的財金英文小學堂開課囉！

透過中英文學習五大財金領域：銀行業務、投資理財、保險商品、會計財稅與金融常識，輕鬆用英文經商、學會理財與理解金融流通...等技巧，自在遨遊財金世界，英文和財金知識100%同步晉級！

與日常生活息息相關的財金英文大揭密

- 翻開【存款業務】篇，解決出國久居，必須用英文到銀行辦理開戶的情況...
- 出差談生意／經商辦理個人貸款，先來熟讀【放款業務】篇內的情境與必背專有名詞...
- 平時習慣收看投資／理財節目的讀者，何不詳閱【投資理財】篇精讀股票、債券......等的英文怎麼說......？
- 保障生命、財產有關的壽險與產險究竟保障了什麼，就透過【保險商品】篇來一窺全貌！
- 讀懂80% 英文財經新聞入門訣竅，就收錄在【金融常識】篇中！

跟著財金界多年經驗的專業人士，吸收**輕量**結合**進階版**的專有名詞解釋、暖身對話填空、多達80組的財金專有名詞整理與20篇短文等單元內容，輕鬆看懂財金文章、通曉理財保險等的小撇步......

這是一本兼顧**財金實務與理論**的參考用書，也是**銀行行員**、**外商會計**、**保險業**等相關工作者英文和工作職務上的必備好幫手！

20%
10%
40%

作者序

由於因緣際會，筆者很幸運於2015年4月自貴社接下了寫財金英文相關的這個案件。雖然，筆者本人在大學和研究所先後專攻的是經濟和企業管理，也在幾個不同的行業有豐富的實務經驗，但是這本《24天就能學會的基礎財金英文》，也算是筆者在財金方面的第一本書。

這本書的特色，是希望藉由會話，加上一些基本資訊、定義、問答的方式和短文，讓讀者克服對財金知識相對較有枯燥難懂的感覺，而能透過每天學習一個主題的方式來漸漸熟悉財金方面的知識。對於在財金方面已經比較有概念，而希望能夠學習或複習財金方面的相關字彙的讀者，本書也可以提供一個基本的參考。

筆者在編列本書遇到比較大的挑戰，主要是在寬廣的財金領域，如何為每一個單元選定一個範圍和方向，讓內容不至於太艱澀困難；同時挑選的英文字彙既要適合準備考新多益的學生們，也要適合一般的社會人士閱讀。尤其，大部分的專有名詞定義都會相對比較制式，所以如何讓讀者們覺得內容恰到好處，也是筆者的另一大挑戰。

最後，筆者感謝貴出版社給予這個寶貴的機會來共同參與這本書的編製，並且也感謝筆者家人的支持，讓這本書能夠順利的完成。

陳和揚

編者序

財務金融英文一直是非此領域出身最頭痛的，什麼是放款、信託業務、共同資金或期貨等，不但一頭霧水，更不用説要用英文來學習了，這樣的難題也帶給想要走口筆譯的英文系學生不少阻礙；對於非英語系，英文基礎不夠厚實，卻又想要走外商財務會計的人，更像是重重的關卡。

本書旨在成為突破這些難關的關鍵，透過精華濃縮5大財金領域知識與中英對照的學習方式，相信讀者能在反覆閱讀，進而熟悉各種專業術語後，漸漸讀出對財金英文的心得和自信。本書並精選出財金相關短文，每篇短文都和該單元有緊密的關聯（如倫敦同業拆放利率（LIBOR）在金融市場所扮演的角色），相信必能加深讀者對該單元的印象。24天有如24堂課，其中穿插4堂課的金融小百科有助讀者稍稍喘口氣放鬆心情，學學數字怎麼説等趣味小常識，然後恍然大悟財金英文和日常生活是息息相關的。

期盼本書成為讀者精通財金英文的一把鑰匙，並藉由本書遨遊財金的世界。

編輯部

目次

CONTENTS

10%
20%
40%

Chapter I
Banking & Money
銀行業務篇

存款業務 Bank Deposits

什麼是存款業務

存款業務是銀行接受客戶存入的資金，存款人亦可隨時提取款項的一種金融業務。存款業務是商業銀行最主要的負債，也是其營運資金的主要來源。大多數商業銀行的存款占其負債總額的 70%以上。

單元暖身小練習 Warm-up conversation and practice

針對以下每個空格，請選一個最適合的字填入。這是協助你對於本主題進行初步的暖身，以利對於後續的介紹可以更有效率的吸收。

(a) which	(b) interest	(c) needed	(d) have to
(e) fill out	(f) can	(g) would like	(h) minimum
(i) would	(j) who	(k) will	

Eric wants to open an account in a bank.

Eric 想要在銀行開戶。

Eric: Good morning, sir.

（你好，早安）

Teller: Good morning! What .....1..... I do for you?

（早安，有什麼我可以協助的嗎？）

Eric: I .....2..... to open an account in your bank.

（我想在你們銀行開個帳戶。）

Teller: No problem. .....3..... type of account .....4..... you want to open ?
（沒問題。你想開什麼樣的帳戶？）

Eric: I would like to open a savings bank account.
（我想開個儲蓄帳戶。）

Teller: Please ......5..... this form and provide your ID card and a secondary identification(ID) document to me.
（麻煩填寫這個表格，然後再提供您的身分證明文件以及第二輔助證件給我。）

Eric: What kind of secondary ID can the bank accept?
（銀行可以接受哪些第二輔助證件？）

Teller: Any kind of ID document or card with a photo that can confirm your personal details. For example: passport, health insurance card, driver's license or student's ID card.
（任何有照片而且可以證明您身份的文件或卡都可以，例如：護照、健保卡、駕照或學生證。）

Eric: How much money is .....6..... to open the account?
（開戶須準備多少錢呢？）

Teller: Currently the .....7..... amount to open a Savings Bank Account is NTD 1000 only.
（目前儲蓄帳戶開戶金額最低新台幣一千元。）

Eric: .....8.....I be able to order a check book with a Savings Bank Account?
（我可以訂購儲蓄賬戶的支票本嗎？）

Teller: You can order a check book if you open a checking account, and you .....9...... deposit at least NTD 10,000 upon opening a checking account.
（如果你想要訂購支票本，那就必須另外再開立支票帳戶。而支票帳戶最低開戶金額不得低於新台幣一萬元。）

Eric: OK, I've got it. Does the bank pay .....10..... on checking account?
（好，我瞭解了。支票存款帳戶有利息嗎？）

Teller: No. Basically, we don't pay interest on checking accounts, but we pay for savings account.
（沒有。基本上我們支票存款不計利息，但是儲蓄存款帳戶有計息。）

Eric: Thanks for this information.
（謝謝你的資訊。）

答案 ANSWERS:

1.f 2.g 3.a 4.i 5.e 6.c 7.h 8.k 9.d 10.b

認識台灣銀行業

按照台灣銀行法的現行條文之規定，除台灣『中央銀行』外可分為：商業銀行、專業銀行和信託投資公司。目前本國銀行總家數為 40 家。外國及大陸銀行來台分行共 30 家。

中央銀行(Central Bank of the Republic of China (Taiwan))，簡稱「央行」：中央銀行屬於國家銀行，直屬於行政院，具部會級地位；目前央行總裁為彭淮南先生。該機構肩負領導國家金融發展、健全銀行制度、維持物價與金融穩定、並積極參與金融體系的建制與改革等重要任務。

商業銀行(Commercial Bank)：以收受支款存款、供給短期信用為主要業務的銀行。主要有：① 一般銀行，包括中小企業銀行以外的專業銀行及各合作金庫，是灣銀行業的主體；② 外國銀行在台分行，目前營業採分行、子行雙軌制。其中有外國銀行在台成立之子行，如:花旗（台灣）銀行、匯豐（台灣）商業銀行、渣打國際商業銀行。

專業銀行(Specialized Bank)：為便利工業、農業、輸出入、中小企業、不動產、地方性等專業信用之供給，經中央主管機關指定或許可設立之銀行，是以特定主體為主要授信對象的銀行。專業銀行共可分成六種：① 工業銀行、② 農業銀行、③ 中小企業銀行、④ 輸出入銀行、⑤ 不動產信用銀行和 ⑥ 國民銀行。

信託投資公司：信託投資公司現在幾乎都存在各銀行的體系裡；雖然先前單獨成立的信託投資公司有三家（台灣土地開發信託公司、中聯信託投資公司、亞洲信託投資公司），但如今也已先後被其他銀行所併購。

一般常見銀行存款業務項目

業務項目 Business Item		
支票存款 **Checking deposit**	支票存款帳戶是銀行帳戶的一種。它一般提供存款人較高的存款流動自由性，所以存款人可以使用支票、自動提款機、電子扣款，以及其他各種方法提領存款。	Checking deposit account is the type of bank account that offers accountholders high liquidity and freedom to withdraw by writing checks, using ATM machines, electronic debits, and other forms of transfers.

	不像儲蓄存款帳戶有時會限制取款和存款的次數，支票帳戶經常允許免費多次取款而且不限制存款的次數。然而，雖然支票存款有較高的流動性，它卻通常不提供利率或利率比較低。	Unlike savings accounts, checking accounts often give the accountholders the option of a certain number of free withdrawals and unlimited deposits per month, whereas savings accounts sometimes limit both. However, even though with high liquidity, checking accounts often offer little or no interests.
儲蓄存款 **Savings deposit**	當您想要開始儲蓄，但還沒有準備好作長期投資的決策時，儲蓄存款是讓您開始為您未來的投資帳戶累積儲蓄的簡單方法。儲蓄存款提供您方便運用的帳戶裡的資金和並且支付利息。儲蓄存款的利息是每日計算，並且利率隨著在儲蓄存款裡的餘額增加而提高。	Savings deposit is a simple way to start saving in investment account when you're not yet ready to make a long-term investment decision. Savings deposit offers easy access to funds and offers interest. The interest is calculated daily, and the rate increases as the balance in the savings deposit increases.
定期存款 **Term deposit**	定期存款是一種保證您投資的100%本金的安全投資方式。	Term deposit is an investment that guarantees 100% of the original amount that you invested.

	您的定期投資在約定的固定時間段內賺取利息，而利息可能是固定利率或變動利率，或根據預先確定的方式。存款人可以在定期存款到期後，通過提供存款證明或其他約定的方式領取本金和利息。	Term deposits give investors either fixed rate or flexible rate interest returns. They can be withdrawn at maturity or by the depositors' requests to terminate the investment before the maturity date.

常用業務例句 Common business terms

1. account 帳戶
withdraw 提款
VISA ATM card VISA 金融提款卡

Sara: Hello, Sir. I've opened a **payroll account** here. May I know if this account offers any benefits?
（你好，先生。我在這家銀行有開立員工薪資帳戶，請問這個薪資帳戶有提供什麼優惠嗎？）

Teller: Sure. We offer various benefits for payroll accounis, including of discounts on mortgage, **free cash withdrawals** at any VISA ATM and etc.
（當然有。我們銀行提供名下有薪資帳戶的客戶多項優惠措施，其中包含房貸利率優惠，以及在各地貼有 VISA 金融卡服務的提款機取款免手續費等等。）

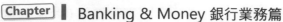

2. savings deposits passbook 儲蓄存款存摺 seal/signature 簽章

(1) **Mr. Lin:** I lost my **savings deposits passbook** yesterday, what can I do to get a new one?
（我昨天遺失銀行活期存款存摺，請問要如何取得新存摺？）

Teller: Don't worry, Mr. Lin. Please provide me your ID card and personal seal, your **signature or seal** should match the original signature or seal on the card of authorized signature,which you provided to the bank when you opened the account.Then later I will make a new passbook for you.
（別擔心，林先生。請先提供您的身份證明文件跟印章，您的簽名或印章都需要跟先前提供的印鑑卡上的樣式一致。然後稍後我會製作一本新的存摺給您。）

(2) I need to check the transaction history of my bank account. Where can I find the passbook update machine?
（我必須查一下我銀行帳戶的交易紀錄，哪裡有補摺機呢？）

3. password / PIN 密碼 E-banking / e-financial service網路銀行

(1) I forget my password of the ATM card; I need to go to the **bank counter** to reset the password in person.
（我忘記提款卡密碼了，看來我需要親自到銀行櫃檯辦理重設密碼。）

(2) You have to change your **e-banking PIN code** frequently; otherwise, the hacker may hack into your account.
（你應該要時常更換網路銀行的密碼，不然駭客有可能會潛入你的銀行帳戶）

4. transfer轉帳

ATM（Automatic teller machine 縮寫）提款機或自動櫃員機

Nowadays, online shopping activities are prevalent and various payment options are available. You can **make payments** through 7-11 stores, or make **transfers** through ATM or online ATM.

（現在線上購物活動很普及且有多種付款方式可以選擇。你可以選擇到 7-11 便利商店繳付款項，或是利用實體 ATM 或是網路 ATM 轉帳完成交易。）

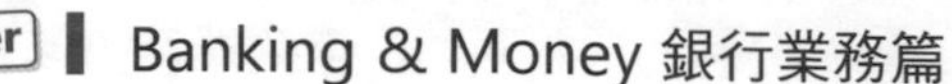

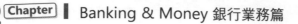

單元短文 Unit reading

Is Saving the Risk-free Investment?
儲蓄是無風險的投資嗎？

Savings usually mean putting money in low risk and interest-earning accounts, rather than high risk investments. Although it is possible to receive higher returns with certain investments, the idea behind savings is to allow the money to grow slowly with little or no associated risk. The emerging of online banking has increased the variety and diversity of savings accounts.

儲蓄通常意味者將金錢存入一個低風險且可產生利息的帳戶，而非所謂的高風險投資。儘管可能因參與某些投資而有可能獲取可觀的報酬，然而儲蓄行為背後所意味的概念卻是在極少風險或甚至無相關風險的情況下，讓所儲蓄的錢慢慢地成長。而網路銀行的興起，則是增加了儲蓄帳戶的多樣性與多元化應用。

常用片語 Common phrases

- save up (存；儲) — I am **saving up** for the coming Summer holiday!（我正為即將到來暑期假期存錢！）

- fill out (填寫) — Please **fill out** this form before depositing your money.（請您在存款前先填寫這張表格。）

重點字彙 Important words to know

名詞 Nouns		動詞 Verbs	
銀行帳戶	bank account	開（帳戶）	open (an account)
儲蓄帳戶	savings account	關（帳戶）	close (an account)
銀行櫃檯人員	teller / cashier	存入（款項）	deposit (money)
存款條	deposit slip	取出（款項）	withdraw (money)
提款條	withdrawal slip	兌現（支票）	cash (a check)
提款卡	ATM card	轉帳	transfer (money)
銀行明細表	bank statement	支付（款項）	make (a payment)
貨幣	currency	做（定存）	make (a deposit)
餘額／結存	balance	換鈔	exchange (note)
利息	interest	查詢（帳戶餘額）	check (account balance)
利率	interest rate		
固定利率	fixed rate		
浮動利率	floating rate		
每年	p.a.*		
存單	certificate of deposit（簡稱CD)		

註 拉丁文 per annum的縮寫

放款業務（個人）－貸款 Personal Loans

什麼是存款業務

放款業務是指銀行在評估客戶償債能力和抵押品的價值之後把資金借給客戶使用而抽取固定、浮動或者混合式利息的融資行為。依目的來分，主要有「經營類」，例如作生意用的營運資金；或者「消費類」，例如購買房屋、汽車或者付學雜費的貸款等兩個主要大類。

單元暖身小練習 Warm-up conversation and practice

針對以下每個空格，請選一個最適合的字填入。這是協助你對於本主題進行初步的暖身，以利對於後續的介紹可以更有效率的吸收。

(a) excited　(b) loans　(c) first　(d) discuss
(e) help　(f) cashier　(g) expenses　(h) chosen
(i) fixed　(j) apply for

Tom wants to apply for a personal loan, so he is meeting a loan officer now.
湯姆想要申請個人貸款，正和貸款專員面談中。

Loan Officer: Good morning, Sir! May I ....1.... you?
（早安，先生！我可以幫您嗎？）

Tom: Yes. I am buying a car, so I would like to ....2.... a personal loan.

（是的，我要買一輛車，所以我想申請個人貸款。）

Loan Officer: Sure. Please take a seat here.
（當然。請這邊坐。）

Tom: Thank you.
（謝謝。）

Loan Officer: Have you ever taken out any ....3.... before?
（您以前有貸款過嗎？）

Tom: No. This is my ....4.... time.
（沒有。這是我的第一次申請。）

Loan Officer: Do you have a job?
（您有工作嗎？）

Tom: Yes, I have been working as a full-time ....5.... at Costco for three years.
（是的，我已經在好市多（Costco）作全職的收銀員有三年了。）

Loan Officer: So you have decided on the car you want to buy?
（所以您已經決定好您想要買的車？）

Tom: Yes, I have ....6.... a brand new Honda Accord, and it will be my first car.
（是的，我已經選擇了一輛全新的本田雅哥，而這將是我的第一輛車。）

Loan Officer: You must be ....7....! How much is the car?
（您一定很興奮！車子多少錢？）

Tom: Yes. The car costs approximately 850,000 dollars, including all taxes, registration fees, and the insurance.
（是的。買車的費用大約NTD850,000台幣，包含所有的稅、登記費和保險費。）

Loan Officer: Do you prefer ....8.... or fluctuating monthly payment?
（您喜歡固定的或浮動的月付款？）

Tom: I prefer fixed payment, so it's easier for me to budget.
（我喜歡固定的月付款，這樣我預算掌控上會比較容易。）

Loan Officer: Right. How much is your salary?
（您的薪水有多少？）

Tom: I get paid 3,000 per month.
（我的月薪是NTD3,000台幣。）

Loan Officer: Do you own or rent your place?
（您住的地方是買的還是租的？）

Tom: I live with my parents, so I can save on the rent.
（我和我的父母一起住，這樣我就可以省下租金。）

Loan Officer: Okay. Do you have any other regular monthly....9...., such as student loan or credit card payment?
（好吧。您有任何其他的每月固定支出嗎？例如學生貸款或者信用卡還款？）

Tom: No. I do have a credit card, but I pay off the outstanding balance every month.
（沒有，我有一張信用卡，但我每個月都還清欠款。）

Loan Officer: Good. Then you just have to fill out the application form and let me photocopy your ID, driver's license, and your pay slip. I will pull out a credit report on you, so we can ⋯.10⋯..more details later.
（好。那您只需要填寫好申請表，讓我影印您的身份證、駕照和薪資證明。我會去把您的信用報告調出來，然後我們待會就可以討論其他更多的細節。)

Tom: Great! Thank you.
（太棒了！謝謝您。）

答案 ANSWERS:
1.e 2.j 3.b 4.c 5.f 6.h 7.a 8.i 9.g 10.d

認識貸款業務

貸款依不同的要素而有以下主要幾個不同的分類方式：

貸款按照其是否有抵押物（Collateral）而分為：

・有抵押貸款（Secured loans）

・無抵押貸款（Unsecured loans）

抵押物的選擇一般是房屋、汽車等資產。而有抵押貸款因為銀行需要承受的風險比較小，所以相對的貸款利息也會比較優惠。房屋貸款和汽車貸款都是常見的有抵押貸款。

無抵押貸款一般是以借款人本身的信用來作為貸款的評估依據，而且銀行要承受的風險相對比較高，所以貸款的利息會比有抵押貸款的利息高很多。信用卡就是典型的無抵押貸款。

貸款可以依照貸款時間長短（Lending Period）而分為：

長期貸款（Long-term）：貸款時間超過5年以上，而其特點是期限長，利率高，風險大。

中期貸款（Mid-term）：貸款時間超過1年而不到5年，而其特點是期限中等，利率中等，風險中等。

短期貸款（Short-term）：貸款時間在1年以下，而其特點是期限短，風險小，利率低。

透支或信用貸款（Overdraft）：沒有固定貸款時間的貸款，風險和利率都

高。

貸款時間長短指的是銀行開始把貸款本金借給借款人直到借款人把貸款還給銀行為止的這一段時間。它是借款人實際使用貸款的時間段。

個人貸款可以按照貸款目的（Lending Purpose）而主要分為：

個人經營類貸款：個人因為要創業而需要的資金可以以個人貸款的方式申請，不過多數的銀行把此類貸款歸於商業貸款的範圍。

個人消費類貸款：一般的個人消費貸款都是屬於這類，例如房屋抵押貸款、汽車貸款和學生貸款等。

貸款可以按貸款利率（Lending Rate）的特性分為：

固定利率貸款：固定利息就是在貸款期間內，貸款利息都是按照約定的固定利率來計算。

浮動利率貸款：浮動利率就是貸款期間內，貸款利息都是隨著市場上利率的調整而變動。

混合利率貸款：混合利率就是結合固定利率和浮動利率，貸款利息是以約定的計算方式的貸款方式。

利率是借款人貸款所支付的代價，亦是銀行借給借款人所獲得的回報。利率通常以一年期利息與本金的百分比計算。

一般常見銀行個人貸款業務項目

業務項目 Business Item		
房屋抵押貸款（房貸） **House mortgages**	房屋貸款，也稱為房屋抵押貸款或者房貸，是由購房者向貸款銀行申請抵押貸款，並提供身份證、收入證明、房屋買賣合同與担保書等。貸款銀行核准房屋貸款之後，並且房地產抵押登記和公證完成之後，銀行就會把所貸出的資金直接匯到售房公司在該銀行的帳戶上。	A house mortgage occurs when an owner pledges his or her home as security or collateral for a loan. He or she needs to provide personal identification, proof of income, property contract, etc. to the bank. After the loan application is approved, and the registration of the mortgage and notarization of mortgage are completed, the bank transfers the money directly to the bank account of the party selling the property.
汽車貸款 **Car loans (auto loans)**	汽車貸款是指銀行借給個人用來購買汽車的貸款業務，包括自用車貸款和商用車貸款。汽車貸款的貸款期限最長不超過5年，其中，商用車和二手車貸款的貸款期限最長不超過3年。	Car loans or auto loans are lent by banks to individuals for the purchase of vehicles, including private use car loans and commercial use car loans. The maximum term for car loans usually does not exceed five years, whereas the term for commercial use car loans and second hand car loans usually does not exceed three years.

學生貸款 **Student loans**	學生貸款，指的是學生為支付學雜費、書籍費及住宿費等就學期間所需的金錢，而向政府或金融機構所申請的貸款，大多在畢業後才需開始清償。有些國家會為申請的學生負擔在學期間的利息，而利率通常較一般商業性質貸款低。與一般貸款一樣，若不依約清償則會造成債信不良，可能會影響日後申請信用卡或其他貸款項目。	Student loans refer to the money students borrowed to pay for tuition fees, books, accommodations and other education related expenses etc., from the government or banks. The repayment normally doesn't start until after graduation. Some countries would even pay the interest for students until they graduate, and the interest rate is usually lower than the normal commercial loans. Like regular loans, if the repayment does not occur according to the contract, the borrower's credit rating would be negatively affected. This would affect the borrower's credit card or other loan applications in the future.
信用卡 **Credit card**	信用卡是一種非現金交易的信貸服務。信用卡是由銀行或信用卡公司依照用戶的信用度與財力發給持卡人，持卡人持信用卡消費時無須支付現金，等到收到帳單時再進行還款。	Credit card is a way of non-cash credit service. Credit cards are issued by banks or credit card companies, based on the cardholders' credit rating and financial capacities. Cardholders can charge expenses to their credit card, and are not required to pay cash at time of purchases until they receive the bills.

常用業務例句 Common business terms

1. expire 到期
credit card 信用卡
replacement 補發

Mary: Good afternoon, Sir. My credit card is **expiring** this week, but I haven't received a new card yet. Could you help me get a new card?
（午安，先生。 我的信用卡這星期就要到期了，不過我還沒有收到新的卡。您可以幫助我拿到新的卡嗎？）

Teller: Sure. Please show me your ID and existing **credit card**, and I will contact the credit card department and get a **replacement** card for you immediately.
（當然。請出示您的身份證和現有的信用卡，我會聯繫信用卡部門，並立即為您申請補發新卡。）

2. pre-authorized 預先授權的
rejected 退回
overdrawn 透支
make up for 彌補

Bessie: I have a car loan with your bank, but my last **pre-authorized** car loan payment was **rejected** as my bank account was **overdrawn** last month. Could you tell me how to **make up** for the missed payment?
（我在您們銀行有汽車貸款，但我上回的汽車貸款無法自動扣款，因為我的銀行帳戶上月透支了。你能告訴我如何補繳費用嗎？）

Teller: Certainly, please tell me your bank account, so I can pull out your car loan details and make a make-up loan payment for you.

（當然，請告訴我您的銀行帳戶，這樣我就可以找出您汽車貸款的細節，並且幫您處理補付貸款的事宜。）

3. re-pay 償還
principal 本金
additional 額外的
outstanding 剩餘未償還的

Mark: I would like to know if it is possible to **re-pay** more **principal** on my house mortgage?
（我想知道是否有可能再多償還我的房屋貸款的本金部分？）

Teller: Sure, please tell me your account number and how much **additional** principal you would like to re-pay?
（當然，請告訴我您的帳號和您想額外多付多少的本金。）

Mark: Could also you let me know what my **outstanding** mortgage principal is before I decide?
（在我決定之前，您可以也讓我知道我目前的貸款本金餘額嗎？）

4. regular 定期的
bi-weekly 每兩週一次的

Alvin: I just graduated and got a job, so I would like to start making payment for my student loan. Could you help me set up **regular** pre-authorized payments from my checking account?
（我剛畢業並且找到工作了，所以我想開始償還我的學生貸款。您能夠幫在我的支票帳戶設置預授權的定期還款嗎？）

Teller: Of course. Would you like to set up **bi-weekly** or monthly payment?
（當然。您希望每兩週或每月支付一次？）

單元短文 Unit reading

Personal loan or Credit card? Which Is A Bigger Monster?
個人貸款或信用卡？何者更可怕？

What's the difference between a personal loan and a credit card? When should we choose a personal loan over a credit card?

Personal loans have lower interest rates than credit cards. But banks do expect loan applicants to have a great credit rating to grant them personal loans. Banks are less demanding about credit rating for credit card applications, but it definitely costs more to use a credit card.

If you need a lump-sum loan with fixed payments (to purchase a home or a car) over a period of time, go for a personal loan. If you need a small amount of cash urgently or prefer flexibility to spend spontaneously from time to time, a credit card is a good option. It is not hard to use your credit card, but you may spend at least 12 percent more when you swipe. So, decide carefully and rationally before you act!

個人貸款和信用卡的區別是什麼？我們何時應該選擇個人貸款而不是信用卡？

個人貸款的利率低於信用卡。但銀行會希望貸款申請人有很好的信用評估才會批准他們的個人貸款申請。銀行對於信用卡申請人的信用評估要求不高，但使用信用卡的利息肯定比較高。

如果您需要在一段時間內固定還款的一整筆的貸款（用來購買房屋或汽車），個人貸款是適合的選擇。如果您需要小額的現金或希望能夠有靈活消費的選擇，信用卡可以提供如此的彈性。信用卡是很容易使用的，但您刷卡花費的利息會比個人貸款高至少12%以上。所以，在您行動之前，請您小心並且做出謹慎的決定！

常用片語Common phrases

- make up for
  彌補

I am sorry I missed your ball game. What can I do to **make** it **up for** you?
（我很抱歉，我錯過了你的球賽。我能夠做什麼來彌補你？）

- pay off
  付清

I prefer to **pay off** my credit card outstanding balance every month.
（我比較喜歡每個月付清我的信用卡餘額。）

重點字彙 Important words to know

名詞 Nouns		動詞 Verbs	
個人貸款	personal loan	申請（貸款）	apply for (a loan)
貸款專員	loan officer	調出	pull out
房屋貸款	mortgage	抵押	pledge
汽車貸款	car loan/auto loan	超過	exceed
學生貸款	student loan	到期	expire
固定的還款	fixed payment	退回	reject
變動的還款	fluctuating payment	設定	set up
抵押物	collateral		
信用卡	credit card		
剩餘的	outstanding		

身分證明	identification		
固定利率	fixed rate		
浮動利率	floating/ variable rate		
信用評估	credit rating		
一整筆的	lump-sum		
全新的	brand new		

放款業務（公司／企業）－貸款 Business Loans

什麼是商業放款

商業貸款是銀行提供工商企業營運用的固定貸款、週轉性支出用的循環貸款，商業信用卡和信用狀等融資服務。商業貸款不超過一年的為短期貸款，超過一年而在七年以下的是中期貸款，而七年以上的是長期貸款。商業貸款一般占商業銀行貸款三分之一以上。

單元暖身小練習 Warm-up conversation and practice

針對以下每個空格，請選一個最適合的字填入。這是協助你對於本主題進行初步的暖身，以利對於後續的介紹可以更有效率的吸收。

(a) purpose	(b) sense	(c) scale	(d) feasible
(e) capital	(f) quotation	(g) available	(h) projection
(i) ambience	(j) renovate		

Melinda wants to apply for a business loan, so she can renovate her boutique chocolate shop.

美琳達想要申請商業貸款，這樣她就可以裝修她的精品巧克力店。

Loan Officer: Good afternoon, Miss Wang! May I help you?

（午安，王小姐！我可以幫您嗎？）

Melinda: Yes, I would like to know about business loans. Could you tell me the options ....1....at your bank?

（是的，我想了解一下商業貸款。您能告訴我您們銀行提供的商業貸款種類嗎？）

Loan Officer: Sure. Please take a seat here.

（當然。請這邊坐。）

Melinda: Thank you.

（謝謝。）

Loan Officer: Would you like to know about small business loans or commercial loans?

（你想了解中小企業貸款或一般商業貸款？）

Melinda: What is the difference between them?

（它們有什麼不同？）

Loan Officer: The main difference is the maximum amount of loans available to the business borrowers. Small business loans usually are in place to provide the initial ....2.... to start a small business, and the maximum amount is not more than NTD 5 million at our bank. If your business is of certain ....3.... and needs a loan exceeding that amount, we would suggest commercial loans to you.

（它們主要的區別是商業客戶可拿到的最高貸款額。中小企業貸款通常是提供中小企業創業的資金，而在我們銀行的最高金額不超過新台幣500萬。如果你的企業有一定的規模且貸款的需求超過這個數額，我們會建議您申請商業貸款。）

Loan Officer: May I know what type of business you are running and for how long? What is the ....4.... to apply for loans?

（我可以知道您經營的是什麼類型的生意並且開業有多久了？您申請貸款的目的是什麼？）

Melinda: I have been running a boutique chocolate shop for 5 years. The reason for my borrowing is to ....5.... my shop. My customers either pick up chocolate from my counter or enjoy tea time at my cafe. The ....6....is important for my business; hence, I decided to redecorate my shop.

（我經營精品巧克力店已經5年了。借款的原因是想重新裝修我的店。我的客戶要不就買巧克力回家，要不也可以在我店裡享受下午茶。氛圍的營造對我的生意很重要，所以我決定重新裝修我的店。）

Loan Officer: That makes....7..... Have you borrowed any money for your business before?

（這是滿有道理的。您以前有為您的生意貸過款嗎？）

Melinda: No. This is my first time. My parents gave me some capital to start my business, so I didn't need to borrow since I started.

（沒有。這是我第一次申請。我的父母給我一些資金創業，所以我從一開始就沒有貸過款。）

Loan Officer: How much would you like to borrow and for how long?

（您想要貸多少和貸多久？）

Melinda: I was thinking about borrowing NTD 500,000 and paying back every month during five years' period. Does that sound....8....?

（我想貸大約新台幣50萬，每月還款在五年內還完。聽起來可行嗎？）

Loan Officer: I would need to do some calculation first. Please give me your personal account number, your company financial statements for the past three years, the ....9.... from your interior designer, and your business ....10.... for the next three years, and fill out this application form, so I can best answer your question.

（我要先計算一下。請給我您的個人帳戶、過去三年中貴公司的財務報表、您的室內設計師的報價和您在未來三年的銷售預測，並填寫申請表，這樣我就可以給您最好的答覆。。）

Melinda: Thank you.

（謝謝您。）

答案 *ANSWERS:*

1.g 2.e 3.c 4.a 5.j 6.i 7.b 8.d 9.f 10.h

認識商業貸款與個人貸款的分別

商業貸款與個人貸款最大的不同之處如下：

抵押物：個人貸款一般用不動產或投資來做抵押，而商業貸款除了用不動產或投資來做抵押之外，還可以用廠房設備、家具、存貨等作為抵押，必要時，股東的個人資產也有可能被銀行要求作為商業貸款抵押物的一部分。

保證人：除了在特殊的情況之外， 銀行對於個人貸款一般不會要求要有保證人。而商業貸款的股東一般都必須作為貸款的保證人，所以，除了公司的資產要作為抵押物之外，股東個人的財產也有可能要為公司的商業貸款承受部分的風險。

支持文件：對於個人貸款，借款人一般只要提供薪資證明、所得稅扣繳憑單加上個人的信用報告，就足夠讓銀行評估個人的基本狀況是否符合貸款的要求。而對於商業貸款，除了公司的信用報告之外，銀行還會要求過去三年經專業會計師所審核的財務報告、報稅單，以及與供貨商、供應商和客戶的合約。

條件：一般來說，個人貸款的利率會比商業貸款低。當然，商業貸款的利率也取決於公司運行的時間長度以及抵押物的種類。 歷史悠久並且有良好又穩定銷售紀錄的公司，較有可能獲得比較低的利率。同時，用不動產抵押的商業貸款也可能會獲得比用其他資產抵押的貸款更低的利率。風險的大小也就是銀行所考慮的因素。

跟進：基本上，個人貸款在貸款發放之後，只要借款人按照約定的方式定期還款，銀行比較不會有特別的跟進。而對於商業貸款，銀行不但要求貸款經理隨時要與借款人聯繫、關心客戶的營運狀況之外，同時每年要對商業客戶作年度審查，並請客戶提供年度財務報表。

不論是個人貸款或者商業貸款，借款人的信用和償債能力是銀行考慮是否通過貸款申請時最主要的因素。

一般常見銀行存款業務項目

業務項目 Business Item		
固定商業貸款 **Term loans**	固定商業貸款一般是為企業提供資本性支出融資，例如構建土地、廠房、營業場所，或更新機器設備等。一般貸款年限為中期（一年以上到七年）或長期（七年到二十年）。貸款通常以不超過需要資金的七成為原則，還款採用本金按月攤還，利息按月繳付。	Term loans are usually provided to support the capital expenditures of business, such as purchase of land, construction of buildings or business premises, or the upgrade of machinery and equipment. Usually the loan period is either medium term (more than one up to seven years) or long term(seven to twenty years). The amounts of loans are usually no more than 70% of total capital needed, and the repayment of principal is on a monthly basis and the interest is paid monthly.
循環商業貸款 **Revolving loans**	循環商業貸款一般是為企業提供週轉性融資的貸款，例如採購原料、生產、加工及運銷過程中所需之週轉資金。	Revolving loans provide funds to companies for the procurement of raw materials, production, processing and distribution process to conduct regular operations.

	貸款額度視實際需要核給，並在額度內循環動用。動用期限最長1年。償還方式依利息按月繳付，本金到期一次清償為原則。一般貸款年限為一年到最多三年為限。	Loan amount depends on the actual needs for operations and is to be used within the limit cycle. The maximum revolving period is one year. The monthly payment includes only interest as the principal repayment is to be paid in full at the loan maturity date. The lending period is usually one year and up to maximum of three years.
商業信用卡 Commercial credit card	如同個人的信用卡，商業信用卡提供企業的信貸服務，方便企業的老闆及員工做便利的無現金消費。而信用卡是由銀行或信用卡公司依照企業的信用度與財力發給持卡人，而持卡人再授權給副卡的持有人。 持卡人持信用卡消費時無須支付現金，等到收到帳單時再進行還款。	Similar to personal credit cards, business credit cards offer business credit services to facilitate business owners and their employees to make convenient cashless spending. Credit cards are issued by banks or credit card companies, based on the businesses' credit rating and financial capacities, and the cardholders authorize certain credit limits to the supplementary card holders. Cardholders can charge expenses to their credit card, and are not required to pay in cash at time of purchases until they receive the bills.

信用狀 **Letter of credit**	信用狀是由銀行開出保證賣方將及時並且正確的收到買方所付的貨款的一份文件。在該買家未能依約付款的情況下，銀行將會有責任支付貨款的全部或餘額。	Letter of credit is a document issued by a bank to guarantee that the seller will receive the correct payment, in a timely manner, from the buyer. In case the buyer fails to make the payments, the bank will be required to pay the full amount or remaining balance of payment.

常用業務例句 Common business terms

1. spread價差
reflect反映
grant發放
relevant 相關的

Melinda: Good afternoon, Sir. Could you tell me how your floating rate is calculated?
（下午好，先生。您能否告訴我您們的浮動利率是如何計算？）

Loan Officer: Sure. At our bank, the floating rates for loans are usually the sum of the bank base rate, the bank's cost margin, and a **spread**. The spread is related to the borrowers' credit rating in order to **reflect** the risk the bank is exposed to by **granting** the loan. And this spread generally refers to the borrower's credit spread, and it is set by assessing the borrower's credit rating, the loan period, the source of

repayment, collateral pledged and the loan's contribution to the Bank's operations, and other **relevant** factors etc..
（當然。我們的銀行所採用的貸款浮動利率通常是銀行基準利率加上銀行的作業成本再加上一個價差的總和。而這個價差是與借款人的信用評級有關的，以用來反映銀行發放貸款所承擔的風險。而這個價差我們一般稱為個別授信加碼幅度，它是在考量客戶之信用評等、借款期限、還款來源、擔保品及對本行業務貢獻度等因素綜合評估後而訂定的。）

2. cost margin 作業成本
domestic國內的
capital 資本

Melinda: What is the bank base rate? And what is the bank's **cost margin**?
（什麼是銀行基準利率？什麼是銀行的作業成本？）

Loan Officer: The bank base rate is basically the average of the annual term deposit interest rates offered by the major **domestic** banks. The bank's cost margin is calculated based on each individual bank's **capital** and operating costs.
（而基準利率基本上是以國內幾個指標銀行每年定期儲蓄存款機動利率的平均數為訂價基礎。所謂的個別銀行的作業成本指的是以個別銀行資金及營運成本為原則訂定的。）

3. qualifying符合條件的
track record記錄
repayment ability償還能力

Melinda: What is considered a mid-term commercial loan, and what

is a long-term commercial loan?
（什麼被是一個中期的商業貸款? 什麼是長期的商業貸款？）

Loan Officer: For commercial loans, when the lending period is not more than one year, it is considered the short-term financing. When the financial period is more than one year but less than seven years, then it is mid-term financing. When it is over seven years, then it is long-term financing.
（對商業貸款而言，融資期一年以下為短期融資。融資期限超過一年而在七年以內者為中期融資，超過七年者為長期融資。）

Melinda: Can anyone **qualify** for mid-term or long-term commercial loans?
（任何人都有資格申請到中期或長期商業貸款？）

Loan Officer: Not really. **Qualifying** applicants for mid-term or long-term financing are usually customers who have good business **track records**, are financially sound and stable, and have good credit rating, and the purpose of the loan, the operation plans, and the **repayment ability** of their business are also taken into consideration.
（不盡然。中長期融資對象一般以客戶有良好的事業經營紀錄、財務健全穩定而信用評估良好者為主，而且參酌借款用途、營運計劃及償還能力等訂定。）

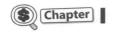

4. comply to 遵守
significant 重大的

Melinda: After I get a commercial loan, do I need to **comply to** any special requirements by the bank every year?
（我申請到了商業貸款之後，每年是否需要遵守任何銀行特殊的要求？）

Loan Officer: For commercial clients, in addition to making regular repayment on time, it is necessary to provide annual financial reports and also inform the bank of any **significant** events related to operations and revenue generation. So, the bank can evaluate and see if there is a need to adjust the current commercial financing in place.
（對於商業客戶，除了每月要按時依合約約定的還款方式還款之外，每年也都要提供正式的年度財務報表，並且隨時向銀行告知會影響公司營運和業務的重大事項，以便讓銀行適時再次評估客戶的償還能力以及是否有調整商業融資的必要性。）

單元短文 Unit reading

借貸俱樂部？貸款的另類選擇？
Lending Club? An Alternative to Money Borrowing?

People often question why there is a huge difference between the interest the banks pay on us on our term deposit (approx. 1.5%) and the interest we are charged on our credit card (approx.18%) ? And after pondering on this question seriously, Mr. Renaud Laplanche co-founded the first Lending Club with Mr. Soulaiman Htite in 2006, and its first loan was given out in 2007. Lending Club is an online company that matches people who want to borrow money with others willing to lend it, and its headquartered is in San Francisco, California.

Lending Club keeps its costs low enough that it can offer rates that are often better than what you pay for your credit card. While these rates have a wide range, Lending Club's average at the end of 2014 was 13.4 percent; credit card borrowers typically pay between 17 and 18 percent.

Lending Club is the world's largest person-to-person lending platform. As of December 31, 2014, the platform has originated $7.62 billion in loans. In August 2014, the firm filed with US regulators for its IPO. It started with personal lending, and in 2014 it also started providing loans to small businesses. Ironically, some of the its major investors are banks.

人們常常有疑問，為什麼銀行付給我們的定存利息和向我們收取信用卡的利率之間有那麼大的差異？在謹慎地琢磨這個問題之後，Renaud Laplanche 先生決定與Soulaiman Htite 先生於2006年共同創立了第一個借貸俱樂部，而其第一筆貸款是在2007年出的。它是一個線上配對借款與貸款者的借貸平台公司，其總部設在加州舊金山市。

借貸俱樂部保持其以低成本的方式營運，所以它可以提供的利率往往比您所支付信用卡的利率還要低。雖然各信用卡公司收取的利率範圍很廣，而借貸俱樂部在2014年底的平均利率約為13.4%；而一般信用卡持卡人通常付17%和18%之間的利率。

借貸俱樂部是世界上最大的個人對個人的網絡借貸平台。截至2014年12月31日為止，該平台已發出76億多美元的貸款。在2014年八月，該公司向美國監管機構提交IPO上市申請。它從個人貸款開始，後來在2014年開始也提供商業貸款。諷刺的是，它的一些主要投資者是銀行。

常用片語 Common phrases

• refer to 參考	When you are in doubt, you can always **refer to** the commercial loan pamphlet for answers. （當您有疑問時您可以隨時參考商業貸款的小冊子裡的答案。）
• Pay back 償還	I am planning to **pay back** my business loan every month. （我打算每月償還我的商業貸款。）

重點字彙 Important words to know

名詞 Nouns		動詞 Verbs	
商業貸款	commercial loan	發放／准許（貸款）	grant (a loan)
小企業貸款	small business loan	反映	reflect
貸款專員	loan officer	抵押	pledge
財務報表	financial statement	超過	exceed
銷售預測	business projection	符合資格	qualify
定期貸款	term loan	遵守	comply to
抵押物	collateral		
信用卡	credit card		
信用狀	letter of credit		
價差	spread		
國內的	domestic		
相關的	relevant		
信用評估	credit rating		
銀行的作業成本	bank's cost margin		
資金	capital		

國際金融 International Finance

什麼是國際金融

國際金融是金融經濟學中處理兩個或以上國家之間的貨幣互動，相關的主題有國際收支、國際匯兌、國際結算、國際投資和國際貨幣體系等。它們之間相互影響、相互制約。國際收支會涉及國際匯兌和國際結算的活動，而國際匯兌中的貨幣匯率對國際收支又有相關的影響，而國際收支的重要項目和國際投資又相互有關聯。

單元暖身小練習 Warm-up conversation and practice

針對以下每個空格，請選一個最適合的字填入。這是協助你對於本主題進行初步的暖身，以利對於後續的介紹可以更有效率的吸收。

(a) denotes　(b) held　(c) drive　(d) merchandise
(e) Certainly　(f) corresponds to　(g) commodities　(h)decades
(i) savings　(j)examples

Amy wants to inquire her university professor about trade surplus.
艾米想向她的大學教授請教貿易順差的問題。

Amy: Good morning, Professor Milton! Do you have a minute?

（早上好，米爾頓教授！您有空嗎？）

Professor Milton: Of course, what can I do for you?

（當然，我能為您做點什麼？）

Amy: I read in the news that our country has a high trade surplus. I would like to know what that means.

（我在報紙上讀到我們國家有高貿易順差的新聞，我想知道這代表什麼。）

Professor Milton: Sure. First of all, trade generally refers to the buying and selling of....1.... In International Trade, buying and selling are replaced by imports and exports. Thus, the Balance of Trade ....2.... the differences of imports and exports of a ....3.... of a country during a fiscal year. Therefore, trade surplus means when a country's exports exceeds its imports. A trade deficit means when a country's imports exceed its exports.

（當然。首先，貿易一般是指商品的購買和銷售。在國際貿易上，購買和銷售由進口和出口取代，因此，貿易平衡是指在一個財政年度當中某商品的進口和出口數量的差異。而貿易順差是指國家的出口量超過了進口量。貿易逆差是指國家的進口量大於出口量。）

Amy: I see. Could you give me ....4.... of countries which are known to have trade surplus? And others with trade deficit?

（我明白了。你能提供給我一些已知有貿易順差國家的案例嗎？還有其他有貿易逆差的國家？）

Professor Milton: ....5.... , countries such as Japan and Germany which have ....6.... surpluses, typically have trade surpluses. China, a high-growth economy, tends to have trade surpluses. A higher savings rate generally ....7.... a trade surplus. Correspondingly, the U.S. with its lower savings rate tends to have high trade deficits, especially with Asian nations.
（當然，擁有儲蓄盈餘的國家像日本和德國，一般都有貿易順差。而像中國這樣一個高速增長的經濟體系，往往也有貿易順差。較高的儲蓄率通常通常有貿易順差。同樣的，美國擁有較低的儲蓄率就會趨向於高的貿易逆差，特別是與亞洲各國之間。）

Amy: Is it bad for a country to have a trade deficit? Could you also give me an example?
（貿易逆差對一個國家是不好的嗎？您還可以提供給我一個案例嗎？）

Professor Milton: A trade deficit is not necessarily bad because it often rectifies itself over time. However, the deficit in the United States has been growing for the past few....8...., which has some economists concerned. This means that large amount of the U.S. dollar are being ....9....by foreign nations, and these countries may decide to sell at any time. A large sale of US dollar can ....10....the value of the currency down, making it more costly to import.
（貿易赤字並不一定是不好的，因為它常常會隨著時間而自行修正。然而，美國的貿易逆差已經在過去的幾十年中越來越大，引起一些經濟學家的擔心。這意味著，外國正在持有大量的美金，而他們可能隨時決定出售手中的美金。大量的拋售美金會引起美金貨幣的貶值，而使進口更加昂貴。）

Amy: I see. Thank you so much. It is now clear to me what a trade surplus means. See you in the class later!

（我明白了。太謝謝您了。現在我清楚什麼是貿易順差了。晚點在課堂上見！）

Professor Milton: See you later!

（晚點見！）

答案 ANSWERS:

1.g 2.a 3.d 4.j 5.e 6.i 7.f 8.h 9.b 10.c

認識國際金融

國際金融是金融經濟學中處理兩個或兩個以上國家之間的貨幣互動，而主要的主題有貨幣匯率、國際貨幣體系、外國直接投資以及國際金融管理的問題，包括涉及管理跨國公司領域本身固有的政治風險和外匯風險。國際金融研究所關注的是總體經濟學，把經濟體作為一個整體而不是一個單獨的市場來看待。從事國際金融研究的國際主體主要有：世界銀行（The World Bank）及其附屬的機構、國際金融公司（International Finance Corporation, IFC）與國際貨幣基金組織（International Monetary Fund, IMF）。

世界銀行（The World Bank）及其附屬的機構：世界銀行（The World Bank）一於1944年成立，而其總部在美國華盛頓特區。目前有屬於國際復興開發銀行的188個國家成員和屬於國際開發協會的173個國家成員。它是聯合國系統國際金融機構（United Nations international financial institution）為發展中國家的資本項目提供貸款的機構；它也是世界銀行集團（World Bank Group）的組成機構之一，然而在某些非正式場合，世界銀行集團也可被簡稱為「世界銀行」。世界銀行的官方目標為消除貧困（宣言：「為一個沒有貧困的世界而努力。」（"Working for a World Free of Poverty"））。根據其有關協定規定，其所有決定都必須旨在推動外商直接投資和國際貿易，以及為資本投資提供便利。

世界銀行（The World Bank）由兩個機構組成：①國際復興開發銀行（International Bank for Reconstruction and Development , IBRD）、② 國際開發協會（International Development Association ,IDA）

世界銀行集團（World Bank Group），是一個聯合國經濟及社會理事會的成員，由五個貸款給貧困國家的機構組成：① 國際復興開發銀行（International Bank for Reconstruction and Development (IBRD)）、② 國際開發協會（International Development Association, IDA）、③國際金融公司

（International Finance Corporation, IFC）、④多邊投資擔保機構（Multilateral Investment Guarantee Agency, MIGA）與⑤國際投資爭端解決中心（International Centre for Settlement of Investment Disputes, ICSID）。

國際金融公司（IFC）：國際金融公司（International Finance Corporation, IFC)，於1956年成立，其目的是發展私人部門和減少貧困，是總部位於美國華盛頓的多邊國際金融機構。 該公司是世界銀行集團的成員，由177個成員國出資設立，目前有184個成員國。 國際金融公司的主要出資股東包括美國、日本、德國、英國、法國。 國際金融公司致力於為發展中國家和新興市場的私營部門提供多樣化的金融支持。

國際貨幣基金組織（IMF）：國際貨幣基金組織（International Monetary Fund, (IMF)），於1945年12月27日成立，其目的是促進國際金融體系穩定，而其職責是監察貨幣匯率和各國貿易情況、提供技術和資金協助，確保全球金融制度運作正常；其總部設在美國華盛頓特區，有188個成員國。

一般常見國際金融名詞解釋

國際貨幣體系 International monetary systems	國際貨幣體系是國際所認定的用來促進國際貿易，跨國境投資和國與國之間資本重新分配的一些規則、慣例和支持機構的總稱。	International monetary systems are certain internationally agreed rules, conventions and supporting institutions, that help international trade, cross border investment and the reallocation of capital between countries.

國際收支 **Balace of payments**	一個國家的國際收支是該國的居民與其他國家之間在某一特定時間內的經濟交易總額的紀錄。國際收支是重要的，因為它能夠告訴你一個國家是否有足夠的儲蓄和其他金融交易來支付它所進口的花費。	The balance of payments of a country is the record of the total of economic transactions between the residents of a country and the rest of the world in a particular period. The balance of payments is important because it will tell you whether a country has enough savings and other financial transactions to pay for its consumption of imports.
國際匯兌 **International exchange**	國際匯兑是指因辦理國際支付而產生的外匯匯率、外匯市場、外匯管制等活動的總和。	International exchange is the total of all activities related to foreign exchange rates, foreign exchange market foreign exchange controls and etc. in order to arrange for international payments.
國際結算 **International settlement**	國際結算是指國際間辦理貨幣收支分配，用來結清不同國家中的買賣雙方之間的交易活動的行為。它主要包括支付方式、支付條件和結算方法等。	International settlement refers to the allocation of monetary payments to settle transactions between two parties from different countries in the international community. It mainly includes payment methods, payment terms , and settlement methods.

國際投資 **International investment**	各國的官方和私人對外國進行的投資總和就是國際投資。國際投資是貨幣資本從一國轉移到另一國，以獲取更多利潤為目的的活動。	The total amount of investment in the foreign countries by the official and private sectors is the international investment. It is the transfer of international capital from one country to another, with getting more profits as the purpose of the activities.

常用業務例句 Common business terms

1. ecological 生態的
footprint 佔地面積
measure 測量

Amy: Good afternoon, Professor Milton. Towards the end of your International Finance class this morning, you briefly mentioned about **ecological footprint**? Could you explain for me what it is exactly?
（米爾頓教授，下午好。您於今天早上的國際金融課接近尾聲時，簡單地提到了「生態需要面積」？您能為我解釋它到底是什麼嗎？）

Professor Milton: Certainly. The ecological footprint is what **measures** human's demand on the Earth's ecosystems. It is a measure of demand for natural resources that may be compared with the planet's ecological regeneration capacity. It shows the amount of biologically productive land and sea area needed to supply the resources for a human population's consumption, and to take in waste thereby created. With this assessment, it is possible to estimate how much of the Earth (or how many planet Earths) it would take to support humanity if everybody followed a given lifestyle.

（當然可以。生態需要面積是一種人類對於地球生態系統需求的測量。它是一種把人類對自然資源的需求與地球生態本身再生的承載力進行比較的測量。它顯示了需要提供人類群體的資源，以及吸收人類所製造廢物的具有生物生產力的土地和海域的面積。使用這種評估，可能可以估計出，若每個人都遵循著特定的生活方式，我們需要多大的地球（或者要多少個地球行星）來供應人類。」。）

2. humanity 人類
lag 延遲

Amy: So, how much is the current ecological footprint measured?

（那麼，目前所測量到的生態需要面積是多少？）

Professor Milton: In 2007, the total ecological footprint for the whole **humanity** was estimated at 1.5 planet Earths; that means, we as humans use the ecological systems 1.5 times as quickly as the Earth can regenerate them. Every year, this measure is recalculated to take into account the three-year **lag** due to the time it takes for the UN to collect and publish statistics and related research.

（拿2007來說，人類的總生態需要面積估計為1.5個地球行星；也就是說，人類使用生態系統的速度比地球自我再生的速度快1.5倍。每年，由於聯合國需要時間收集和發布統計數據和相關研究，所以這個數字會納入三年的延遲後再重新計算。）

3. consumed 消耗

Amy: Professor Milton, could you give a real life example related to ecological footprint?

（米爾頓教授，您能不能給我一個現實生活中有關於生態需要面積的例子？）

Professor Milton: Of course. For example: The Mainland China supplies almost all natural resources to Hong Kong; therefore, the ecological footprint for Hong Kong also includes the resources **consumed** and the investment and development required to provide for Hong Kong.

（當然。例如：香港幾乎所有的天然資源都由中國大陸供應，因此香港的生態需要面積亦包括為提供香港所消耗的資源而作的投資及開發。）

4. household 家庭
indicator 指標
disposal 處置

Amy: Could we also apply the ecological footprint to the **household** unit?

（我們也可以把生態需要面積運用到以家庭為單位嗎？）

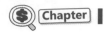

Professor Milton: Through the same way, we can also calculate the household footprint. Household footprint is an **indicator** of green living. It can be calculated as: Sum up the total of a household's daily garbage **disposal**, electricity and water consumed daily, and the daily traffic expenditures, then convert the sum into the area required to occupy in order to provide all of the former items, and divide it by the actual area the household owns, then we get the household footprint.

（透過相同的方法，我們也可以計算一個家庭生態需要面積。家居需要面積是一種綠色生活的指標。方法就是：透過把一個家庭每日所丟棄的垃圾、消費的電力和食水以及每日的交通消費，換算成為要提供這所有所得需要所佔用的土地面積，除以家居實際的面積而得出的數值便是家庭生態需要面積。）

單元短文Unit reading

Which countries have the highest government debts in Eurozone?

在歐元區內，哪些國家的政府債務最高？

The countries that had the highest government debt to GDP ratios in the Eurozone were Greece (168.8%), Italy (135.1%) and Portugal (129.6%), according to a recent news release for the first quarter of 2015. However, the Greek government debt also recorded the highest decrease compared to the first quarter of 2014, dropping by 5.5%.

In contrast, the largest increase in public debt within the Eurozone was recorded in Italy, amounting to 135.1% from 132.1%, followed by France at 97.5% from 95,6%.

In comparison, the Eurozone as a whole had a Government Debt to GDP of 91.90% of the areas GDP in 2014. Government Debt to GDP in the Eurozone was in average approximately 75.17 % from 1995 until 2014, then reaching an all time high of 91.90 % in 2014 and a record low of 66.20 percent in 2007.

Nevertheless, Germany, Cyprus and Portugal were listed as the countries whose government debt to GDP ratio decreased in 2014.

根據最近針對2015年第一季度的統計數據新聞發布，在歐元區裡，政府債務對國民生產毛額的比率最高的國家是希臘（168.8%）、意大利（135.1%）和葡萄牙（129.6%），然而，希臘政府債務的下降比率也創下了新高，與2014年的第一季度比較起來整整下降了5.5%。

相對照之下，在歐元區內國家公共債務增加最多的是意大利，從132.1%增加到135.1%，其次是法國，從95.6%提高到97.5%。

相比之下，歐元區整體的政府債務占歐元區生產總值的91.90%，而在1995年到2014年之間，歐元區的平均政府債務約占區內生產總值的75.17%，直到2014年才達到91.90%的歷史高點，而目前的紀錄低點則是在2007年的66.20%。

然而，德國、塞浦路斯和葡萄牙則被列入國家的政府債務佔國民生產毛額比例下降的其中幾個國家。

常用片語 Common phrases

- transform into 把……轉變成
  Typically, these fresh corns **are transformed into** cans of corns, and might be exported to other countries.
  （通常情況下，這些新鮮的玉米會被轉變成玉米罐頭，並可能出口到其他國家去。）

- inquire about 詢問
  Amy wants to **inquire about** her country's financial status in the international community.
  （艾米想詢問她的國家在國際上的財務狀況。）

重點字彙 Important words to know

名詞 Nouns		動詞 Verbs	
國際金融	international finance	代表	denote
商品	merchandise	對應於	correspond to
大宗商品	commodities	往往	tend to
十年	decade	納入	incorporate
貿易順差	trade surplus		
貿易逆差	trade deficit		
貨幣	monetary		
慣例	conventions		
機構	institution		
重新分配	reallocation		

金融工具	financial instrument		
結算	settlement		
國際收支	balance of payments		
簡要地	briefly		
支出	expenditure		

匯款 Remittance

什麼是匯款

匯款是付款方通過銀行或相關的金融機構將款項轉給收款方的結算方式。匯款一般主要是用來付貨款、預付款、佣金等，是支付款項最簡便的方式之一。傳統的匯款主要有票匯（demand draft，D/D）、信匯（mail transfer，M/T）和電匯（telegraphic transfer，T/T）三種方式。但現今較常用的匯款方式是透過電子網路，或在銀行電匯或以郵件完成。

單元暖身小練習 Warm-up conversation and practice

針對以下每個空格，請選一個最適合的字填入。這是協助你對於本主題進行初步的暖身，以利對於後續的介紹可以更有效率的吸收。

(a) Here (b) exactly (c) legitimate (d) input
(e) remit (f) amounts (g) drawn (h) remitter
(i) exchange (j) beneficiary

Garrett wants to send a remittance to his supplier as the full payments for the merchandises he ordered yesterday.
加勒特想要匯款給他的供應商用來支付他昨天所訂的商品的全額貨款。

Bank teller: Good morning, Sir. May I help you?
（早上好，先生。我可以幫你嗎？）

Garrett: Yes, I would like to ....1.... USD 10,000 to this company in Los Angeles.
（是的，我想匯1萬元美元到洛杉磯的這個公司。）

Bank teller: Sure, may I see your bank account number and your ID first？
（當然，我可以先看一下您的銀行帳號和您的證件嗎？)

Garrett: ....2.... you are.
（在這，給您。）

Bank teller: Thank you. Would the ....3.... be yourself or your company?
（謝謝您。請問匯款人是您自己或您的公司？）

Garrett: It would be my company, Grand Pharmacy Co., Ltd., and here is my company address.
（匯款人將是我的公司，宏昇藥局有限公司，而這是我的公司地址。）

Bank teller: Would the funds be ....4....from your personal account or business account?
請問匯款的金額是從您的個人帳戶或公司賬戶裡出帳呢？

Garrett: It would be from my business account, so I can list it as a ....5.... item for cost of goods sold in the financial statement. And here is the ....6.... of the remittance and its bank account details, including the SWIFT code.
（從我的公司帳戶裡出帳，這樣我就可以將它列在財務報表裡作為合法的銷貨成本的項目之一。這是收款人和收款人銀行帳戶的詳細信息，包括收款銀行的SWIFT代碼。）

Bank teller: Thank you! Would you be paying for the remittance fees or would the beneficiary be responsible for the fees?

（謝謝！請問是由您支付匯款費用或由收款人付費用？）

Garrett: I would be paying for all the fees as I want my supplier to receive USD 10,000....7.....

（我將支付所有的費用，因為我想要我的供應商收到剛好10,000美元。）

Bank teller: No problem. The current ....8....rate to exchange NTD for USD is 30.35, but the best exchange rate I can offer you is NTD 30.30/USD. Are you ok with it?

（沒問題。目前的新台幣兌美元的匯率是30.35，但我可以給您的最好的匯率是新台幣30.30／美元。可以嗎？）

Garrett: Great. Thank you.

（太棒了。謝謝您。）

Bank teller: And there is a remittance fee of NTD 200 from our end and another USD 40 from the paying bank, so the total ....9.... to NTD 304,412. Could you sign on this debit memo, so I can deduct this amount from your business account

（我們這邊的匯款手續費是新台幣200元，而收款行會收40美元，所以匯款總金額為新台幣304,412元。麻煩您簽這個取款憑證，所以我就可以從您的公司帳戶中扣除此金額。）

Garrett: Sure.

（當然。）

Bank teller: Would you like to add any information on the note section for your supplier?
（您想要在備註欄裡填寫任何信息給您的供應商嗎？）

Garrett: Yes, please ....10.... this merchandise order number there for me.
（是的，請幫我在那裡填寫這個商品訂單號。）

Bank teller: Sure. Please first check the details and sign on this remittance form, and I will be getting my supervisor to authorize this wire transfer. I will be right back.
（當然。首先請檢查這個匯款單上細節並且簽字，然後我現在要去請我的主管授權發放此匯款。我馬上就會回來。）

Garrett: Thank you!
（謝謝您！）

答案 ANSWERS:
1.e 2.a 3.h 4.g 5.c 6.j 7.b 8.i 9.f 10.d

認識匯款

匯款是付款方透過金融機構的協助把款項付給收款方的結算方式。一般是用網路，電匯或郵件等方式進行，而且通常是用來付貨款或費用。其他常見的匯款例子有：外籍勞工把薪金匯款給家鄉的父母，消費者郵購外國雜誌、時裝等，先匯款後收貨，以及跨國企業，公司內部，例如分店銷售產品之後，把收入匯兌交回外國的總公司。

傳統的匯款方式可分為信匯、電匯和票匯三種：

信匯（Mail Transfer）

信匯是指匯出銀行應匯款人的申請，將信匯付款委託書寄給收款銀行，授權解付指定的金額給收款人的匯款方式。它的優點是費用較為經濟，但信匯送達的時間較長。

電匯（Telegraphic Transfer）

電匯是指匯出銀行應匯款人的申請，採用SWIFT（環球銀行間金融電訊網路）等電訊方式將電匯付款委託書給收款銀行，指示解付指定的金額給收款人的匯款方式。它的優點是收款人可迅速收到匯款，但費用較高。

票匯（Remittance by Banker's Demand Draft）

票匯是指匯出銀行應匯款人的申請，代匯款人開立銀行即期匯票（Banker's Demand Draft），支付一定金額給收款人的匯款方式。

一般常見匯款名詞解釋

匯款人Remitter	匯出錢的人，一般是進口商。	The party who remits money; it is usually the importer.
收款人 Payee/ Beneficiary	收到款項的人，也叫受益人，一般是出口商。	The party who receives the remittance; it is also known as the beneficiary; it is usually the exporter.
匯出銀行 Remitting bank	辦理匯出款的銀行。	The bank which sends out the remittance.
收款銀行 Receiving/ Beneficiary bank	匯出行委託支付匯款的銀行，一般是收款人的銀行。	The bank which the remitting bank entrusted to release the remittance to the beneficiary; it is generally called the receiving bank or the beneficiary bank.

環球銀行金融電信協會 **SWIFT Codes (Society for Worldwide Interbank Financial Telecommunication)**	SWIFT代碼是銀行識別代碼（BIC）的標準格式，它也作為一個銀行或金融機構的獨特的標識碼。它們是銀行之間轉移資金時使用的，特別是針對國際電匯時。它們也用來傳輸金融機構和銀行之間的消息。它們可以是8或11位數長，8位數字代碼指的是主要辦公室。 SWIFT代碼的格式如下： AAAA BB CC DDD	SWIFT code is a standard format of Bank Identifier Codes (BIC) and serves as a unique identifier for a bank or financial institution. They are used when transferring money between banks, particularly for international wire transfers. They are also used to transmit messages between financial institutions and banks. They can be either 8 or 11 characters long and 8 digits code refers to the primary office. The format of SWIFT Code is as follows; AAAA BB CC DDD
	前4個字母（“AAAA”）代表銀行。只有字母是允許的。 再下來的2個字母（“BB”）代表國家。它使用了ISO 3166-1α-2國家代碼的格式。 接下來的2個字母（“CC”）代表城市。字母和數字是允許的。 最後3個字母（“DDD”）指定分支。這是一個選項的。	The first 4 characters ("AAAA") specify the bank. Only letters are allowed. The next 2 characters ("BB") specify the country. It uses the format of ISO 3166-1 alpha-2 country code. The next 2 characters ("CC") specify the location. Letters and digits are allowed. The last 3 characters ("DDD") specify the branch. This is an optional.

常用業務例句 Common business terms

1. charges 費用
transaction 交易

Garrett: Good afternoon, Sir. I make remittance to my supplier regularly to pay for merchandise for my business, almost every month or so, so I would like to know if there is any way I could save the remittance **charges**?
（下午好，先生。我幾乎每個月固定要匯款給我的供應商來支付我公司的商品，所以我想知道是否有什麼辦法可以節省匯款費用？）

Bank teller: Certainly, I would suggest to set up online banking for your business account, so you can remit the payments online in the future. That would save you at least half of the **transaction** fees and save you a lot of time as well.
（當然，我會建議您為您的公司帳戶設定網上銀行，這樣您今後就可以在　網上匯款。這將節省您至少一半的交易費用，同時也會節省和您大量的時間。）

Garrett: I see. That is a great idea. Thank you! Please set it up for me.
（我明白了。這是一個好主意。謝謝您！請您為我設定。）

2. nowadays 如今
instantaneously 瞬間

Garrett: Could you tell me how much time it takes for my supplier to receive the remittance ?
（您能告訴我需要多少時間我的供應商才能收到匯款？）

Bank Teller: It used to take 3 to 5 business days maybe even a week, but

nowadays most of the time, it takes only 1 business day and sometimes only a few minutes if the remittance is sent from and received by major banks in major cities. When you provide the correct SWIFT cod, it can sometimes arrive **instantaneously**!

（過去需要3至5個工作日甚至於一個星期，但現在大部分只需要1個工作日，如果匯款是從主要的城市的主要銀行發送和接收的，有時只需要幾分鐘的時間。當您提供正確的SWIFT，它有時瞬間就到達！）

3. livelihood 生計
prosperous 富裕的

Garrett: Professor Milton, I recently heard that remittances play an increasingly large role in the economies of many countries. Why is that?

（米爾頓教授，我最近聽說匯款對於許多國家的經濟扮演著越來越重要的角色。這是為什麼呢？）

Professor Milton: Remittances contribute to economic growth and to the livelihoods of less prosperous people. According to World Bank statistics, remittances totaled US$404 billion in 2013, more than 75% of which went to developing countries that involved 192 million migrant workers. For some individual recipient countries, remittances can be as high as a third of their GDP.

（匯款有助於經濟的增長以及比較不富裕的人們的生計。根據世界銀行的統計，在2013年匯款總額高達4.04千億美金，其中75%以上流向了開發中國家並且涉及

1.92億的農民工。對於一些個別的收款國，該匯款額可能高達其國民生產總值的三分之一。）

4. recipient 接收者
major 主要的

Garrett: Professor Milton, could you also tell me which countries are the main source of remittances and which ones are the main remittance **recipient** countries?
（米爾頓教授，您能不能也告訴我哪些國家是匯款的主要來源國，而哪些又是主要的匯款接收國？）

Professor Milton: The US has been the **major** source of remittances globally every year since 1983. Russia, Saudi Arabia, and Switzerland have been the next largest senders of remittances since 2007. As for the recipients, a majority of the remittances from the US have been sent to Asian countries like India, China, the Philippines, Bangladesh, and Pakistan.
（自1983年以來，美國每年一直是全球匯款的領先來源國。自2007年以來，俄羅斯、沙特阿拉伯和瑞士已成為匯款的第二大發送國。 至於接收國，大部分來自美國的匯款都是到亞洲國家，例如印度、中國、菲律賓、孟加拉國和巴基斯坦。）

單元短文 Unit reading

Remittance's contribution to poverty reduction
匯款對扶窮的貢獻

Based on forecast statistics released by a senior official of the U.N. agricultural bank in Feb, 2015, an estimated 230 million migrants will send $500 billion in remittances back to their home countries in 2015. Ten percent of the world's people in the developing countries are directly affected by this money. This amount could play a key role in facilitating food production and solving famine problems affecting 805 million people by allowing families to buy or harvest their own foods.

According to the estimates by United Nations, one ninth of the global population have too little to eat. Approximately 80 percent of the the rural residents receiving remittances do not have access to regular banking services. Therefore, setting up mobile network and other new banking access could help rural residents to use financial services when they collect their remittances, giving them better access to all financial products which could help them improve productivity.

The projection of $500 billion in remittances going to poor countries in 2015 is a significant jump from the $404 billion in such remittances the World Bank recorded in 2013.

The estimation of $500 billion's remittances to poor countries in 2015 is a significant increase from $404 billion in 2013 as recorded by the

World Bank. The global remittances are four times as much as all international development aid provided by wealthy countries.

根據由聯合國農業銀行的一位高級官員在2月2015年發表的統計預測，估計在2015年有2.3億的移民將寄送 5千億美金的匯款匯到他們自己的母國。世界上在開發中國家有百分之十的人們直接受到這筆錢的影響。這筆金額可以通過讓許多家庭能夠買糧食或生產自己的糧食以及消除8.05億人面臨的飢荒問題，而起了關鍵性的作用。

聯合國估計， 全球有九分之一的人口有太少的東西可以吃。據估計，80%的在農村的匯款收款人們無法獲得一般的銀行服務。設定移動網路等連接銀行的新方法，可以幫助農村居民獲得到金融服務，方便他們收取他們的匯款，能運用到金融產品，以用來幫助他們提高生產率。

2015年預計有5千億美金將被匯到貧窮國家，而其與世界銀行在2013年所記錄的4.05千億相較之下是一個很明顯的增長。目前全球的匯款金額是富裕國家所提供的國際發展援助金額的四倍。

常用片語 Common phrases

• draw...from 從……領取	Every month, a lump-sum **is drawn from** my checking account to repay my car loan. （每個月，會有一筆金額從我的支票帳戶領取來償還我的汽車貸款。）
• amount to 合計；成為	I would like to thank my parents for believing that I would **amount to** something great one day! （感謝我的父母相信有一天我會成就偉大的事！）

重點字彙 Important words to know

名詞 Nouns		動詞 Verbs	
匯款	remittance	促進	facilitate
匯款人	remitter	消除	eliminate
匯款銀行	remitting bank	匯（款）	remit
收款人/受益人	payee/beneficiary		
收款銀行	beneficiary bank		
收款銀行	receiving bank		
電報	telegraph		
中介銀行	intermediary bank		
生計	livelihood		
接收者	recipient		
預估	forecast		
途徑	approach		

信託業務 Trust Services

什麼是信託

信託是一種財產管理制度，一般是由「委託人」（提供財產的人）透過「受託人」（銀行）的規劃和安排來確保「受益人」（委託人想照顧的人）權益的制度。通常是針對有需要協助作財產規劃的人，用以幫他們以更有效率而且安全的方式達到財產管理的目標。委託人將財產權移轉給受託人後，受託人須依信託契約所約定的條款照顧受益人之利益或完成特定目的來管理或處分該筆財產。

單元暖身小練習 Warm-up conversation and practice

針對以下每個空格，請選一個最適合的字填入。這是協助你對於本主題進行初步的暖身，以利對於後續的介紹可以更有效率的吸收。

(a) trustee (b) will (c) distributing (d) beneficiary
(e) estate (f) property (g) effective (h) pamphlets
(i) arrangement (j) setting up

Stephen wants to inquire about setting up a trust at the bank.
斯蒂芬想在銀行打聽設立信託的事宜。

Financial advisor: Good morning, Sir. May I help you?
（早上好，先生。我可以幫你嗎？）

Stephen: Yes, many of my friends said they had already set

up trusts for their children, so I would also like to inquire about your bank's trust services.
（我很多朋友說他們已經為自己的小孩設立了信託，所以我也想打聽您們銀行的信託服務。）

Financial advisor: Certainly, please take a seat here.
（當然，請這邊坐。）

Stephen: Could you first tell me what a trust means?
（您能不能先告訴我信託是什麼？）

Financial advisor: Sure, a trust is an ....1.... in which someone's ....2.... or money is legally held or managed by someone or by an organization, namely the ....3.... (such as a bank) , for usually a set period of time for the benefit of the designated ....4.....
（當然，信託是安排讓某人的財產或金錢合法由某人或某組織持有或管理，即受託人（如銀行），通常是在一定的時間段內，為指定受益人的利益而運作。）

Stephen: Why would I need a trust?
（我為什麼需要信託？）

Financial advisor: Setting up your own trust can have significant impacts on your ...5.... planning. It allows you to designate your assets to an individual or organizations, and still retain control over how the assets are managed, whether it's during your lifetime or through your ....6..... It can also be an ....7.... way to provide income for yourself and your future generations, while minimizing taxes, costs and delays when it comes to ....8.... the

assets to your beneficiaries.
（設立信託能在遺產規劃方面發揮重要的作用。它可以讓您轉移您的資產給個人或組織，並保有如何使用資產的控制權，無論是您在世時，或透過您的遺囑（遺囑信託）執行。它也可以是一種為自己和後代子孫提供收入的有效方式，同時降低稅賦、費用和延誤，在涉及到分配資產給您的受益者時。）

Stephen: What can your bank do for me?
（您的銀行能為我做什麼呢？）

Financial advisor: Whether you're ....9.... a trust for yourself or have been named a trustee, we can help protect the interests and requirements of the trust—through our experience and expertise in all aspects of trust management.
（無論您是為您自己設立信託或您已經被命名為信託的受託人，透過我們信託管理各方面的經驗和專業知識，我們可以幫助您保護您的信託的利益和要求。）

Stephen: Thank you. Please give me these ....10.... for me to take home and discuss with my wife before we make decisions.
（謝謝您。請給我這些冊子讓我帶回家和我的妻子進行討論後再作決定。）

Financial advisor: You are welcome, sir.
（不用客氣，先生。）

答案 ANSWERS:

1. i 2. f 3. a 4. d 5. e 6. b 7. g 8. c 9. j 10. h

認識信託業務

信託是指委託人將其財產或財產權利委託給受託人設定信託，而由受託人根據委託人設定信託的規定和目的，由受託人管理和處置該財產或財產權利，從而為委託人和受益人維護利益, 並且同時達到財產保護，資產增值或節稅等功能。

成立信託的兩個主要重點：

1）信託財產的移轉或作其他處分：成立信託的第一個重點，是委託人要將財產權移轉給受託人。信託的標的物，必須是可依金錢計算價值的權利，像現金，股票，不動產等有形的權利，以及專利權，著作權或其他無形的財產權，都是財產權，均可作為信託的標的物；所謂「移轉」，是指發生財產權的直接變動，例如將股票信託移轉登記給受託人；所謂「其他處分」，是指在財產權上設定擔保物權等，例如將其不動產設定抵押權等予受託人。

2）信託財產的管理或處分：成立信託的第二個重點，是受託人依照信託的條款管理或處分信託財產。信託的目的除了保護受益人的權益之外，也要遵照委託人對信託財產管理或處分的本意，例如委託人將其工廠設備信託給受託人，根據信託的本意只能出租而不得出售，如果受託人將工廠設備出售給第三方，則是違反信託本意。

設定信託的相關人

1. 委託人（Client or Principal)：是指設立信託的一方。當委託的一方想為受益的一方作財務規劃，而將資產以信託方式交由信託業者進行管理時，該委託方便成為信託關係的委託人。

2. 受託人（Trustee）：是委託人賦予權力管理委託人資產的另一方。受託

人自委託人手上接受信託財產的移轉，而在法律上成為財產的名義所有人，並且負擔以信託本意來管理信託財產的義務。

3. 受益人（Beneficiary）：是指委託人設立信託來保障其權益的那一方。換而言之，受益人也可以說是委託人所設定的資產信託的繼承人，同時也是委託人想以信託財產加以照顧的對象，可能是子女或其他親人，也可以是自己，或是特定目的下之適當團體或個人。

成立信託的好處

1. 獨立性與安全性：信託資產由於受到「信託法」的保護，不受任何一方的之債權人強制執行或抵銷不屬於該信託財產之債務，因此可以讓委託人的財富不因任何狀況而受到影響。

2. 財產公平分配：委託人可以透過信託來決定所有受益人利益分配的比例，並在受託人的嚴格執行下，避免產生財產分配的問題。

3. 合法節稅：依傳統的贈與方式，每人每年只有一定金額的免稅贈與額度，超出的部份就必須繳納贈與稅；但是透過信託，利用稅法上對於部分信託權利的贈與，以折現方式計算，可以將贈與總額降低，讓財產移轉的稅負減到最少。

4. 財產掌控權：財產交付信託後，委託人仍保有信託財產運用的決定權，亦得隨時終止信託契約，避免將財產贈與子女後子女揮霍無度之困擾。

5. 照顧家族：信託的規劃，可將委託人的財產依照委託人的遺志，使受託人依約管理並分配給委託人的家人與後代子孫。

一般常見信託服務種類解釋

遺產規劃 **Estate planning**	遺產規劃指的是在個人喪失決定能力或者死亡之前進行個人資產的整理和管理計畫，包含贈與遺產給繼承人和遺產稅的結算。遺產規劃一般是由資深的律師協助進行。主要的計畫項目有：擬訂遺囑，以受益人的權益設定信託，為家屬制定一個監護人，選定一個遺囑執行人，決定喪禮的內容，設定每年贈與資產來減少應稅的遺產，選定授權人來管理其他的資產和投資等。	Estate planning refers to organizing and managing a plan for personal assets prior to incapacitation or death, including handling the bequest of assets to heirs and the settlement of estate tax. Estate planning is generally carried out with the assistance of an experienced lawyer.The major items to consider include: draft a will, set up a trust in the interests of the designated beneficiaries, choose a guardian to take care of the family, choose an executor of the will, make decision on funeral related matters, set up annual bequests of assets to heirs to reduce taxable estate, choose power of attorney to manage other assets and investments, etc.

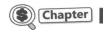

資產管理 **Asset management**	資產管理指的是由金融服務公司對客戶的投資進行管理，而一般通常是由投資銀行來管理。該公司將代表其客戶為客戶投資，並讓他們能夠得到比一般投資者更廣大範圍的各項傳統和新式投資產品的選擇。	Asset management refers to the management of a client's investment by financial services company, and this is usually by an investment bank. The company will invest on behalf of their clients, and allows them to access to a wider range of traditional and alternative investment products than what the average investors would have.
企業信託服務 **Corporate trust services**	企業信託服務讓公司能夠把資產的管理交給其他專業的公司負責。一般來說，銀行和各種類型的金融服務是能夠提供這樣的資產處理的單位。	Corporate trust services allow companies to hand over its assets to another professional company to manage. In general, banks and all types of financial services are entrusted to provide such kind of corporate trust services.
房地產投資信託 **Real Estate Investment Trust (REIT)**	房地產投資信託是一種直接投資在房地產或抵押貸款的證券，並且像股票一樣在主要交易所場交易。房地產投資信託在稅收方面有特殊的優惠，而且通常為投資者提供高流動性的收益。	Real Estate Investment Trust is a type of security that directly invests in real estate or mortgage securities, and trades on major exchanges, just like stocks. REITs are under a special tax scheme, and generally provide returns with high liquidity for investors.

常用業務例句 Common business terms

1. distribute 分發
confidential 機密的
tax-effective 節稅的

Stephen: Could you tell me the benefits of setting up a trust?
（您能告訴我設立信託的好處是什麼嗎？）

Financial Advisor: Certainly, setting up a trust ensures your assets are **distributed** to your family, or people you care about, according to your specific wishes, in a **confidential**, **tax-effective** way. The benefits are the following: Provide for yourself, your spouse, children or other minor family members. Protect the future of family members with a physical or mental disability. Donate to a charitable cause. Maintain confidentiality when it comes to your financial affairs. Achieve certain tax advantages.
（當然，設立信託確保您的財產能分給您的家人，或者您關心的人，根據您的具體願望，以保密的、節稅的途徑。設立信託的好處如下：提供給您自己、您的配偶子女或其他未成年人的家庭成員；保護有身體或精神殘疾家庭成員的未來、捐贈給慈善事業、保持涉及到您的財務狀況的機密性達到一定的節稅目的。）

2. assess 評估
capacity 能力

Stephen: What type of people need a trust?

（什麼樣的人需要信託？）

Financial Advisor: Whoever has property management needs can consider to set up a trust. Trust companies charge fees to provide trust services, so those who are interested can **assess** their own financial conditions, such as, the condition of their property and their financial **capacity** ... and so on. We recommend that you contact the bank you are familiar with in advance, and inquire about their trust-related business and relevant handling charges.

（凡有財產管理需要的人，均可以考慮以信託方式辦理。信託業者在辦理信託業務時，會收取一定的手續費用，有心想以信託方式理財的人，可以先就自己的條件預做評估，例如：財產狀況與經濟能力……等。我們建議您事先聯絡熟悉的往來銀行，洽詢信託相關業務的處理方式和收費標準。）

3. **security** 保障
regulations 規範
inevitably 不可避免地

Stephen: What kind of **security** do I get by setting up a trust thorough the trust company?

（透過信託業者辦理信託，有什麼保障？）

Financial Advisor: If the trustee of your trust is a trust company, it is under the Trust Enterprise Act **regulations** and the supervision of the competent authorities, so your property is more secure. And now the trust companies are usually the banks, so if your assets are handled by professional financial experts it would better ensure that the purpose of your trust is achieved. If there are several types of assets involved, the process is **inevitably** complicated, so it would be better to achieve a multiplier effect by having the bank's trust division manage and act for you.

（信託的受託人如果是信託業者，則是由信託業法規範及主管機關監督，您的財產將會更有保障。而且目前信託業通常是銀行，交由這些專業的金融專家為您進行資產管理，更能確保您的信託目的的達成。如果您的資產項目眾多，處理過程勢必複雜，交由銀行信託業者管理處分的話，您更能達到事半功倍的效果。）

4. qualities 特質
administer 採取行動
empathetic 同理心

Stephen: What are the **qualities** of a good trustee I should look for?

（那些是我所該尋找的一個好的受託人的特質？）

Financial Advisor: A good trustee should be someone who knows trust laws well, has professional experiences with trusts, can **administer** and manage trust reliably on an ongoing basis, has good integrity, can maintain **empathetic** relationships with beneficiaries, understands the complexity involving investment of trust assets, can be available when needed by beneficiaries.

（一個好的受託人應該是熟知信託法，具備信託方面的專業經驗，能夠持續不斷的可靠地執行和管理信託，具有誠信，能夠與受益人維持有同理心的關係，了解投資信託資產的複雜性，以及能夠在受益人需要時投入時間協助。）

單元短文 Unit reading

5 Questions You Should Pay Attention to in Estate Planning

您在遺產規劃時所要注意的五個事項

There is no perfect estate plan, as we can't plan for everything, but if we take some time to think about the most important things, plan for them and double check that the right people are responsible for the right tasks, it can go a very long way in the end. Here are a few estate planning questions we should pay attention to:

1）Are we too young to start planning?

If we wind up in the hospital with difficulty to communicate, we would wish we had designated a Power of Attorney to decide on our treatment or at least write down how we prefer to be taken care of at the end of our life.

2）Keeping our will a secret?

In most cases, estate planners recommend telling our family exactly what they can expect before we pass away.

3）Are we leaving too much money to the wrong people?

Using a trust can be a smart way to leave money to our relatives, since it is administered by a trustee who must distribute the cash exactly how and when we tell them to.

4）Forgetting to minimize estate taxes? One way experts recommend getting around high estate taxes is to carefully plan ahead which assets we will leave to certain family members and friends.

5）Remember to update our plan along the way? Life is far from predictable, which means our estate plan, like any financial plan, should be updated as our financial and personal circumstances change. It is highly recommended that we go to a professional to help draft and review our estate plan as needed.

世上沒有完美的遺產規劃，因為我們無法為每一件事做規畫，但如果我們花一些時間來做最重要的大事，仔細的規劃它們並且確認正確的人負責正確的事情，最後就可以起很大的作用。下面是一些我們必須注意的有關遺產規劃的問題，：

1）我們現在就規劃是否還太年輕？

如果我們最後進了醫院而且再也無法與人溝通，我們就會希望我們早已經指定了授權人來代我們決定如何治療或者至少記下我們希望在我們的生命接近終點時如何被照顧。

2）把我們的遺囑視為秘密？

在大多數情況下，遺產規劃師建議我們告訴我們的家人，在我們過世之後，他們可以期待得到什麼。

3）我們是否留下太多現金給錯的人？

設立信託可能是一個把錢留給親戚的聰明辦法，因為它是由受託人必須依照我們所告訴的方式和時間來分配現金的管理人。

4）忘記儘量降低遺產稅？

專家推薦對抗高額遺產稅的方法之一，就是要儘早認真規劃未來我們會留給家人和朋友的資產。

5）記得隨時修改我們的規劃？

人生是很難預測的，這意味著我們的遺產規劃，就如同任何的財務計劃，必須因應我們的財務和個人情況的變化而作更新。強烈的建議我們尋求專業的協助來起草和複審我們的遺產規劃。

常用片語 Common phrases

- be named as... 被命名為
  Trust companies **are** often **named as** the executors in people's wills and testaments.
  （信託公司時常被命名為人們的遺囑執行人。）

- engage in 從事，進行
  Stephen **is** good at **engaging in** conversations with strangers.
  （斯蒂芬善於與陌生人進行交談。）

重點字彙 Important words to know

名詞 Nouns／形容詞 Adjectives		動詞 Verbs	
信託	trust	解決	settle (claims)
委託人	principal	交代	account for
受託人	trustee	分配	distribute
受益人	beneficiary	結構	structure
遺產規劃	estate planning	遺囑認證的	probate
信託服務	trust services	捐贈	donate
指定的	designated	評估	assess
小冊子	pamphlet	修改	edit
執行人	executor		
代表	representative		
遺囑	will／testament		
遺產稅	inheritance taxes		
監護人	guardian		
保護人	conservator		
保管	safekeeping		
信託的	fiduciary		
破產	bankruptcy		
理財顧問	financial advisor		

保管業務 Custody Services

什麼是保管業務

保管業務是指當金融機構（保管人）持有幫客戶保管的資產和證券（以電子或實物形式），以盡量減少資產和證券被盜或丟失的風險。除了保管之外，保管人還提供其他各種服務，包括帳戶管理、交易結算、代收股息和利息、稅務服務和外匯管理。各保管人所收取的費用不同，一般取決於客戶所期望的服務，而保管費用一般是基於所保管的資產的總價值按季度收取。

單元暖身小練習 Warm-up Conversation and Practice

針對以下每個空格，請選一個最適合的字填入。這是協助你對於本主題進行初步的暖身，以利對於後續的介紹可以更有效率的吸收。

(a) sales　(b) prepare　(c) activities　(d) appropriate
(e) Absolutely　(f) behalf　(g) available　(h) investment
(i) charge　(j) authority

Jessica wants to know the types of custody services available at her bank.
傑西卡想要知道她的銀行有那些保管業務。

Financial Planner: Good morning, Madam. May I help you?
（早安，女士，我可以幫您嗎？）

Jessica: Yes, I heard that many types of custody services are ....1..... here. Could you tell me what they are?
（是的，我聽説您們這裡有多種類型的保管服務。您能告訴我是哪些嗎？）

Financial Planner:....2...., our bank can act as a custodian, also known as an agent, to exercise legal ....3.... over the financial assets of an individual or company.
（絕對的，我們的銀行可以作為保管人，也被稱為代理人，對個人或公司的金融資產行使法定權力。）

Jessica: How does it work?
（那是如何運作的？）

Financial Planner: A custodian usually deals with various ....4...., including safekeeping equities and bonds, settling purchases and....5.... , recording and reporting the status of all assets, taking care of tax compliance and reporting, and managing the client's accounts and transactions. For example, a bank may act as a custodian for a client's ....6.... activities, including transferring funds to brokerage accounts, looking for ....7.... investment alternatives, instructing brokers to buy or sell securities, overseeing the investment activities within the account, and reporting account activity to the client. The custodian may also ....8.... the tax filings on behalf of the client, based on the activities within the account.

（保管人通常會處理各式各樣的活動，包括保管股票和債券、結算買入和賣出、紀錄和報告資產的狀況、負責符合稅務要求和報告，以及管理客戶的帳戶和交易。例如，銀行可以作為客戶的投資活動的保管人，包含將資金轉入經紀帳戶、尋找合適的投資選項、指示經紀人買入或賣出證券、監督該帳戶內的投資活動，並向客戶報告帳戶的活動。保管人也可以根據帳戶內的活動，代表客戶準備必要的稅務申報。）

Jessica: Can your bank be anyone's custodian?
（您的銀行可以作任何人的保管人嗎？）

Financial Planner: Certainly, in addition to acting on ....9....of people of legal age, custodians may be appointed to hold control of assets of a minor or an incapacitated adult.
（當然，除了作法定年齡的人的代表之外，託管人可以被任命代表未成年人或無行為能力的成年人持有資產的控制權。）

Jessica: Who else offers similar custody services ?
（還有誰提供類似的保管服務？）

Financial Planner: The custodian role is often held by banks, law firms, or accounting firms which usually ....10.... additional fees for the services.
（保管人的角色往往是由銀行，律師事務所或會計師事務所扮演的，而他們通常收取額外的服務費用。）

Jessica: I see. Thank you. Now I have some idea what custody services mean.
（我明白了。謝謝您。現在，我有一點概念保管業務代表什麼了。）

Financial Planner: You are welcome!
（不客氣！）

答案 ANSWERS:

1.g 2.e 3.j 4.c 5.a 6.h 7.d 8.b 9.f 10.i

認識保管業務

一般大眾所知道的保險箱業務只是（銀行所提供的保管業務）其中的一小塊。大部分銀行真正的保管業務包含受託保管證券投資信託基金及其他各項保管業務。

常見的銀行保管業務如下：

國內基金保管——國內基金保管主要是用來服務國內的證券投資信託公司。服務的內容包含辦理證券投資信託公司委託銀行保管之證券投資信託基金之證券開戶，買賣交割，交易確認，投資證券保管，庫存資產管理，買入證券之權利行使，稅捐申報等各項事宜。

全權委託保管——主要是服務自然人或法人的投資者。服務內容主要是辦理自然人或法人的投資者委託銀行保管之投資資產之證券開戶，買賣交割，交易確認，投資證券保管，庫存資產管理，買入證券之權利行使，稅捐申報等各項事宜。

外資保管——主要是服務境外外國機構投資人，境外華僑及外國自然人等外資。而服務的內容主要是由銀行代理外資向台灣證券交易所辦理投資我國有價證券登記，及辦理後續國內證券買賣開戶，認購股份申請，買入證券之權利行使，結匯之申請，交易確認，買賣交割，投資證券保管，繳納稅捐及資料申報等事宜。

投資型保單保管——主要是服務保險公司。而服務內容主要是辦理由保險公司（委託人）之投資型保單所投資之證券投資信託基金受益憑證，共同信託基金受益憑證，政府債券，銀行定期存單或其他經核定之投資標的，委託由銀行辦理下單，買賣交割，保管及款項匯付等各項事宜。

有價證券保管——主要是服務證券商，票券商，公債交易商，壽險業等法人。而服務內容只要是辦理法人委託銀行保管之國內有價證券（包括公司債，金融債券，中央登錄債券等有價證券）之買賣交割，存提等作業。

擔任海外存託憑證保管機構——主要是服務證券交易所上市或在證券商營業處所買賣之公開發行公司。而服務內容為代為保管存託憑證所表彰之股票，依存託機構指示於台灣股票市場代為賣出股票，或依投資人、其代理人或存託機構指示買入股票，並對上開股票行使股東權利，並協助存託機構與發行公司核符存託憑證所表彰之股票餘額與實際集保股數餘額。

一般常見保管服務內容解釋

代理記帳 **Bookkeeping**	代理記帳是以系統的方式以及按照時間順序來紀錄所有財務交易的行為。	Bookkeeping is the an act of keeping the records of all financial transactions according to a systematic way and in a timely order.

代理投票 **Proxy voting**	代理投票是一種投票的形式，由機構的成員授權給同一機構的其他成員在他們缺席時代理他們投票。接受委託投票權的人被稱為“代理人”，而指定代理人的人被稱為“授權人”。	Proxy voting is a type of voting whereby some members of an organization may delegate their voting power to other members of the organization to vote in their absence. A person who is delegated to vote is called a "proxy" and the person delegating the proxy is called a "principal".
現金管理 **Cash management**	現金管理指的是現金的收集，處理和使用的。它也涉及到評估市場流動性，現金流和投資。在銀行業的現金管理，或稱財務管理，指的是有關提供現金流給大型企業客戶為主的服務。	Cash management refers to the collection, handling, and usage of cash. It also involves assessing market liquidity, cash flow, and investments. In banking, cash management, or treasury management, is a term for the services related to cash flow offered primarily to larger business customers.
證券借貸 **Securities lending**	證券借貸指的是由一方把債券借貸給另一方。它一般會要求債務人以價值等於或大於所借的證券的現金、政府債券，或信用狀作為借貸證券的抵押品。	Securities lending refers to the lending of securities by one party to another. It requires that the borrower provides the lender with collateral, in the form of cash, government securities, or a letter of credit of value equal to or greater than the loaned securities.

	至於貸款的付款方式，雙方會協商以所借出證券價值的百分比來計算年度收費。證券的主要債權人包括共同基金，保險公司，養老金計劃和其他大型投資組合。	As payment for the loan, the parties negotiate a fee, quoted as an annualized percentage of the value of the loaned securities. Key lenders of securities include mutual funds, insurance companies, pension plans and other large investment portfolios.

常用業務例句 Common business terms

1. minor 未成年人
custodian 保管人
relinquish 放棄；交回

Jessica: Who else can be the custodian for the **minor**?
（還有誰可以成為未成年人的保管人？）

Financial Planner: Any adult with legal status may act as the **custodian** for a minor. An adult or parent sets up the account on behalf of the minor and serves as the custodian, retaining the legal authority and direction over the custodial account. When the minor becomes an adult, the custodian **relinquishes** his or her authority over the account.
（任何具有合法身分的成年人都可以作為未成年人帳戶的保管人。成人或家長可以代表未成年人設立帳戶，並作為其帳戶的保管人，維持對所保管帳戶的法律權力和方向。當未成年人成為成年人之後，原保管人就放棄他或她對所保管帳戶的權力。）

2. absentee 不在場
substantial 大量
compliance 法規遵從

Jessica: Typically, who can take advantage of your custodian services?
（通常情況下，什麼樣的人需要信託？）

Financial Planner: Custodian services are useful for "**absentee**" owners who are either not interested or unable to be involved in the day-to-day management activities of their accounts. People who need help with more complex transactions, management of substantial assets, timely reporting and compliance, and tax management strategies can also use custodian services.
（保管業務對於不感興趣的或者不能夠參與他們的帳戶每天日常管理活動的"不在場"的帳戶持有者是有用的。需要協助來處理比較複雜的交易，大量資產的管理，及時投資報告和法規遵從，和稅務管理策略的人也適用信託服務。）

3. safekeeping 妥善保管
proxy 代理
reclaim 退回

Jessica: What kind of custody services does your bank provide?
（您們銀行提供什麼樣的保管業務？）

Financial Planner: Our custody business includes a range of security

services, such as **safekeeping** and settlement, reporting, corporate actions, dividends collection and distribution, **proxy** voting, tax **reclaim** services, fund administration and providing market news and information.
（我們的保管業務包含了一系列的安全性服務，包括保管和結算、資產報告、企業行為、股利徵收和分配；代理投票、退稅服務、資金管理和提供市場新聞和信息。）

4. outstanding 脫穎而出
devoted 專注的
sub-custodian 附屬保管人（在某銀行沒有業務的國家代表某銀行提供保管服務的機構）

Jessica: What makes you custody services **outstanding**?
（是什麼讓您們的保管業務脫穎而出？）

Financial Planner: We understand that **devoted** investment professionals constantly need to lower risk, improve competitiveness and benefit from increased operational efficiencies. In addition, the risk management of our **sub-custodians** has always been of key significance to us as a global custodian. We place a strong emphasis on the selection and ongoing monitoring of our sub-custodian network to ensure appropriate monitoring is in place to continually assess and review the performance of each of our sub-custodians and for the safeguarding of clients' assets.
（我們了解，專注的投資專業人士需要不斷降低風險、提高競爭力以及從增加運營效率中獲益。此外，我們的附屬保管人的風險管理，對我們作為一個全球託管人一直是至關重要。我們強調慎選和持續監督我們的附屬保管人的網絡，以確保適當的監督已到位，以便不斷評估和審查我們的每個附屬保管人的績效和客戶資產的保護。）

單元短文 Unit reading

Don't let investments fees eat away our investment returns!

別讓投資費用吞噬掉我們的投資回報！

In an environment where a diversified portfolio is only expected to offer a return of 6% annually, any fees will have a significant impact on our investment results.

To show this, here's an example: If we invested $10,000 in a fund that produced a 10% annual return before expenses and had annual operating expenses of 1.5%, then after 20 years we would have roughly $49,725. But if the fund had expenses of only 0.5%, then we would end up with $60,858. That's a huge difference!

Investment-related fees come in the following categories:

1) Management/advisory fees and commissions are those we expect to pay for someone to manage our investment, and they including the management fee (0.05% – 0.50% for ETFs, and 0.40% – 1.50% for mutual funds) on ETFs (Exchange Traded Funds) and mutual funds, the advisory fees (0.25% – 1.5% of our account holding value) ,and the commissions ($0.10－$8.95 per share) we pay our brokers at traditional brokerage firms.

2) Administration charges include wire transfer fees ($25 – $40 per transfer), record keeping fees ($25 - $90 per year), and custodian Fees ($0 – $95 per year for accounts below the minimum.),

3) Other charges include the lost spread on our outstanding cash balance as the brokerage firms make returns on our cash balances but give us very little interest back.

在一個風險分散的多元投資組合每年只預計有6%的回報的環境中，任何費用都會對我們的投資結果有顯著的影響。

為了說明這一點，這裡有一個例子：如果我們投資了10,000 美金在一個扣掉費用前有10%的年收益的基金，而每年的運營費用是1.5%，那麼20年後我們將有大約49,725美元。但是，如果該基金只有0.5%的年費用，那麼我們最終就會有60,858美元。這是一個多麼巨大的差別啊！

與投資相關的費用有下列三種類型：

1）管理費／諮詢費和是那些我們僱人來管理我們的投資而預期要支付的費用，而它們包含管理年費（指數股票型基金每年收取帳戶價值的0.05%—0.50%，共同基金每年收取帳戶價值的 0.40%—1.50%），諮詢費用（帳戶價值的 0.25%—1.5%），和我們付給傳統經紀公司仲介的佣金（每股收取 0.10—8.95美金）。

2）行政費用包含電匯費（每次電匯時收25—40美金），記錄保存費（每年收　25—90美金）和保管費（每年向帳戶餘額低於最低限額的投資者收取 0—95美金）。

3）其他費用包含我們帳上的現金餘額所損失的利差，因為證券商拿我們帳面上的現金去投資並且賺取利潤，但是給我們的利息非常低。

常用片語 Common phrases

- take advantage of Investors can **take advantage of** banks' custody services to take care of their investments.
  利用 （投資者可以利用銀行的保管業務來打理他們的投資。）

- act on behalf of Custodians **act on behalf of** their clients.
  代表……行動 （監護人代表他們的客戶採取行動。）

重點字彙 Important words to know

名詞 Nouns		動詞 Verbs	
保管	custody	代表	delegate
保管人	custodian	放棄，交回	relinguish
權力	authority	回收	reclaim
股票	equities	奉獻	dedicate
債券	bonds	減低	mitigate
稅務合規定	tax compliance	吞噬	eat away
報稅	tax filling	評估	assess
未成年人	minor		
無行為能力的	incapacitated		
代理	proxy		
妥善保管	safekeeping		
財務	treasury		
回扣	rebate		

金融小百科 1 財經英文數值表達要點
Financial Tips (1) - Highlights of Financial and Economical Numerical Expressions in English

基數（Cardinal numbers）

0	**zero**	**10**	**ten**		
1	one	11	eleven		
2	two	12	twelve (一打 a dozen)	20	twenty
3	three	13	thirteen	30	thirty
4	four	14	fourteen	40	forty
5	five	15	fifteen	50	fifty
6	six	16	sixteen	60	sixty
7	seven	17	seventeen	70	seventy
8	eight	18	eighteen	80	eighty
9	nine	19	nineteen	90	ninety

在 21 到 99 的數字當中，當個位數字不是零時，通常要用連字符（－）分隔兩個數字的單詞。

21	**twenty-one**	56	fifty-six	82	eighty-two
26	twenty-six	68	sixty-eight	98	ninety-eight
33	thirty-three	78	seventy-eight		

英語中的「百」和「千」是完全規則的，無論它前面的數目是多少，「百」和「千」保持在單數形式。

100	**one hundred**	...	...
200	two hundred	900	nine hundred

1,000	**one thousand**
2,000	two thousand
...	...
10,000	ten thousand
11,000	eleven thousand
...	...
20,000	twenty thousand
21,000	twenty-one thousand
30,000	thirty thousand
75,000	seventy-five thousand
100,000	one hundred thousand
999,000	nine hundred and ninety-nine thousand nine hundred ninety-nine thousand
1,000,000	one million
10,000,000	ten million

在美國，當四位數字裡的十位數和個位數不同時是 0 時，數值的表示經常使用的「百」的倍數，結合十位和個位的數字：“1,001＝one thousand one”，“1,103＝eleven hundred three”，“1,225＝twelve hundred twenty-five”，“4,042＝four thousand forty-two”，或“9,999＝ninety-nine hundred ninety-nine”。在英國，這種用法只有針對的 1,000 和 2,000 之間 100 的倍數（如：1,500＝fifteen hundred)，但不適用於高於 2,000 的數字。

在美國，當四位數字裡的十位數和個位數都不是 0 時，他們常用不説「千」或「百」，而四個數字分成兩組兩位數字來發音，如果十位數是 0 時，則加入“0＝oh”，oh 是用來代表零的。例如：“2,659＝twenty-six fifty-nine”或“4,105＝forty-one oh five”。這種用法可能是由年份的表示法延伸來的；如：“1981 年＝nineteen-eighty-one”，或者是美國的電話號碼系統的用法。但是當數字小於 2500 時，會避免這種表示法以免和上下文的時間混淆。如：“1010＝ten ten”或“1204＝twelve oh four”。

	常見英式英語	常見美式英語	常見英式英語
	“How many balls do you have?”	“What is your postal code?”	“Which bus goes to the city hall?”
101	“A hundred and one.”	“One-oh-one.”	“One-oh-one.”
109	“A hundred and nine.”	“One-oh-nine.”	“One-oh-nine.”
110	“A hundred and ten.”	“One-ten.”	“One-one-oh.”
117	“A hundred and seventeen.”	“One-seventeen.”	“One-one-seven.”
120	“A hundred and twenty.”	“One-twenty.”	“One-two-oh.” or “One-two-zero.”
152	“A hundred and fifty-two.”	“One-fifty-two.”	“One-five-two.”
208	“Two hundred and eight.”	“Two-oh-eight.”	“Two-oh-eight.”
334	“Three hundred and thirty-four.”	“Three-thirty-four.”	“Three-three-four.”

中間數不同的讀法取決於它們的用途，用於計數的數字或者用在標記時。備註：當開支票時，100 總是被寫為“one hundred”，而從來不會寫為“a hundred”。

在美式英語中，一般不會用“and”這個詞來表示數字的整數部分，所以在十位數和個位數時是不使用的。只有在表示複合數字時才作為一個口頭分隔音。因此，“373”不是“three hundred and seventy-three”，而是“three hundred seventy-three”。

當數字大於百萬時，有兩種不同的系統。

		常見的美式英文，但現在也常見於英式英文	英式英文，但是現在漸漸少用了
1,000,000	一百萬	one million	one million
1,000,000,000	十億	one billion a thousand million	one milliard a thousand million
1,000,000,000,000	一萬億	one trillion a thousand billion	one billion a million million
1,000,000,000,000,000	一千萬億	one quadrillion a thousand trillion	one billiard a thousand billion
1,000,000,000,000,000,000	一百萬的三次方	one quintillion a thousand quadrillion	one trillion a million billion
1,000,000,000,000,000,000,000	一千的七次方	one sextillion a thousand quintillion	one trilliard a thousand trillion

這裡有一些大的複合數字的美式英語寫法和讀法：

	寫法	讀法
1,200,000	1.2 million	one point two million
3,000,000	3 million	three million
250,000,000	250 million	two hundred fifty million
6,400,000,000	6.4 billion	six point four billion
23,380,000,000	23.38 billion	twenty-three point three eight billion

乘積的副詞（Multiplicative adverbs）

one time	once
two times	twice
three times	thrice

負數（Negative numbers）

負數的表示方式為在相應的正數前面加“minus”或“negative”。因此-8.2 是“minus eight point two”或“negative eight point two”。對於溫度，美國人通常說“below”作為“below zero”的縮寫，所以-5° 的溫度是“five below”（與此相反，例如：2 度就說”two above”）。

序數（ Ordinal numbers）

序數是指在數字一系列上的位置。常見的序數包括：

0th	zeroth	10th	tenth		
1st	first	11th	eleventh		
2nd	second	12th	twelfth	20th	twentieth
3rd	third	13th	thirteenth	30th	thirtieth
4th	fourth	14th	fourteenth	40th	fourtieth
5th	fifth	15th	fifteenth	50th	fiftieth
6th	sixth	16th	sixteenth	60th	sixtieth
7th	seventh	17th	seventeenth	70th	seventieth
8th	eighth（只有一個 t）	18th	eighteenth	80th	eightieth
9th	ninth（沒有 e）	19th	nineteenth	90th	ninetieth

序數如第 21、第 33 等，都是由一個十位數的基數與一個序號單元組合而成。

21th	**twenty-first**	**65th**	**sixty-fifth**
26th	twenty-sixth	78th	seventy-eighth
33th	thirty-third	84th	eighty-fourth
58th	fifty-eighth	99th	ninety-ninth

10%
20%
40%

2 Chapter

Investment
投資理財篇

股票 Stocks

什麼是股票

股票是有價證券的一種。擁有股票就代表擁有公司的所有權，並且對公司的資產和部分盈餘有權利分享。股票的擁有者（股東）同時也要承擔公司運作所帶來的風險。它主要有兩種類型：普通股（Common Share）和特別股（Preferred Share）。普通股的股東在股東大會上有投票權和也可以獲得股息。特別股一般沒有投票權，但對資產和盈餘比普通股有更高的優先權。

單元暖身小練習 Warm-up conversation and practice

針對以下每個空格，請選一個最適合的字填入。這是協助你對於本主題進行初步的暖身，以利對於後續的介紹可以更有效率的吸收。

(a) alternatives (b) fluctuate (c) objective (d) potential
(e) saving up (f) brokerage (g) duration (h) comply
(i) capitalization (j) tolerate

Linda wants to invest in stocks.
琳達想要投資股票。

Investment Specialist: Good morning, Madam, may I help you?
（早安，女士，我可以幫您嗎？）

Linda: Yes, I would like to open a ....1.... account to buy and sell stocks. What kinds of accounts

do you have?
（是的，我想開一個經紀帳戶買賣股票。您有什麼樣的帳戶？）

Investment Specialist: Before I explain the types of accounts we have here, I would like to ask you a few KYC (Know Your Client) questions to ....2.... with the bank regulations. You wouldn't mind, would you?
（在我解釋我們這裡的帳戶類型之前，我想請教您幾個（了解您的客戶）問題，以符合銀行的規定。您不介意吧？）

Linda: No problem.
（沒問題。）

Investment Specialist: Have you ever invested in stocks before?
（您以前有投資過股票嗎？）

Linda: No, this is my first time.
（沒有，這是我第一次投資。）

Investment Specialist: What is your main investment....3.... ?
（您投資的主要目標是？）

Linda: Well, my term deposit doesn't give me very high interest, so I was looking for ....4.... which would help me earn more return.
（嗯，我的定存利息並不高，所以我一直在尋找能夠讓我獲得更多的回報的替代方案。）

Investment Specialist: I see. How long are you planning to invest in stocks? Will you be needing the money invested very soon?

（明白了。您計劃投資股票多久？您將會很快需要所投資的錢嗎？）

Linda: I am ....5....for an apartment, so I probably won't need this money within five years.
（我正在為買房子而存錢，所以我五年之內可能不會需要用到這筆錢。）

Investment Specialist: Good. Then how much risk can you....6.... ? The prices of stocks ....7.... over time, so do you consider yourself a conservative investor, or an aggressive investor? Or somewhere in the middle?
（好的。那麼您能承受多大的風險？股票的價格會隨著時間上下波動，所以您認為自己是保守的投資者，還是激進型的投資者？或者是中庸的？）

Linda: I think I can take some risk. I understand that stocks that have ....8.... for higher return may also be more risky. I think my heart is strong enough to bear with some short-term fluctuations.
（我想我可以承受一些風險。據我所知，有高回報潛力的股票也可能會有較高的風險。我覺得我的心臟應該夠強到足以承受一些短期波動。）

Investment Specialist: Good. Although you are willing to take some risk, the ....9..... you will invest in is only mid-term and not long term. If you insist on investing in stocks, I would suggest that you choose stocks carefully. You might also want to consider the blue-chip stocks.

（好的。雖然您願意承擔一定的風險，您的投資期間只是中期的，而不是長期的。如果您堅持投資股票，我建議您謹慎選擇股票。您可能也會想要考慮藍籌股。）

Linda: What are blue-chip stocks?

（什麼是藍籌股？）

Investment Specialist: They are stocks of a company that has a long track record of profitable financial results, and usually has a market ....10.... of millions. It is also often one of the top players in its industry. Blue-chip companies are also known for having paid stably increasing dividends over the years.

（他們是一個長期以來在財務上有獲利記錄的公司股票，並且通常擁有數以百萬的市值。它們也常常是行業裡的佼佼者。藍籌公司一般也被認知為多年來紅利持續穩定增長的公司。）

Linda: Ok. Thank you for your advice.

（好的。謝謝您的建議。）

答案 ANSWERS:

1.f 2.h 3.c 4.a 5.e 6.j 7.b 8.d 9.g 10.i

什麼是股票

最早的股票制度源於1602年的荷蘭東印度公司。當時該公司在每次出海前向投資人集資，航程完成後再將投資人的出資以及該航次的利潤還給投資者。1613年起該公司改為每四個航次才分派一次利潤。這就是股東和派息的前身。

股票是有價證券的一種。擁有股票就代表擁有公司的所有權，並且對公司的資產和部分盈餘有權利分享。股票的擁有者（股東）同時也要承擔公司運作所帶來的風險。它主要有兩種類型：普通股和特別股。普通股的股東在股東大會上有投票權和也可以獲得股息。特別股一般沒有投票權，但對資產和盈餘比普通股有更高的優先權。

台灣的股票分類

－ 依股東的權利，可分為普通股（Common）和特別股（Preferred）。

－ 依股票的狀況，可分為普通股和全額交割股。

－ 按交易的方式，可分為上市股票、上櫃股票、興櫃股票（即將上市上櫃的股票）和未上市上櫃股票。

中國大陸的股票分類

－ 依票面形式，可分為記名股票，無記名股票和有面額股票。

－ 依上市交易所和買賣主體，可分為A股（上海和深圳）、B股（上海和深圳，其中上海B股以美元結算；深圳B股以港元結算）、H股（大陸的公司在香港聯交所交易）和紅籌股（在香港或境外登記註冊，但實際經營活動在中國大陸的公司）。

－ 依持股的主體，在2005-2006年的股權分置改革以前，可分為國家股、法人股和個人股。

－ 依公司的業績，可分為績優股和垃圾股。

－ 依股東的權利，分為優先股和普通股。

－ 依流通的狀況，分為流通股和非流通股。

國際股票的分類

— 依權利及分紅情況，可分為優先股、普通股（A股）、B股。

普通股和特別股的最大分別是：

1）普通股必須在公司有盈餘的時候才能分配股利，但特別股則視公司規定而決定。

2）普通股在開會時有表決權；而特別股沒有表決權。

3）當公司破產清算時，特別股對剩餘財產的分配權優於普通股的股東。

另外，還有增資股，所謂增資股就是公司增加新資金時所發行的股票。

擁有普通股的權利和優點包括

1）有權獲得普通股股利

2）股利收入和資本收益有稅務減免優惠

3）流動性高 - 可以很容易買賣持有的股份

股票交易一般以委託方式進行，而委託可分為下列幾種形式：

1）填交易單委託 — 填寫並遞交交易單委託轉移股權。

2）電話委託 —用電話委託仲介轉移股權。

3）委託機委託 — 用特殊的交易所接入設備委託轉移股權。

4）網上委託 — 用股票軟體委託中介機構對股權進行轉移。

股票交易費用一般包含託管費、佣金、印花稅（交易稅）、過戶費（手續費）和轉託管費等。

一般常見股票術語解釋

初次公開發行 **Initial Public Offerings (IPO)**	首次公開發行是指私人公司第一次向大眾開放出售公司股票。首次公開發行可以是由小的公司尋求擴大資本而進行的，也可以是大型私人公司希望公開上市而發行的。	IPO refers to when a private company sells its shares to the public for the first time. IPO may be conducted by small companies to expand their capital, or by large-scale private companies that may wish to issue publicly traded shares.
開盤價 **Opening price**	開盤價是有價證券在交易市場開市時的第一筆買賣成交價格。	Opening price refers to the first trading price of a security when the stock exchange opens on a given trading day.
收盤價 **Closing price**	收盤價是指有價證券在某個交易日於交易所所成交的最後一筆交易的價格。	Closing price refers to the final price a security trades at the exchange on a given trading day.
壓力線 **Resistance level**	壓力線是技術分析中所用的一個術語，它指的是一個有價證券很少能夠超越的價格上限。	Resistance level is a term used in technical analysis, and it refers to a certain price ceiling that a security rarely rises above.
支撐線 **Support level**	支撐線是技術分析的一個名詞，而它是指有價證券的價格如果要低於這個價格點應是比較困難的，也就是說，在這個價格點上的需求多於供給。	Support level is a term used in technical analysis, and it refers to a certain price level that a security rarely falls below it. That means at that price level the demand for the security is greater than its supply.

K線圖 **Candlestick charts**	K線圖是一種用來標示有價證券在一定的時間的開盤價、收盤價、最高價和最低價的方法。白色方框表示證券價錢向上移動的趨勢，而黑色方框代表證券價錢向下移動的趨勢。方框的頂部和底部代表的是開盤價或收盤價。	Candlestick chart is a method used to chart a security's opening price, closing, highest price and lowest price during a given period. The white boxes represent upward movements of the security, and the black boxes represent downward movements of the security. The top and bottom of the boxes are either the opening or closing prices.
美國線 **Open-High-Low-Close chart (OHLC chart)**	美國線是技術分析的圖表，它顯示一個有價證券在一個交易日裡的開盤價、最高價、最低價和收盤價。它是技術分析師用來追蹤證券在短期內的趨勢的圖表。	OHLC Chart is a technical analysis chart, and it shows a security's opening price, the highest price, the lowest, and closing price on a given trading day. It is used by the technical analyst to track the trend of a security in the short term.
牛市 **Bull market**	牛市又稱為多頭市場，指的是有價證券在持續的幾個月或幾年的期間內價格不斷上漲的現象。牛市通常用來形容股市的狀況，但它也可以用來形容其他的市場，如房地產或外匯市場。它的相反是熊市，代表證券價格持續的下跌。	A bull market refers to the phenomenon when securities continue to rise over a period of months or years. Bull is usually used to describe the condition of the stock market, but it can also be used to describe the stock markets. Its opposite is bear market, and it refers to the continuous falling of security prices.

熊市 **Bear market**	熊市，又稱為空頭市場，指的是有價證券在持續的幾個月或幾年的期間內價格不斷下跌的現象。熊市通常用來形容股市的狀況，但它也可以用來形容其他的市場，如房地產或外匯市場。它的相反是牛市，代表證券價格持續的上漲。	A bear market refers to the phenomenon when securities continue to fall over a period of months or years. Bear is usually used to describe the condition of the stock market, but it can also be used to describe the stock markets. Its opposite is bull market, and it refers to the continuous rising of security prices.
多頭 **Bull position or Long position**	多頭是指當投資者普遍認為市場將看好，所以用「買入並持有」的態度，在價格下降時買入並持有等到當價格上升時才賣出。	A bull or long position refers to the phenomenon when investors generally believe that the market will be bullish, so have the "buy and hold" attitude to buy when the prices fall and hold to sell when prices go up.
空頭 **Bear position or Short position**	空頭是當投資者賣出他或她還沒有持有的股票的現象。所賣出的股票必須在出售前借來，並且在約定的日期交付給買方。賣出的股票還是必須買回來平倉。這種情況通常發生在投資者認為股票價格將下降時。	Short position refers to the phenomenon when investors sell the stocks he or she does not own yet. The stocks must be borrowed before they are sold and delivered to the buyer at the agreed time. The stocks sold should be bought back to balance the short position. This usually happens when investors believe the stock price will fall.

指數 **Index**	指數指的是測量經濟或金融市場變化的統計數據，而它往往以一年或一個月裡的百分比變化來表示。指數可以用來測量股票市場、債券市場或商品市場的變化起伏，而以市場價格和加權指數來表示。	Index refers to the statistical measurement of changes in economic or financial markets, and it is usually expressed by percentage change in a year or a month. It can be used to measure the changes in the stock market, bond market or commodity market, and can be expressed by the market price and weighted index.

常用業務例句 Common business terms

1. KYC (Know Your Client) 了解你的客戶
mandate 規定

Linda: What does **KYC** mean? Why is it necessary to answer the KYC questions?
（KYC 代表什麼？為什麼有需要回答 KYC的問題？）

Investment Specialist: KYC means Know Your Client, and it is a client identification program that verifies and maintains records of the identity and address of investors. It is necessary as it is **mandated** by most regulatory authorities when opening a new bank account to buy securities.
（KYC代表著了解您的客戶，這是檢證和維護投資者身份和地址記錄的客戶識別程序。它是必要的，因為它是大多數監管部門對於開設新的銀行帳戶來買賣證券時規定要完成的。）

2. self-directed 自己管理的
broker 經紀

Investment Specialist: Now we have completed the KYC questions; I can explain the types of accounts available for you. Would you like to manage your own account or would you prefer to have your account managed by our **broker**?
（現在，我們已經完成了KYC的問題，我可以為您解釋不同類型的帳戶。您想管理您自己的帳戶，或者您希望由我們的經紀人管理您的帳戶？)

Linda: If I prefer to manage my own account, what type of account should I open?

(如果我比較希望自己管理自己的帳戶，我應該開什麼類型的帳戶？)

Investment Specialist: If that is the case, then we can open a **self-directed** investment account for you.

(如果是這樣的話，我們可以為您開一個自己管理的投資帳戶。)

3. dividend 股利
surplus 盈餘
allocate 分配

Linda: What does **dividend** mean?

(股利代表什麼？)

Investment Specialist: A dividend is a payment paid to a company's shareholders, usually as a distribution of profits. When a company earns a profit or **surplus**, it can either re-invest it back in the business (retained earnings), and pay a portion of the profit as a dividend to its shareholders. Dividend can be paid in cash or by the issuance of shares or share repurchase. A dividend is **allocated** as a fixed amount per share based on the shareholders' shareholding.

(股利是公司付給股東的款，而該款項通常是利潤的分配。當一個公司有額外的利潤或盈餘時，它可以再投入到公司的運作（保留盈餘），並且把盈餘的一小部分作為股利分配給股東。股利可以用現金支付或者用額外的股份或者發行股份回購。股利的分配是以股東的持股作為依據而按每股的固定數額來分配的。）

4. marketability 市場化

Linda: I was told that **marketability** is an advantage of common share ownership, why is that?
（有人告訴我，市場化是擁有普通股股票的優勢，這是為什麼？）

Investment Specialist: Marketability is a measure of the ability of a security to be bought and sold. Marketability is an advantage of common shares because it indicates that the security can be bought and sold easily.
（市場化是一個證券能夠進行買賣的能力的測量。市場化是普通股的優勢，因為它表示該股票可以很容易的買入和賣出。）

單元短文 Unit reading

How Stock Market Bubbles Burst？
股市泡沫如何爆破的？

When people look back and try to think about how the tech bubble and credit bubble burst, they probably only remember the stock market was going straight up to an inflection point then plunging relentlessly.

In reality, the stock price movements weren't that simple and straightforward. When stock market bubbles come to an end, they make wild swings both upwards and downwards. For investors, it's extremely difficult to tell if the market is still in a bubble or if that bubble is in the middle of bursting itself.

Watching the recent volatility we've been experiencing, we can't help but wonder if the stock market is in the process of bursting.

The volatile market movements - sharp plunges and even sharper surges - are just like the movements seen prior to the market tops in 2007 and 2000. It'll be a few months before we can be sure whether or not we've been experiencing the beginnings of a stock market crash.

當大多數人回想而試著去想起科技泡沫和信貸泡沫到底是如何爆破時，他們可能只記得當時股市直線上升到一個轉折點之後就毫不留情的暴跌。

在現實中，股票價格波動並不是那麼簡單和直接。當股市泡沫到了盡頭，它們會向上和向下劇烈的波動。對於投資者來說，非常難分辨到底市場還在泡沫當中或者泡沫正在爆破當中。

看著我們最近已經經歷的波動，我們不禁懷疑股市正瀕臨爆破的階段。

市場狂躁的動向—極速的暴跌和暴漲 - 這就像是在2007年和2000年時在主要市場到頂之前所看到的主要動向。可能還要再幾個月我們才可以確認是否我們已經在經歷股市大跌的前奏。

* **A stock market bubble** refers to when market participants drive stock prices above their value in relation to some system of stock valuation.

* **股市泡沫**指股票交易市場中的股票價格超過其內在的投資價值的現象。

常用片語 Common phrases

- think back 回想
  I began to **think back** which stocks I have invested so far.
  （我開始回想起我有投資過那些股票。）

- go straight up 向前走
  Go straight up this street, you will see the bank on the right.
  （在這條街上向前走，你會看到銀行在右邊。）

重點字彙 Important words to know

名詞 Nouns／形容詞 Adjectives		動詞 Verbs	
股票	stocks	波動	fluctuate
股票	equity	分配	allocate
股份	shares	捕捉	capture
經紀	brokerage	暴跌	plunge
股本	capitalization	激增	surge
普通股	common shares	崩潰	crash
優先股	preferred shares		
KYC（了解你的客戶）	KYC (Know your client)		
規定	regulations		
積極的	aggressive		
保守的	conservative		
IPO（首次公開發行）	IPO (Initial Public Offering)		
壓力線	resistance level		
K線圖	candlestick charts		
股利	dividend		
盈餘	surplus		
市場化	marketability		
波動	volatility		
狂躁的	manic		

債券 Bonds

什麼是債券

債券是一種由投資者借款給企業或政府的債權投資，而貸款的時間是設定好的，而利率可以是浮動的或固定的。企業和政府通常會用債券來籌集資金和資助各種項目和活動。債券的持有人是債券發行人（bond issuer or debtor）的債權人（creditor）。根據發行方不同，債券可分為政府債券、金融債券以及公司債券。

單元暖身小練習 Warm-up conversation and practice

針對以下每個空格，請選一個最適合的字填入。這是協助你對於本主題進行初步的暖身，以利對於後續的介紹可以更有效率的吸收。

(a) maturing	(b) classified	(c) safe	(d) categories
(e) stable	(f) length	(g) taxes	(h) default
(i) issued	(j) maturity		

Erica wants to buy government bonds.
艾瑞卡想要購買政府債券。

Investment Specialist: Good morning, Miss Wang, may I help you?
（早安，王小姐，我可以幫您嗎？）

Erica: Yes, I would like to buy some government bonds. Could you tell me how many kinds

of government bonds are available?
（是的，我想購買一些政府債券。您能告訴我有幾種政府債券可以選擇？）

Investment Specialist: Sure. In general, there are three main ....1.... of government bonds according to the ....2....of time before maturity.
（當然。一般說來，政府債券依到期前的時間長度分三大類。）

Erica: Really? What are they?
（真的嗎？它們是？）

Investment Specialist: Bonds are ....3.... as a type of fixed-income or debt security. When the bonds are ....4.... in less than one year, it is called Bills. When the bonds are maturing in one to 10 years, it is called Notes. When it is maturing in more than 10 years, it is called Bonds.
（債券歸被歸類為固定收益證券或債務證券。當債券離到期日不到一年時，它被稱為所謂的票據（Bills）。當債券的到期日是一年到10年之間，它被稱為票據（ Notes）。當它要超過10年以上才到期時，它就被稱為債券（Bonds）。）

Erica: I see. I have heard about T-bill. What is that?
（明白。我聽說過國庫券。那是什麼？）

Investment Specialist: Marketable securities ....5.... by the government are collectively known as Treasuries and based on their maturity, they

are called Treasury bonds, Treasury notes and Treasury bills (T-bills). Technically speaking, T-bills aren't bonds because of their short....6.....
（政府發行的有價證券統稱為國債 - 根據它們的到期日而各別稱為國債，國家票據和短期國債（國庫券）。技術上來説，國庫券因為他們的期限很短而不是真正的債券。）

Erica: Are government bonds relatively....7....?
（政府債券是否相對的算是安全的？）

Investment Specialist: All debt issued by the American government is regarded as extremely safe, as is the debt of any ....8.... country. Nevertheless, the debt issued by many developing countries can be substantially risky. Like companies, countries can default on payees.
（由美國政府發行的國債都被認為是非常安全的，就像是任何穩定的國家所發行的的債務。然而，許多開發中國家的債務的確有相當大的風險。就如同公司一樣，有些國家可以也會拖欠借款人。）

Erica: What kinds of risks are typically associated with buying government bonds?
（通常購買政府債券會有什麼樣的風險？）

Investment Specialist: Typically, there would be three types of risks. **Credit risk, currency risk** and **inflation risk. Credit risk** refers to the risk that a borrower will ....9.... on any type of debt by failing to make required payments. Government bonds in a country's own currency are sometimes taken as an approximation of the theoretical risk-free bond, because it is assumed that the government can raise ....10.... or create additional currency in order to redeem the bond at maturity. There have been incidents when a government defaulted on its own domestic currency debt, such as Russia in 1998 (the "Ruble crisis"). **Currency risk** refers to the risk when the value of the currency a bond pays out will decline compared to the bondholder's reference currency. As for **inflation risk**, it is the risk that the value of the currency a bond pays out will decrease over time. Investors expect some level of inflation, so the risk is that the inflation rate will be higher than what the investors expected.

（通常情況下，會有三種類型的風險。**信用風險**、**匯率風險**和**通貨膨脹風險**。**信用風險**是指借款人拖欠任何類型的債務而未能做出必要的支付償還的風險。當一個國家以自己本國的貨幣發行政府債券時，在理論上可以被視為近似無風險的債券，因為我們可以假設政府能夠為了贖回債券而在到期日前提高稅收或者印製額外的貨幣。已經有政府拖欠其國內貨幣債務的實例，比如俄羅斯在1998年（「盧布危機」）。**貨幣風險**指的是當債券所支付貨幣的價值與持有人的參考貨幣相較下會下降的風險。至於**通貨膨脹風險**，那就是債券支付的貨幣的價值將隨著時間而貶值的風險。投資者預期有一定程度的通貨膨脹，所以通貨膨脹風險是當通貨膨脹率將高於投資者所預期的。）

Erica: I see. That was very informative. Thank you.（明白了。真是非常詳盡的訊息。謝謝您。）

答案 ANSWERS:

1.d 2.f 3.b 4.a 5.i 6.j 7.c 8.e 9.h 10.g

認識債券

債券為發行期限一年以上的債務。當投資者購買債券時，他或她等於是借錢給發債人（債券的賣方）。而發債人同意在指定時間內償還本金的貸款和利息。債券本身是投資者憑以在約定日期獲得利息，並且在到期日拿回本金及利息的證書。發債人須按期支付早前承諾的利息，並且在到期日依指定價格向債券持有人歸還本金並且贖回債券。

債券根據發行方的性質，可分為政府債券、金融債券以及公司債券。

投資者購入債券，就如同借出資金給政府、大企業或其他債券發行機構。這三者中政府債券因為有政府稅收作為保障，因而風險最小，但收益也相對最小。

公司債券風險最大，可能的收益也最大。

債券持有人是債權人（Creditors），發債人為債務人（Debtors）。與銀行信貸不同的是，債券是一種直接債務關係，而銀行的信貸要先通過存款人到銀行再由銀行到貸款人而形成了間接的債務關係。債券不論是何種形式，大都可以在市場上進行買賣，並因此形成了所謂的債券市場。

由於投資者尋求躲避通貨膨脹的威脅，所以也有債券是以負利率出售的。2010年時美國政府第一次以負利率出售債券。投資者其所購買的每100美元債券要支付105.50美元。他們願意付錢給政府來換取向政府貸款的權利。但是，投資者這樣做的目的仍然是希望能從債券中賺錢，因為這些債券提供了抵制通貨膨脹的保障。

債券的特點

－償還性：對於償還期限有規定，所以發行人必須按債券約定條件償還本金並支付利息。

－流通性：債券一般都可以在流通市場上自由買賣。

－安全性：與股票相比，債券通常規定有固定的利率。因其與企業績效沒有直接聯繫，收益比較穩定，風險較小。此外，在企業破產時，債券持有者享有優先於股票持有者對企業剩餘資產的索取權。

－收益性：債券的收益性主要表現在兩個方面：

－利息收入：投資債券可以給投資者定期或不定期地帶來利息收入

－價格差額：投資者可以利用債券價格的變動來買賣債券賺取差額。

債券的基本票面要素

・發行年限

・利率

・發行量

・發行人

・承銷商

・起息日

・繳款日

・兑付日

債券的風險

債券投資的風險，主要包括信用風險、價格風險、利率風險、購買力風險、流動性風險、政治風險和操作風險等。

債券的基本要素

債券雖有不同種類，但基本要素卻是相同的，主要包括債券面值、債券價格、債券還本期限與方式和債券利率四個要素。

債券面值

債券面值包括兩個基本內容：一是幣別，二是票面金額。面值的幣別可用本國貨幣，也可用外幣，這取決於發行者的需要和債券的種類。債券的發行者可根據資金市場情況和自己的需求選擇適合的幣種。債券的票面金額是債券到期時償還債務的金額。不同債券的票面金額大小相差十分懸殊，但現在考慮到買賣和投資的方便，多趨向於發行小面額債券。面額印在債券上，固定不變，到期必須足額償還。

債券價格

債券價格是指債券發行時的價格。理論上，債券的面值就是它的價格。但實際上，由於發行者的種種考慮或資金市場上供求關係，加上利息率的變化，債券的市場價格常常不同於它的面值，有時高於面值，有時低於面值。也就是說，債券的面值是固定的，但它的價格卻是經常變化的。發行者計息還本，是以債券的面值為依據，而不是以其價格為依據的。

債券利率

債券利率是債券的利息與債券面值的比率。債券利率分為固定利率和浮動利率兩種。債券利率一般為年利率。債券利率直接關係到債券的收益。影響債券利率的因素主要有銀行利率水平、發行者的資信狀況、債券的償還期限和資金市場的供需等。

債券還本期限與方式

債券還本期限是指從債券發行到歸還本金之間的時間。債券還本期限長短不一，有的只有幾個月，有的長達十幾年。還本期限應在債券票面上註明。債券發行者必須在債券到期日償還本金。債券還本期限的長短，主要取決於發行者對資金需求的時限、未來市場利率的變化趨勢和證券交易市場的發達程度等因素。

債券還本方式是指一次還本還是分期還本等，還本方式也應在債券票面上註明。

債券除了具備上述四個基本要素之外，還應包括發行單位的名稱和地址、發行日期和編號、發行單位印記及法人代表的簽章、審批機關批准發行的文號和日期、是否記名、記名債券的掛失辦法和受理機構、是否可轉讓以及發行者認為應說明的其他事項。

債券交易程式

1．證券交易所債券交易的一般程式

⑴投資者委託證券商買賣債券，簽訂開戶契約，填寫開戶有關內容，明確經紀商與委託人之間的權利和義務。

⑵證券商通過其在證券交易所內的代表人或代理人，按照委託條件實施債券買賣業務。

⑶辦理成交的手續。成交後，經紀人應於成交的當日，填制買賣報告書，通知投資人按時將交割的款項或交割的債券交付委託經紀商。

⑷經紀商核對交易記錄，辦理結算交割手續。

2．櫃臺交易市場的交易分為自營買賣和代理買賣兩種。

⑴自營買賣是指證券公司作為交易商為投資人買賣債券，賺取價差。

⑵代理買賣是指證券公司作為經紀人，根據客戶的委託，代理客戶買賣債券，賺取佣金，即手續費。

債券交易方式

1）現貨交易：是指交易雙方在成交後立即交割或在極短的期限內交割的交易方式。

2）信用交易：又稱保證金交易，是指交易人憑自己的信譽，通過交納一定數額的保證金取得經紀人信任，進行債券買賣的交易方式。

3）回購交易：是指賣出（或買入）債券的同時，約定到一定的時間後以規定的價格再買回（或賣出）這筆債券，實際上就是附有購回（或賣出）條件的債券買賣。

4）期貨交易：是指交易雙方約定在將來某個時候按成交時約定的條件進行交割的交易方式。

5）期權交易：期權是指持有期權者可在規定的時間里，按雙方約定的價格，買入或賣出金融資產的權利。

一般常見債券術語解釋

本金 **Principal**	本金就是債券上的面額，也是發債人向債券持有人借的金額，同時也是發債人付利息給債券持有人個的依據。	Principal is the face value on a bond. It is also the amount the bond issuer borrows from the bondholder, and the basis on which the bond interest is calculated.
到期日 **Maturity Date**	到期日指的是債券發行人必須歸還本金給債券持有人並且贖回債券的日期。	Maturity date refers to the date when the bond issuer shall pay back the principal amount to the bondholder and redeem the bonds.
票面利息 **Coupon**	票面利息指的是債券發行人因發行債券給債券持有人而應該付的利息。	Coupon refers to the interest that the bond issuers shall pay the bondholders for issuing the bonds.

保證債券 **Guaranteed Bond**	保證債券指的是有得到第三者信用保證的債券。	Guarantee bond refers to the bond that is guaranteed by a third party with a strong credit rating.
擔保債券 **Secured Debenture**	擔保債券指的是債券發行人所發行的債券是由特定的資產所擔保的。	Secured debenture refers to the bonds which are secured with issuers' specific assets.
無擔保債券 **Unsecured Debenture**	無擔保債券指的是沒有特定資產擔保的債券。	Unsecured debenture refers to the bonds which are not secured with any of issuers' specific assets.
次信用債券 **Subordinated Debentures**	次信用債券指的是受償順序在債券持有人請求資產償付的權利時，比信用債券更次一級的債券。	Subordinated debt refers to the type of debit, in the case of default, the bondholder of which would not get paid until after the more other senior debt holders are paid in full first.
平價 **Par Value**	平價指的是當債券的賣價與面額相同時的狀況。	At par value refers to the situation when the selling prices of bonds are the same as the face value of the bonds.
溢價 **Premium**	溢價指的是當債券的賣價高過面額時的狀況。	Premium refers to the situation when the selling prices of the bonds are higher than the face value of the bonds.
折價 **Discount**	折價指的是當債券的賣價低於面額時的狀況。	Discount refers to the situation when the selling prices of the bonds are lower than the face value of the bonds.

機會成本 **Opportunity Cost**	機會成本是經濟學上用來計算成本效益分析的名詞。它指的是當某資源已經決定用在某一用途上時，所必需放棄把該資源運用在其他途徑的可能回報。它也代表如果您把相同的資源用在其他不同的用途上所可能得到的回報。	Opportunity cost is an economic term used in cost benefit analysis. It refers to the return of an alternative that must be forgone in order to pursue a certain action. It also refers to the benefits you could have received by taking an alternative action.
有效報酬 **Effective Return Rate**	有效報酬指的是投資完成後的實際效益回報率 。	The effective return rate is the actual rate of return received from completing an investment when all factors impacting the investment are considered.
現值 **Present Vale**	現值指的是未來所能收到的現金或回報的總和換算到現在的價值。未來的回報總和用折現率來計算現在的價值；貼現率越高，則未來的回報綜合的現值越低。選擇適當的折現率是評估未來回報總合的關鍵，無論是計算盈利或債務的現值。	Present value is the current worth of the sum of future cash received or total return, given a specified discount rate. Future total return is discounted at the discount rate to calculate the current value; and the higher the discount rate, the lower the present value of the future total return. Choosing the appropriate discount rate is the key to properly evaluating the future total return, whether it is for earnings or debts.

資本增值 **Capital Gains**	資本增值指的是當資產的賣出價格大於買入價格時的差額，但資本增值要等到資產實際賣出後才能真正產生。	Capital gains refer to the situation when the selling price of a capital asset is higher than its purchase price, but the capital gain is not realized until the asset is sold.
收益率 **Yield rate**	收益率指的是投資者在購買證券時所得到的利息或股利收益，通常是以收益金額除以其所投資證券的成本或面額而得到的年百分率來表示。	Yield rate refers to the interest or dividends the investor receives from investing in a security, and it is usually expressed as an annual percentage based on the investment's cost, its current market value or its face value.
到期收利率 **Yield to Maturity**	到期收益率指的是債券持有人願意持有債券直到債券到期的投資報酬率。	Yield to maturity refers to the rate of return which the bondholder expects to receive from a bond if the bond is held until its maturity.
贖回收益率 **Yield to Call** **（YTC）**	贖回收益率指的是債券直到被提前贖回之投資報酬率。贖回收益率只有在債券實際有被提前贖回時才有效。	Yield to call refers to the yield of a bond if it were to be held the security until its call date. This yield is valid only if the bond is called prior to maturity.

債券信用評級 **Bond credit rating**	債券信用評級就是針對發債人的財務實力或及時支付債券本金和利息的能力的評估。它是一種債券評級，是用來表明債券信用質量的參考。最常見的私人的獨立評級服務機構有標準普爾，穆迪和惠譽等。	Bond credit rating is a grade given to evaluate bond issuers' financial strength or its ability to pay a bond's principal and interest in a timely fashion. It indicates a bond's credit quality and can be used by investors for credit reference . The most common private independent rating services are Standard & Poor's, Moody's, Fitch and etc.
百分點 **basis point (bp)**	百分點是計算利率與金融報價之基本單位。一個百分點代表1%。	A basis point, or abbreviated as bp, is a common unit used to measure interest rates or the percentage change in financial instruments. One basis point is equal to 1/100th or 1%.

常用業務例句 Common business terms

1. inflation 通貨膨脹

inflation-indexed 通貨膨脹保值的

consumer prices index 消費物價指數

Erica: How does the government protect investors against **inflation** risk?

（政府如何保護投資者免受通貨膨脹的風險？）

Investment Specialist: Many governments issue **inflation-indexed** bonds, which protect investors against inflation risk by linking both interest payments and maturity payments to a **consumer prices index**.

（許多國家的政府發行通貨膨脹保值債券，藉著把利息付款和到期付款與消費物價指數連結來保護投資者免受通貨膨脹的風險。）

2. securities 證券
stake 股份
stockholders 股東
bankruptcy 破產
Consols 統一公債

Erica: What are the major differences between bonds and stocks?

（什麼是債券和股票主要的區別？）

Investment Specialist: Bonds and stocks are both **securities**, but the major difference between them is that **stockholders** are equity holders of the company (i.e. they are the investors of the company), whereas bondholders have creditors of the company (i.e. they are lenders). Being creditors of the company, bondholders have the absolute priority and will be repaid before the stockholders (who are owners of the company) in the event of a **bankruptcy**. Another major difference is that bonds usually have a definite term, or maturity, after which the bond is redeemed, whereas stocks are typically outstanding indefinitely. An exception is an irredeemable bond, such as **Consols**, which is a perpetuity, i.e. a bond with no maturity.

（債券和股票都是證券，但兩者之間的主要區別是，股東是公司股權的持有者（股東是公司的投資者），而債券持有人是公司的債權人（他們是貸款給公司的人）。作為債權人，在公司破產時，債券持有人擁有絕對的優先權，他們將在股東（公司老闆）之前得到償還。另一個區別是，債券通常有預先設定的期限，或到期日，債券在到期日後被贖回，而股票一般是無限期有效。也有例外的無贖回日債券，如統一公債（Consols），它是一個永續年金，即無到期日的債券，是英國政府1751年開始發行的長期債券。）

3. yield 投資收益

expressed 表達

face value 面值

par value 面值

coupon rate 票面利率

Erica: What is the **yield** rate of a bond?

（什麼是債券的投資收益率？）

Investment Specialist: The yield rate of a bond is the income return on a bond. It refers to the interest received from a bond and is usually **expressed** annually as a percentage based on the bond's cost, its current market value or its **face value**.

（債券的投資收益率是債券的收益回報。它指的是從債券收到的利息，通常依每年用債券的成本、市場價值或者面值的百分比來表示。）

Erica: What is the coupon rate of a bond?

（什麼是債券的票面利率？）

Investment Specialist: The coupon rate of a bond is simply the annual **coupon payments** paid by the issuer divided by the bond's face or **par value**.

（債券的票面利率就是由債券發行者支付的年利息除以債券的面值所得到的百分數。）

4. in a timely fashion 及時地
combinations 組合
differentiate 區分

Erica: How do we know if a bond has good credit quality?

（我們怎麼知道一個債券是否有良好的信用質量？）

Investment Specialist: The private independent rating services, such as Standard & Poor's, Moody's and Fitch, evaluate a bond issuer's financial strength, or its ability to pay a bond's principal and interest **in a timely fashion**. After the evaluation, a grade is given to bonds to indicate their credit quality. Bond ratings are expressed in letters ranging from 'AAA', which is the highest grade, to 'C' ("junk"), which is the lowest grade. Different rating services use the same letter grades, but use various **combinations** of upper- and lower-case letters to **differentiate** themselves from the others. For example, the Standard & Poor's format:

AAA and AA : High credit-quality investment grade

AA and BBB : Medium credit-quality investment grade

BB, B, CCC, CC, C : Low credit-quality (non-investment grade), or "junk bonds"

D:Bonds in default for non-payment of principal and/or interest

（私人的獨立評級服務機構，例如標準普爾、穆迪和惠譽都會評估債券發行人的財務實力，或及時償還債券本金和利息的能力。他們作了評估之後，會給予一個債券評級來標示他們的信用品質。債券評級用字母表示：“AAA”代表最高等級，而"C"（「垃圾」）代表最低的評級。各評級服務機構會使用相同的字母來表示不同的評級，但它們會使用字母大小寫與不同的字母組合來和其他的評級服務機構作區分。例如，標準普爾格式：

AAA和AA：高等信用品質投資評級

AA和BBB：中等信用品質投資評級

BB，B，CCC，CC，C：低等信用品質（非投資評級），或「垃圾債券」

D：債券違約而拖欠本金和/或利息）

Erica: Thank you. Now I have some idea about bond credit rating.
（謝謝您。我現在對債券的信用評級有一些概念了。）

單元短文 Unit reading

The Largest Global Bond Market
全球最大的公債市場

The sizes of government bonds

When people wonder where the largest bond market is, we would simply assume it is in the USA. In fact, the largest bond market is in the Eurozone. Factors that help contribute to the booming of Eurozone bond market are the increasingly liquid Euro currency, the low-inflation phenomenon in the recent years, the low interest situation, and the continuous launch of new kinds of bond products. If we would compare the Euro bond market with the American bond market, up to June 2005, there were a total of 3.4 trillion Euro long-term government bonds outstanding, and it is almost twice the size of the American government bonds (approximately 1.8 trillion in Euro).

Bond Issuance

Since the inception of Euro currency, the monthly bond issuance in the eurozone has also greatly increased. From January to July 2005, the total circulation of euro-zone government bonds was 5.7 trillion euros, showing that a substantial growth of 2.5 times over the same period in

1999 and that the expansion of debt during this period was phenomenal.

公債的規模

當有人想知道全球最大的公債市場在哪裡時，我們很有可能很容易就假設是美國。事實上，全球最大的公債市場在歐元區。有助於歐元區公債市場的蓬勃發展的因素有：歐元貨幣的流動性增加、歐洲近年來的低通膨環境和低利率，再加上新的債券商品不斷推出。我們如果比較歐元公債市場與美國公債市場，我們會發現，截至2005年6月，歐元區在外流通的長期公債的金額高達3.4兆歐元，幾乎是美國公債市場規模（大約1.8兆歐元）的兩倍多！

債券發行量

自歐元開始發行後，歐元區每月債券發行量也顯著的增加，從2005年1月到7 月這段期間，歐元區國家債券的總發行量是5.7兆歐元，較1999年同期大幅成長達2.5倍，顯見此段期間債券市場快速的擴張。

常用片語 Common phrases

- is regarded as 被認為是
  My uncle's company's shares **are regarded as** a good long-term investment options options.
  （我叔叔公司的股票被認為是良好的長期投資選擇。）

- be associated with 與……相關聯
  Bonds with low credit rating **are** usually **associated with** higher risk.
  （信用評級低的債券通常與高風險相關聯。）

重點字彙 Important words to know

名詞 Nouns／形容詞 Adjectives		動詞 Verbs	
債券／債券	Bond/ debenture	拖欠	default
政府債券	government bonds	追求	pursue
類別	category	影響	impact
固定收益	fixed income	確定	determine
債務證券	debt security	連結	link
國庫券	treasury-bill	贖回	redeem
大量的	substantial		
近似值	approximation		
理論的	theoretical		
實例	instance		
下降	decline		
債券持有人	bondholder		
面值／面值	face/par value		
發行者	issuer		
規定的	defined		
優先	priority		
優先	senior		
永久	perpetuity		

共同基金 Mutual Funds

什麼是共同基金

共同基金是由專業的投資公司聚集投資人的錢，依不同的投資目標而提供不同種類的基金項目來管理投資的方式。投資者根據基金公司公佈的目標及投資章程來選擇適合自己投資的項目。某些保守型的基金， 例如貨幣市場基金，有相對比較穩定的定期投資回報，其風險也相對比較小；還有一些高風險的基金項目， 例如高科技基金，雖然投資風險會比較高，但相對的，投資者也會預期有得到更高的回報的機會。有些基金在買賣時會收取手續費，而有一些不收手續費。

單元暖身小練習 Warm-up conversation and practice

針對以下每個空格，請選一個最適合的字填入。這是協助你對於本主題進行初步的暖身，以利對於後續的介紹可以更有效率的吸收。

(a) restrictions (b) buy back (c) common (d) hybrid
(e) principal (f) oversees (g) securities (h) traded
(i) trustees (j) portfolio

Virginia wants to know what mutual funds are.
維吉尼亞想知道共同基金是什麼。

Investment Specialist: Good morning, Miss Lin, may I help you?
（早安，林小姐，我可以幫您嗎？）

Virginia: Yes. I would like to know what a mutual fund is.
（是。我想知道共同基金是什麼。）

Investment Specialist: Sure. A mutual fund is a pool of stocks, bonds and other ....1.... held in trust on behalf of individual investors. When you invest in a mutual fund, you purchase units in a professionally managed ....2.... of securities, with each unit representing a share of ownership in the portfolio.
（共同基金是以信託的方式匯集投資人的資金和代表投資人持有股票、債券和其他證券等投資項目。當您投資在共同基金時，您等於是購買由專業管理人管理的投資組合的單位，而每單位代表投資組合所有權的股份。）

Virginia: How many types of mutual funds are there?
（共同基金的種類有哪些？）

Investment Specialist: There are two types of mutual funds—open-end funds and closed-end funds. The most ....3.... type, the open-end fund, does not have ....4.... on the amount of shares the fund will issue. If the demand is high enough, the fund will continue to issue shares no matter how many investors there are. Open-end funds also ....5.... shares when investors wish to sell. A closed-end funds usually have a pre-determined

CHPATER 1 CHPATER 2 CHPATER 3 CHPATER 4 CHPATER 5

number of shares to issue to the public through an initial public offering (IPO), after which funds are ....6.... on a stock exchange, just like stocks. The unit prices of closed-end funds are determined by market demand, so they can either be below their net asset value or above it.

（基本上有兩種類型的共同基金，開放式基金和封閉式基金。開放式基金是最常見的基金類型，而且其發行量沒有特定的上限。如果需求足夠的話，無論有多少投資者想要投資，基金都可以繼續發行。開放式基金也會在投資者希望賣出基金時回購基金。封閉式基金通常已經有事先預定好的最高發行量，而且是透過首次公開發行（IPO）來發行的，在基金發行了之後，它就像股票一樣在證券交易所交易。封閉式基金的單位價格是由市場需求決定的，所以價格可能高於或者低於資產淨值。）

Virginia: Can they be classified into different categories?

（它們也有被分類為不同的類別？）

Investment Specialist: Mutual funds are generally categorized by their ....7.... investments. The main categories of funds are: money market funds, bond or fixed income funds, stock or equity funds, and ....8.... funds. Funds may also be categorized as index（passively

managed) or actively managed types.
（共同基金一般以他們的主要投資項目而分類。基金的主要類別是貨幣市場基金、債券或固定收益類基金，股票或股票型基金和混合型基金。基金也可以被歸類為指數（被動管理）基金，或主動型基金等種類。）

Virginia: Who ....9.... mutual funds?
（誰負責監督共同基金？）

Investment Specialist: Open-end and closed-end funds are supervised by a board of directors (if organized as a corporation) or board of ....10.... (if organized as a trust). The Board is responsible for ensuring that the fund is managed in the best interests of the fund's investors and for hiring the fund manager and other service providers for the fund.
（開放式和封閉式基金是由董事會（如果組織為法人機構）或受託人董事會（如果組織為信託）來監督。董事會負責確保該基金是以基金投資者的最佳利益而管理，並且負責招聘基金經理和其他為基金服務的供應商。）

Virginia: I see. Thank you for your explanation.
（我明白了。謝謝您的解釋。）

答案 ANSWERS:

1.g 2.j 3.c 4.a 5.b 6.h 7.e 8.d 9.f 10.i

認識共同基金

世界上的第一個基金是荷蘭國王威廉一世在 1822 年所創的私人基金。在 1868 年英國也創立了倫敦國外及殖民政府的信託，其主要目的是投資海外殖民地的公債，也是最早的證券投資信託公司。而目前所見的基金，則要首推 1924 年麻薩諸塞公司設立的麻薩諸塞投資信託基金（ MIT ）。到了 1940 年，美國更訂定了投資公司法，奠定了日後共同基金發展的良好基礎。

據美國投資公司協會統計，至2004年底，全球40多個國家的投資基金規模約有16.06萬億美元。

共同基金依基金公司之組織型態，可分為以下二種：

⑴ 契約制

由基金公司，保管銀行和投資人三方共同訂立信託契約，並受其契約規範，由基金公司發行受益憑證給投資人，並管理基金；保管銀行則負責保管基金的資產；投資所產生的利潤歸投資人。

⑵ 公司制

由公司發行股份，讓投資人購買公司的股票，進而成為股東，股東可以行使公司組織中的各項權利，等基金達成立規模後再和基金公司訂約，委託其管理及運作該基金。

基金按交易方式來分類：

共同基金按交易方式可分為開放式基金、封閉式基金及股票交易所交易基金。

1）開放式基金 - 對於此類基金，投資人可以直接向基金公司或其代理機構買入及賣出基金，以基金資產淨值作為買入或賣出的價格，開放式基金的規模會隨著投資人的買入和賣出而增加。

2）封閉式基金 - 這類基金在一開始募集完事先設定的發行量之後，就不再由投資人直接或間接向基金公司購買，而是在股票市場上進行交易，因此基金的規模不會因為買賣而增加或減少。此外，這類基金的單位價格會由於市場上的需求而變動，所以實際買賣的價格可能會高於或低於基金淨值。

3）股票交易所交易基金 - 又稱作 ETF（exchange traded fund），這類基金大致上與封閉式基金類似，但增加了以基金與實物可交換（例如：股票基金可以與股票交換）的機制。這一機制使得單位價格與資產淨值的差異不會像封閉式基金那麼大。另一方面，資產變動雖不如開放式基金那麼大，但也會因交換機制而有所變化。

基金按不同操作方式來分類

基金按操作方式一般可分為主動型基金及指數基金。

1）主動型基金 - 此類基金的操作策略和買進賣出等都由基金經理人或團隊來作決定，希望能獲得最好的績效，市面上多數的基金屬於此類。

2）指數型基金 - 此類基金的基金經理人運用追縱技術，使得基金的表現能與相對應股價指數相近。一般而言，這類基金的收費較便宜，因此實際上績效並不輸給主動型基金。目前市面上大多數ETF都屬此類型。

基金按資產類別區分

依照資產類別，共同基金大致可分為：

—股票型基金：又可依投資地域或產業再分類。

—債券型基金：又可依債券類型或地域再分類。

—貨幣型基金：可依貨幣幣種再分類。

—混合型基金：可同時持有多種類別資產的基金。

投資基金的相關機構及人員

1）投資者：購買基金單位的法人或個人

2）基金管理公司：負責基金的具體運作，並收取一定的管理費，但不直接承擔基金風險的公司。

3）基金託管銀行：負責對基金進行託管，執行基金管理公司的命令及其他監督工作

4）政府管理機構及其他服務組織：包括證券交易所、會計師事務所、律師事務所、評級機構等。

正常情況下，投資基金之所以能有高的回報率在於：

1）規模效應：由於投資基金的規模較大，可以對某一項目進行資金的追加，從而降低成本，彌補某些投資方向上的損失，獲得較高收益。

2）分散風險：由於投資基金的運作遵循追求穩定成長的股票，分散投資的策略，能夠最大可能地降低個人投資時單一股票很高的風險。

3）專家理財：投資基金都由專業的基金公司運作，匯集了熟悉資本市場的人員，能夠彌補個人投資者投資知識的不足。

一般常見共同基金名詞解釋

基金單位資產淨值 **Net Asset Value （NAV） per share**	基金單位資產淨值是基金的每單位買賣價格。基金單位資產淨值 = 基金淨資產總值/已經發行並且還在市面上流通的基金單位總數。開放式基金的申購和贖回都以這個單位價格進行交易。	NAV is a mutual fund's price per unit. It is calculated by dividing the total value of the fund's net asset by the total number of fund units outstanding. The open-end funds are traded based on this unit price.
認購 **To subscribe**	認購指的是投資者在基金發行期內申請購買基金的行為。	To subscribe refers to the action by which an investor confirms his or her intent to buy mutual funds prior to the fund issuance date.
申購 **To purchase**	申購指的是投資者在基金已經發行之後向基金公司提出申請購買基金的行為。	To purchase refers to the actions by which an investor buys units of mutual funds after the fund units have been issued.
贖回 **To redeem**	贖回指的是在開放式基金已經發行之後，已持有基金的投資者向基金公司提出要賣出基金的行為。	To redeem refers to the actions by which an investor expresses his or her intention to sells units of mutual funds after the fund units have been issued and purchased.

公開說明書 **Prospectus**	公開說明書是相關的基金監管機構為了確保投資人投資基金之前，能夠清楚了解基金的投資目的和相應的風險而要求基金公司提供給（準）投資人的正式文件。公開說明書中必須告知基金的管理公司、保管機構，以及說明基金的投資目標與策略，並評估可能的風險、解釋相關的費用、買賣的方式等。	A prospectus is a formal legal document that is required by the relevant mutual fund authority for fund companies to provide details about their funds to （potential）investors before they invest in mutual funds. A prospectus should contain facts including the fund manager, the fund custodian, fund objectives and strategies, the estimated risks, the explanation of related fees, the distribution policy, etc.
基金經理人 **Fund manager**	基金經理人負責執行基金的投資策略和投資組合買賣的活動。經理人可以是個人或者一個團隊。經理人收取基金平均資產的特定百分比的金額作為管理基金的費用。	The person or team responsible for implementing a fund's investing strategy and managing the portfolio trading activities. A fund can be managed by one person or by a team. Fund managers are paid a fee for managing the funds, and the fee is usually a percentage of the fund's average assets under management.

股利 **Dividend**	股利是公司的某一部份盈利的分配。一般是由董事會來決定發放的辦法。股利的發放方式可以是現金或者股票或公司其他的資產。	A dividend is a distribution of a portion of a company's earnings. The distribution details are usually decided by the board of directors, and it can be distributed in cash, stocks or other assets.
管理費 **Management fee**	管理費指的是指基金公司支付給基金經理的費用。費用是作為補償基金經理人花費時間和專業在投資、營運和管理基金的費用。管理費有時也包含基金的其他行政費用。	Management fee is the amount that a mutual fund pays its manager for managing the fund. The management fee is intended to compensate the managers for spending their time and expertise on investing, operations, and management. It can also include other items like the administration costs of the fund.
投資組合 **Portfolio**	投資組合一般是由投資經理設計以及管理的包含多種不同投資工具的投資配置。它們可以包含股票、債券、基金和與現金等值的資產等。	Portfolio is usually a composite of financial assets created and managed by investment managers. They can include stocks, bonds, mutual funds, and cash equivalents etc.

申購手續費 **Front-end load**	申購手續費是投資人在認購基金時需要支付的費用，它主要是用來補償基金銷售中介(經紀、理財專員、投資顧問等）所提供服務，協助投資人挑選合適基金的費用。	Front-end load is a commission or sales charge that the investors pay at the time of the initial purchase of mutual funds. It is meant to be paid to investment intermediaries (brokers, financial planners, investment advisors) as fees for providing their services in making sales and helping investors choose suitable funds.
贖回手續費 **Back-end load**	贖回手續費是投資人在贖回（賣出）基金時需要支付的費用，它主要是用來補償基金銷售中介(經紀、理財專員、投資顧問等）所提供服務，協助投資人挑選合適基金的費用。	Back-end load is a commission or sales charge that the investors pay when they sell mutual funds within a specified number of years. It is meant to be paid to investment intermediaries (brokers, financial planners, investment advisors) as fees for providing their services in making sales and helping investors choose suitable funds.

平攤手續費 **Level-load**	平攤手續費基本上是以基金的資產淨值的百分比來收費的。它通常是在投資人持有基金的時間段內每年直接從投資人的帳戶裡扣除，主要是用來支付投資仲介的費用，投資人要一直支付直到基金賣出為止。	Level-load is an annual charge that is usually calculated based on a fixed percentage of the investors' average mutual fund holdings and is deducted from an investors' mutual fund account for as long as the investors hold the funds. It is mostly used to pay the investment intermediaries for their services.

 常用業務例句 Common business terms

1. diversification 分散，多樣化
liquidity 流動性
portfolio 投資組合

Virginia: What are the advantages of mutual funds?
（共同基金的優勢是什麼？）

Investment Specialist: Mutual funds have advantages over investing directly in securities individually because of:

(1) More **diversification**: A fund normally holds a variety of securities; diversification decreases risk.

(2) High **liquidity**: Investors can sell open-end funds every day at a price equal to the closing net asset value of the funds.

(3) Professional **portfolio** management: Mutual funds hire portfolio managers to manage the

fund's investments.

(4) Access to investments that may otherwise be available only to larger investors.

(5) Ease to compare results: All mutual funds are required to report the same information to investors, and that makes them easy to compare.

（共同基金比直接投資在個別證券的優勢有：

（1）更加多樣化：一個基金通常持有多種證券，而分散降低風險。

（2）高流動性：投資人每日都可以以每交易日收盤時的淨資產值的等值價格賣出其所持有的開放式基金。

（3）專業的投資組合管理：基金聘請專業的基金經理管理基金的投資。

（4）能夠投資在原本可能只提供給大規模投資者的項目。

（5）容易比較：所有基金都必須報告相同的信息給投資者，這使得它們很容易作比較。）

2. disadvantages 缺點
recognition 認定
predictable 可預料的
customize 客製化

Virginia: What are the **disadvantages** of mutual funds?
（共同基金的缺點是什麼？）

Investment Specialist: Mutual funds have disadvantages including:

(1) Fees

⑵Less control over timing of **recognition** of gains

⑶Less **predictable** income

⑷No opportunity to **customize**

（共同基金的缺點，包括：

（1）費用

（2）對於確認收益的時間有較少的控制權

（3）比較難預料收入

（4）無法作客制化的投資）

3. qualification 資格

according to 按照

registered investment adviser 註冊登記的投資顧問

Virginia: What do the fund managers do? What is their necessary **qualification**?

（基金經理的工作是什麼呢？他們需要符合什麼樣的資格？）

Investment Specialist: The fund managers take care of all matters related the trading of the fund's investments **according to** the fund's original investment objective. A fund manager must be a **registered investment** adviser.

（基金經理負責按照該基金的投資目標而為基金的投資進行交易。基金經理必須是已註冊登記的投資顧問。）

4. outstanding 已發行的

Virginia: How do we calculate a mutual fund's price per share?
（我們要如何計算共同基金的單位價格？）

Investment Specialist: A mutual fund's Net Asset Value (NAV) per share is calculated by dividing the total net value of all the assets in the portfolio by the total number of fund shares **outstanding**. All mutual funds' buying and selling are calculated at the closing Net Asset Value on the trade date. However, we must wait until the following day to get the actual price.
（共同基金的單位資產淨值是以其投資組合內所有資產的總價值除以已發行而且還在市場上流通的基金單位總數來計算的。所有共同基金的買入和賣出都是以交易日收盤時的資產淨值來計算的，然而，我們必須等到第二天才能得到真正的交易價格。）

單元短文 Unit reading

Are No-Load Funds (NLF) really not as good as Loaded funds?
免手續費的基金真的不如有手續費的基金嗎？

A no-load fund is the type of mutual fund without a front-end, back-end or level sales charge. However, even if the fund's prospectus says that there is no-load fund, there still might be a small charge because security regulations allow a fund to charge up to 25% for services and still consider itself a no-load fund.

Being without a transaction cost means that an investor's entire investment goes into the fund. For example, if Virginia invests $10,000 in a NLF, all of her $10,000 investment will make return in the fund. If, on the other hand, Virginia invests in a loaded fund with a 3% sales commission, then Virginia will only have the $9,700 to invest in the fund. Even without sales commission, an annual charge of 1% will lower Virginia's return because each year for as long as she owns the funds, she will pay $100 to the fund company.

However, statistics has shown that no-load funds generally perform as well as loaded funds. Thus, the additional fees don't always mean additional returns.

免手續費基金是一種沒有申購手續費（front-end load）、贖回手續費（back-end load）或平攤手續費（level-load）的共同基金。即使基金的公開說明書聲明該基金是一個免手續費的基金，仍可能會有一小筆費用產生，因為證券法規允許基金最多收取25%的服務費而仍然稱自己為免手續費基金。

在沒有交易費用時的情況下，代表的是投資者的所有的投資都用來購買基金。如果維吉尼亞購買了價值1萬美金的無手續費基金，她所投資的所有1萬美金都將在基金中賺取收益。反過來説，如果維吉尼亞購買的是有收取3%的銷售手續費的基金，則維吉尼亞只有9700美金可以投資在基金中。即使她不用付銷售手續費，而只是付1%的年費，維吉尼亞的回報也會是比較低的，因為每一年只要她繼續持有基金，她將需要支付100美金給基金公司。

然而，統計調查顯示，免手續費資金和有手續費的基金通常會提供投資人相同的回報率。因此，多付費用並不一定代表會有額外的回報。

常用片語 Common phrases

• be classified into 被分類為	Mutual funds **are** usually **classified into** three different types. （共同基金通常被分為三種不同類型。）
• be charged with 負責	The Board of Directors are **charged with** ensuring that the fund managers invest according to the pre-set investment objective. （董事會負責確保基金管理人根據預先設定的投資目標去投資。）

重點字彙 Important words to know

名詞 Nouns		動詞 Verbs	
共同基金	mutual fund	監督	oversee
投資組合	portfolio	認購	subscribe
混合式	hybrid	贖回	redeem
開放式基金	open-end fund	申購	purchase
封閉式基金	closed-end fund		
基金單位淨值	net asset value (NAV)per share		
公開說明書	prospectus		
基金經理人	fund manager		
基金持有人	fund holder		
有申購手續費基金	front-end load fund		
有贖回手續費基金	back-end load fund		
免手續費基金	no-load fund		
有平攤手續費基金	level-load fund		
分散，多樣化	diversification		
流動性	liquidity		
負債	liabilities		

期貨
Futures

什麼是期貨

期貨是一種金融合同，能讓買賣雙方約定在未來的交易日期以約定好的交易價格和數量來交易資產，交易的資產可以是實物商品或金融工具。期貨合約裡的細節包含日期、標的物的質量、數量和金額都被標準化，以方便在期貨交易所進行交易。有些期貨合約可能會要求用實物商品交割，而另外有一些則要求以現金結算。

單元暖身小練習 Warm-up conversation and practice

針對以下每個空格，請選一個最適合的字填入。這是協助你對於本主題進行初步的暖身，以利對於後續的介紹可以更有效率的吸收。

(a) hedge　(b) speculators　(c) deliver　(d) fix
(e) mitigate　(f) unfavorable　(g) derivative　(h) yield
(i) advantageous　(j) commodities

Lucy wants to know what futures are.
露西想知道期貨是什麼。

Investment Specialist: Good morning, Miss Shih, may I help you?
（早安，施小姐，我可以幫您嗎？）

Lucy: Yes, I would like to know what futures are.
（是，我想知道期貨是什麼。）

Investment Specialist: Sure. A futures contract is a type of ....1.... instrument, or financial contract, in which the buyer and the seller agree to trade financial instruments or physical ....2.... for future delivery at an agreed price. If you buy a futures contract, you are basically obligated to buy something that a seller has not yet produced, for a set price. However, participating in the futures market does not always mean that you will be obliged to receive or ....3.... large quantity of physical commodities - as players in the futures market primarily enter into futures contracts to ....4.... risk or speculate rather than to trade physical goods. That is why futures are used as financial instruments by not only producers and consumers but also ....5.....

（當然。期貨合約是一種衍生工具或者金融合約，其中買賣雙方同意以金融工具或實物商品的期貨在未來以約定的價格交易。如果您買了一個期貨合約，您基本上有責任以一個特定價格購買賣方尚未產生的東西。然而，參與期貨市場並不一定意味著您總是有義務接收或交付大量的實物商品 - 因為在期貨市場裡的參與者簽訂期貨合約主要是用來降低損失的風險或用來投機，而不是真正要交易實物商品。這就是為什麼除了生產者和消費者之外，投機者也同時把期貨作為金融工具來運用。）

Lucy: What was the original use of the futures?
（什麼是期貨最原始的用途？）

Investment Specialist: The original purpose of futures contracts was to ....6.... the risk of price or exchange rate movements by allowing the participants to ....7.... prices or rates in advance for future transactions. This could be ....8.... when one party expects to receive payment in a foreign currency in the future, and wishes to guard against an ....9..... movement of the currency in the period before payment is received. However, futures contracts also offer the opportunities for speculators, who predicts that the price of an commodity will move in a particular direction, can enter into a contract to buy or sell it in the future at a price which will ....10.... a profit.
（期貨合約原來的目的是透過讓參與者可以事先鎖定未來交易的價格或利率，來減輕價格或匯率變動的風險。當一方預計未來將收到外幣的貨款，同時希望在收到款項之前能夠防範貨幣往不利的方向變動，這可能是有效的方式。但期貨合約也提供投機者們機會，讓預測資產的價格會往一個特定方向移動的投機者可以訂立合約，在未來購買或出售將會產生利潤的價格。）

Lucy: I see. Your explanation was very clear. Thank you!
我明白了。您的解釋非常清楚。謝謝您！）

答案 ANSWERS:

1.g 2.j 3.c 4.a 5.b 6.e 7.d 8.i 9.f 10.h

認識期貨

傳統的交易方式是「一手交錢，一手交貨」，而期貨的交易方式則是「一手交錢，未來交貨」。由期貨的英文Futures可知，期貨就是"未來的商品"之意。所以買賣期貨，就是買賣未來東西的一個契約。歷史上最早的期貨市場是江戶幕府時代的日本。由於當時的白米價格對經濟及軍事活動造成很重大的影響，所以米商會根據白米的生產量以及市場對白米的需求而決定庫存白米的買賣。

中國古代也已經有由糧棧和糧市構成的商品信貸及遠期合約制度。在民國年代，中國上海曾出現多個期貨交易所。滿洲國政府也曾經在東北大連、營口、奉天等15個城市設立期貨交易所，主要經營大豆、豆餅、豆油的期貨貿易。1949年後，期貨交易所在中國大陸絕跡幾十年，到1991年深圳設立期貨交易所，才又展開另一波期貨熱炒風潮，最多曾經一度同時開設超過50家期貨交易所，超過全球其他國家期貨交易所數目的總和。中國大陸在1994年及1998年，兩次大力收緊監管，暫停多個期貨品種，勒令多間交易所停止營業。

自1998年後，中國大陸合法的商品期貨交易所只剩下上海 、大連 、鄭州三所，前者主要經營能源與金屬商品期貨，後兩者經營農產品期貨。到2006年9月8日，中國金融期貨交易所在上海掛牌成立，並於2010年4月16日推出其首項產品，滬深300股指期貨。以歐美國家來說，在1848年美國成立芝加哥期貨交易所時，期貨的交易方式便具體成型了。

期貨並非貨物，只是一張承諾買進或賣出貨物的合約，此外，為了維持市場流通，集中在交易市場交易，期貨合約必須符合幾項條件：1）將合約標準化，針對合約的訂定統一標準，方能夠集中競價。2）採取每日結算制度並由結算所統一負責，以降低違約風險。3）以公開競價的方式決定合約價格，期能使參與者根據最新資訊作出判斷。

所謂標準化合約是指將標的物的規格與品質，合約價值，價格計算方式，與結算時間統一化，使合約之間除價格之外完全相同，以利合約集中競價交易，提高流動性。

由於期貨交易僅須支付合約價值一定百分比的保證金即可，因此，具有以小搏大的高槓桿特性。若依期貨的標的來看，則期貨可分為商品期貨及金融期貨，期貨肇始於商品期貨，但目前金融期貨的交易比重已達到 78% 成為主流。而金融期貨中利率期貨佔6成多，股價指數期貨則佔24%左右，匯率期貨則佔不到一成。

參與期貨交易者之中，避險者 (Hedgers) 透過買賣期貨，鎖定利潤與成本，減低時間帶來的價格波動風險。投機者 (Speculators)則透過期貨交易承擔更多風險，伺機在價格波動中牟取利潤。

期貨就是一種法律合約，所以，任何一張期貨合約內容都必須包含五種條件：

1）在哪一個期貨交易所交易

2）何種商品

3）商品的數量，規模

4）何時到期

5）如何交割

期貨是一種衍生工具，按現貨標的物之種類，期貨可分為商品期貨與金融期貨兩大類。但是期貨演變至今天，可以交易的可不是只有買商品而已。像是股票市場上的許多金融指數也都可以變成期貨做交易。

期貨的種類

商品期貨：

－ 農產品期貨：如棉花，大豆，小麥，玉米，白糖，咖啡，豬腩，菜籽油，天然橡膠、棕櫚油，紅酒，家禽，家畜。

－ 金屬期貨：如銅，鋁，錫，鋅，鎳，黃金，白銀。

－ 能源期貨：如原油、汽油、燃料油。新興品種包括氣溫、二氧化碳排放配額。

金融商品：

－ 股票期貨，公債期貨。

－ 指數期貨 ，台指期貨，金融期貨，電子期貨，英國FTSE指數，德國DAX指數，東京日經平均指數，香港恆生指數，等。

－ 利率期貨：利率期貨是指以債券類證券為標的物的期貨合約，它可以避免利率波動所引起的證券價格變動的風險。利率期貨一般可分為短期利率期貨和長期利率期貨，前者大多以3月期利率為標的物，而後者大多以5年期以上長期債券為標的物。

－ 外匯期貨。

期貨買賣過程（建倉到交割）

一般我們買股票的單位是「張」。擁有一張股票，代表你擁有這間公司的一小部分的權利。但在期貨的世界，買賣的單位是「口」，擁有一口期貨，代表你可以在未來買到約定數量的貨物。

在期貨交易的整個過程中，業界習慣用「倉」來表示

－ 今天我買了一口大豆期貨 → 建倉

－ 我持續抱著這口期貨半年 → 持倉

－ 到期日當天，我拿合約換大豆 → 交割

－ 若在到期日前，我就先把這口期貨又賣給別人 → 平倉

概念分析

先買後賣

先買：是指與他人簽訂一份在未來以一定價格買入一種商品的協議，或從他人手中接受這種類型的協議。 後賣：指在中途將這份協議轉讓給他人，或者到期平倉。

先賣後買

先賣：是指與他人簽訂一份在未來以一定價格賣出一種商品的協議。或從他人手中接受這種類型的協議。 後買：指在中途將這份協議轉讓給他人，或者到期平倉。

期貨市場與股票市場的分別

－ 期貨市場是「零和遊戲」，同一段時間內所有贏家賺的錢，加上交易費用等於所有輸家賠的錢；期貨市場是針對現貨市場風險的一個保險市場，以期貨市場投機者的金錢為現貨市場經營者提供經濟保險，從而保障經濟的穩定發展。投入股市的錢則不同，透過商業機構的營運業務增長，可以創造新的經濟價值，若經濟環境穩定，大部分人可以同時賺錢，一般回報較期市慢，風險較期市低。

－ 期貨買賣以槓桿操作，只需要在期貨戶口存入某百分比的開倉保證金（Initial Margin，常見為5-10%），作為應付商品或相關資產價格波動之儲備，就可以買賣價值100%的期貨合約，獲利與風險比例均比股票高。當市場劇烈波動時，買賣股票者最多賠光所有投入資本，戶口價值為零。但買賣期貨者獲利或虧損的幅度，卻可以是本金的數十以至數千倍。每日收盤後，期貨結算所會根據收盤價，計算每日結算價（Settlement Price），來釐定未平倉合約價值，並在保證金內調整未實現盈利／虧損。如未實現虧損含保證金跌低於維持水準（Maintenance Margin），持倉者就需追繳保證金（Margin Call），否則需平倉止蝕（俗稱砍倉）。

全球主要的期貨交易所

- 芝加哥商品交易所（CME）
- 芝加哥期貨交易所（CBOT）
- 倫敦金屬交易所（LME）

・紐約商品期貨交易所（NYMEX）

・紐約期貨交易所（NYBOT）

・上海期貨交易所（SHFE）

人工喊價與電子交易

－ 人工喊價是指交易廳內的交易代表，透過手勢與喊話途徑，進行交易。芝加哥CBOT是早期最有代表性的人工交易池，每個品種由交易代表在八角形的梯級範圍內，進行頻繁的喊話與手勢交易。

－ 電子交易是指市場採取中央電腦交易系統，根據交易規則、買賣指令的價格與先後次序，自動撮合買賣合同。交易員在認可的電腦系統前下單即可，毋須擠到特定的空間內人工喊價。

一般常見期貨名詞解釋

開倉 **Open position**	新建期貨合約的交易行為稱為開倉。	An open position refers to the opening of new futures contracts.
未平倉合約 **Open interest**	持倉是指到期貨市場收盤為止，還沒有沖銷或到期交割的剩餘合約量。	Open interest refers to the total number of remaining futures contracts that are not closed or delivered on a particular day.
平倉/沖銷 **Cover/Offset**	平倉是指賣出先前買進的部位。或以等量但相反買賣方向沖銷原有的契約稱之為平倉。	To cover or offset refers to executing a futures transaction that is the exact opposite of an open position.

交割 **Delivery**	交割指的是期貨合約的賣方與買方將合約所載的商品所有權按規定進行轉移或以現金方式進行結算的行為。	Delivery refers to the action by which a futures contract is tendered and completed by the seller and the buyer of the contract.
口 **Lot**	計算期貨合約的單位，一口表示一張期貨合約。	Lot is the unit used to calculate futures contracts. One lot means one unit of futures contract.
風險預告書 **Risk Disclosure Statement (RDS)**	開立期貨交易帳戶者，於開戶時簽署一份表示瞭解期貨交易風險的聲明文件。	RDS is the legal document which the account holders are asked to sign upon opening a futures account to specify that they understand the risks involved with futures trading.
對作 **Bucket**	接受客戶的委託買賣卻未下單到交易所進行撮合交易之行為，或擅自挪用客戶保證金之行為。	Bucket refers to the behavior of traders accepting customers' purchase or sell orders and failing to match the orders at the futures market, or the unauthorized use of customers' margin.
套利 **Arbitrage**	買入一個商品契約同時又賣出另外一個商品契約，以獲取兩個契約間的差價為目的一種交易。	Arbitrage refers to the transactions of buying a commodity contracts while selling another commodity contract, with the purpose to acquire the difference between the two contracts to make a profit.

避險 **Hedging**	避險指的是現貨市場的買家或賣家，利用在期貨市場上買進或賣出與自己手上要買入或賣出相同數量的同樣期貨商品，來降低現貨市場價格波動對其不利的影響。	Making an investment to reduce the risk of adverse price movements in a particular commodity. Normally, a hedge consists of taking an offsetting position in a related future contract.
原始保證金要求 **Initial Margin Requirement**	期貨商要求期貨交易人於下單委託買賣前，必須存入帳戶的交易保證金。	The percentage of the purchase price of securities (that can be purchased on margin) that the investor must pay for with his or her own cash or marginable securities.
結算價 **Settlement Price**	結算價指的是在每日期貨交易市場開盤時和收盤後計算的平均交易價格。	The settlement price is the average price at which a contract trades, calculated at both the open and close of each trading day.

常用業務例句 Common business terms

1. unified 統一的

open cry system 人工喊價

matched electronically 以電子交易方式匹配

Lucy: What is a futures market?

（什麼是期貨市場？）

Investment Specialist: The futures market is a **unified** marketplace for buyers and sellers from around the world who

meet and enter into futures contracts. Prices can be set based on an **open cry system**, or buying and selling orders can be **matched electronically**. The futures contract will state the transaction price and the delivery date. But almost all futures contracts end without the actual physical delivery of the commodity.
（期貨市場是一個為來自世界各地的買家和賣家提供了會面並簽訂期貨合約的統一的市場。定價可以以人工喊價，或者買賣需求可以以電子交易方式進行匹配。該期貨合約會註明交易價和交貨日期。但是，幾乎所有的期貨合約最終都沒有用商品的實際實物交割。）

2. short position 空頭部位
long position 多頭部位

Lucy: What is a futures contract?
（什麼是期貨契約？）

Investment Specialist: A futures contract is an agreement between two the buyer and the seller: a **short position** - the party who agrees to sell a commodity - and a **long position** - the party who agrees to buy a commodity. In the scenario of a wheat farmer versus a bread maker, the farmer would be the holder of the short position, while the bread maker would be the holder of the long position. In every futures contract, all details are specified:

the quantity and quality of the commodity, the price per unit, and the date and method of delivery.

（期貨合約是由買賣雙方達成的協議：空頭部位 - 同意賣出商品的一方 - 和多頭部位 - 同意買入商品的另一方。在種小麥的農民相對於麵包師傅的情況下，農民將是空頭部位的持有人，而麵包師傅將是多頭部位的持有人。在每一個期貨合約裡，所有的細節都規定好了：交貨數量和貨物品質，每單位的價格，以及交貨的日期和方式。）

3. adjustments 調整

Lucy: How are the profits and losses of futures contracts calculated?

（期貨合約的利潤和虧損是如何計算的？）

Investment Specialist: The profits and losses of a futures contract depend on the daily movements in the market for that contract, and are calculated on a daily basis. As the market moves every day, **adjustments** are made accordingly. Unlike the stock market, futures positions are settled on a daily basis, which means that gains and losses from a day's trading are deducted or credited to each individual's account each day.

（期貨合約的利潤和損失取決於該合約每天在市場上的變動，並且是每天計算的。隨著市場每天的變動，而作相應的調整。不同於股市，期貨部位是每天結算的，這表示當天的交易中的收益和損失會從每個持有人的帳戶裡增加或扣除。）

4. price discovery 價格探索

Lucy: I have heard people talking about **price discovery** related to the futures. What does it mean?
（我有聽過人家談論與期貨相關的價格探索？它是什麼意思？）

Investment Specialist: Price discovery is a method used to determine the prices of a certain commodity or security through the market related supply and demand factors. It is the general method used to determine spot prices. For example, if the demand for a certain commodity is greater than the supply of the commodity, the price of the commodity usually increases (and vice versa).
（價格探索是一種透過市場相關的基本供需因素來決定特定商品或證券的價格的方法。它是決定現貨價格所使用的一般方法。例如，如果某一商品的需求大於供給時，它的價格通常會增加（反之亦然）。）

單元短文 Unit reading

Hedgers and Speculators
避險者和投機者

Hedgers

Producers and merchants can all be hedgers. A hedger buys or sells in the futures market to secure the future price of a commodity he or she intends to sell at a later date in the cash market. This helps protect him or her against price risks.

The long position holders in futures contracts will try to secure a price as low as possible. The short position holders will try to secure a price as high as possible. The futures contract, however, provides a definite price certainty for both parties, which reduces the risks associated with price volatility. Hedging by means of futures contracts can also be used as a means to secure a certain price margin between the cost of the raw material and the retail price of the final product sold.

Speculators

Speculators are the market players who aim to benefit from the risks involved in the futures market. They profit from the risks that the hedgers try to find means to mitigate. Hedgers aim to reduce their risks no matter what they invest in, while speculators want to increase their risks and thereby make their profits.

Speculators who tend to buy low in order to sell high in the future would most likely buy the future contracts from hedgers selling low expecting prices to fall in the future.

Unlike the hedgers, the speculators does not really mean to buy any commodity. Rather, they participate in the market hunting for profits by offsetting rising and declining prices through the buying and selling of contracts.

避險者

生產者和商人都可以是避險者。避險者在期貨市場買入或賣出，以確保他或她日後打算在現貨市場銷售的商品的未來價格。這有助於他或她防範價格風險。

期貨合約的多頭部位持有者，總是盡可能的努力爭取最低的價格。而期貨合同的空頭部位持有者則會盡可能的努力爭取最高的價格。然而，期貨合約為雙方提供了一個明確的價格確定性，從而減少因價格波動帶來的風險。用期貨合同的方式避險也可以用來鎖定原料的成本和最終產品銷售的零售價錢之間的可接受的範圍。

投機者

投機者是志在從期貨市場的風險中獲利的市場參與者。他們從避險者想要找辦法降低的風險裡獲利。避險者希望無論他們在投資什麼都要將風險降低，而投機者想要增加風險來因此獲利。

傾向於買低而在未來賣高的投機者，是最有可能去向預期未來價格會下降而賣低的避險者買期貨合約。

與避險者不同的是，投機者並不是真的有意購買任何商品。相反的，他們進入市場只是想要透過買入和賣出合約用來抵消上升和下降的價格而謀利。

常用片語 Common phrases

・parallel to 平行	This road is roughly **parallel to** the border. （這條路與邊境大致上是平行的。）
・merge into 合併	Eventually, everything **merges into** one and a river runs through it. （最終，一切都融合為一，而有一河流穿過它。）
・close out 平倉拋售	They are prepared to **close out** their business. （他們準備結清他們的業務。）

重點字彙 Important words to know

名詞 Nouns		動詞 Verbs	
期貨（合約）	Futures (contract)	避險	hedge
避險者	hedger	投機	speculate
投機者	speculator	平倉／沖銷	cover/offset
減輕	mitigate	合併	merge
衍生產品	derivative	對作	bucket
開倉	open position	套利	arbitrate
未平倉合約	open interest		
交割	delivery		
口	lot		
保證金	margin		
結算價	settlement price		
多頭部位	long position		
空頭部位	short position		
開倉保證金	initial margin		
追繳保證金	margin call		
保證金下限標準	maintenance margin		

金融小百科 2 數字與單位的趣味小知識
Financial Tips (2) - Fun Bits and Pieces of Numbers and Units

數字和單位 (Numbers and Units)

所有低於10的數字（包括0）都應該用字母表示，除了以下的例外之外：年齡、時間、日期、頁碼、百分比、錢、比例和測量單位。大於9的數字則用阿拉伯數字表示。

例如：

one robot（一個機器人）

two containers（兩個容器）

three team members（三名隊員）

eight workstations（8台工作站）

zero chance（零機率）

例外：

2 seconds（2秒鐘）

$3（3美元）

4:00AM（清晨4點）

8 percent（8%）

9 years old（9歲）

如果有兩個以上的數字一起表達時，則要把所有的數字用阿拉伯數字表示。這會讓您的數字表達一致、整齊且容易理解。但是，如果所有的數字都低於10時，則全部用字母表示。

例如：We used 4 worm gears, 15 pulleys, and 3 motors.。或者：We used four worm gears, two pulleys, and three motors.

當數字和計量單位是用來修飾名詞時，則要用連字符號（hyphenation）來表示。

例如：

a 4-year-old boy（一個4歲的男孩）

a 12-inch-long pipe（一個12英寸長的管道）

an 8-pound baby（8磅重的嬰兒）

如果數字是一個近似值，則用字母表示出來。

例如：

twice as much（兩倍多）

half finished（已完成一半）

我們一般不用數字作為句子的開頭，如：16 years after the project began, funding was cut.

而是會用字母表示數字或改寫句子，將數字放在句中。因此以上述句子為例，要改寫成：Sixteen years after the project began, funding was cut.（將16改為字母表示）或改寫成：Funding was cut 16 years after the project began.（將數字放在句子中間）。

日期（Dates）

一週的每一天及其縮寫（The days of the week and their abbreviations）：

The working week					The weekend	
Monday	Tuesday	Wednesday	Thursday	Friday	Saturday	Sunday
Mon	Tue	Wed	Thu	Fri	Sat	Sun

The working week					The weekend	
星期一	星期二	星期三	星期四	星期五	星期六	星期日

一年的所有月份及其縮寫（**The months of the year and their abbreviations**）：

January	February	March	April	May	June
Jan	**Feb**	**Mar**	**Apr**	**May**	**Jun**
一月	二月	三月	四月	五月	六月
July	**August**	**September**	**October**	**November**	**December**
Jul	Aug	Sep	Oct	Nov	Dec
七月	八月	九月	十月	十一月	十二月

日期用數字和字母表示（**Dates expressed in figures and in words**）：

In figures	In words	In figures	In words	In figures	In words
1st	the first	11th	the eleventh	21st	the twenty-first
2nd	the second	12th	the twelfth	22nd	the twenty-second
3rd	the third	13th	the thirteenth	23rd	the twenty-third
4th	the fourth	14th	the fourteenth	24th	the twenty-fourth
5th	the fifth	15th	the fifteenth	25th	the twenty-fifth
6th	the sixth	16th	the sixteenth	26th	the twenty-sixth
7th	the seventh	17th	the seventeenth	27th	the twenty-seventh

8th	the eighth	18th	the eighteenth	28th	the twenty-eighth
9th	the ninth	19th	the nineteenth	29th	the twenty-ninth
10th	the tenth	20th	the twentieth	30th	the thirtieth
				31st	the thirty-first

年份的表示方式（**Expressing the year**）：

年份的寫法（**How we write the year**）	2008	1900	1959	2000
年份的說法（**How we say the year**）	Two thousand and eight	Nineteen hundred	Nineteen fifty-nine	The year 2000

日期的表示方式（**Expressing the date**）：

日期的寫法（**How we write the date**）	1st January 2004	07/09/1959	August 12 2003
日期的說法（**How we say the date**）	The first of January Two thousand and four	The seventh of September Nineteen fifty-nine	August the 12th Two thousand and three

日期的介詞 **(Prepositions for dates)**：

對於單獨的日子和日期，我們用"on"。

例如：

I was born **on** the 7th of the month.

My birthday is on September the 7th.

對於月份，我們用“in”。

例如：

I was born **in** September.

如何詢問星期幾和日期（How to ask the day or date）

例如：

What day is it please?（請問今天是星期幾？）It's Tuesday.（今天是星期二。）

What date is it please?（請問今天的日期是？）It’s the 1st of April.（今天是四月一日。）

What's the date today please?（請問今天的日期是？）It's the 1st of April.（今天是四月一日。）

與日期表示相關的字彙（Vocabulary Relevant to Dates）

AD（Anno Domini）代表公元（拉丁語意為「在我們的主的年份」），簡稱AD。它一般用來代表耶穌出生的時代。它用在英語時，表示這個時間開始後的年份。

BC（Before Christ）代表基督之前（古希臘語的耶穌），縮寫為BC。它用在英語時，表示這個時間開始前的年份。有一些不承認基督教的內涵的非基督徒也使用了縮寫 AD 和 BC，但有些人更喜歡 **CE**（Common Era －紀元）和 **BCE**（Before Common Era －紀元前），認為他們是比較中性而不具宗教色彩的術語。

A millennium（複數 millennia）指的是為期一千年的期間。

A century 指的是為期連續一百年的期間。世紀的表示使用是配合序數來表示的。 例如：19世紀＝the **nineteenth** century

A decade 指的是為期十年的期間。

年代的用法（Expression of years）

在1920年至1929年的這幾十年，被稱為 "the Twenties”（二十年代）⋯

"the Sixties"「六十年代」等。但在當前的十年還沒有普遍接受的特別名稱。有人指這十年為“twenty hundreds”，也有人指其為“two thousands”。在寫法上，也可能被表示為“the ‘00s”（00年代）或“the 2000s”（2000年代）。但是，寫為”the 2000s”或者乾脆說”the two-thousands”可能會產生混淆，因為這可能指的是整個21世紀，甚至整個一千年。

英國英語和美國英語對於日期有不同的表示法（British English vs. American English）

在表示2007年9月7日時，英國人會寫DD/ MM / YY (07/09/07)，而美國人會寫MM / DD/ YY（(09/07/07)。這往往會造成很大的困惑。比較清楚的寫法是把日期全部寫出來（7th September 2007 或者 September 7th 2007）。

非特定數字（Empty number）

在日常英語裡，有三個字尾和一個字首可以用來組合以表示非特定數字。我們在數字有不確定性時或當確切數目並不重要時可以使用它們。非特定數字可以代表某個可能範圍內的數字。

字尾：

-teen：用於表示在10和20之間非特定的數字。

-ty：用來表示在20和100之間非特定的數字。

-illion：用來表示超過1,000,000以上的非特定的數字（或者只是表示某物非常大）。

字首：

ump-：這個字首一般只被添加到字尾-teen或-ty的前面，而從不用來添加到字尾 -illion的前面。其他字首則會被添加到-illion的前面。

例如：

“I called the store **umpteen** times before someone answered the phone.”

“There were **umpteen** people in front of her in line when she started waiting.”

在上面這兩個句子裡，我們知道其所提到的是10～20之間的數字，但我們不知道確切的數字是多少，而我們也不需要知道。

例如：

“There are **umpty** some ways to get there from here.”

“**umpty**”是英文裡很少使用的字；相對之下，**umpteen**比較常見，而且在適當時機是，它會更適於表示非特定數字。

字尾-illion通常用來表示非常非常大的數字或非常大的數字的概念。它也可以用來誇大東西，而且它也有強調的效果。字尾-illion也可以用來代表實際的數字，例如 billion（十億）和 million（百萬）。它也可以用來與數字“zillion”一起用，這通常代表任何大於（a billion）十億的數字。該-illion 字尾也可以和一些人們虛構的字首一起使用，來表示真正的大的數額。字尾有-illion的單詞是用來作形容詞的，即修飾名詞。不定冠詞“a”經常會在以-illion 作為結尾的字的前面使用。

例如：

“I swear there are a **babillion** people here!”

“There must be a **gazillion** stars in the sky.”

通常，當人們使用字尾-illion創建一個非特定數字時，他們只是編造一個字首（例如：gag-, baz-, tr-）來加在字尾-illion的前面，就像上面的例句。

下面的例句裡同時採用了兩個非特定數字：

“There were **umpteen zillion** people at the concert.”

在這個例句中，您可以肯定它試圖表達的是有很多很多人。此外，請注意在“zillion”的前面沒有“a”，因為它的前面緊接著“umpteen”，而umpteen並不需要有一個“a”在它前面。

最後，還有另一種方式用英語編造非特定數字。它是在“some”之前或之後加一個結尾有0的整數，例如30，100，2000，120 000。當以這種方式表達時，它通常是在小於1000的整數的後面，或者在超過1000的整數的前面。

例如：

“After 30-some years, I am reuniting with my best friend from elementary school.”

“I attended high school with some-1,000 other people.”

“James has 400-some friends on Facebook.”

總之，非特定數字是用於表達一個非特定範圍號碼的；它們一般都是非正式和強調的用法。

10%
20%
40%

3 Chapter

Insurance 保險商品篇

壽險 Life Insurance

什麼是壽險

人壽保險是一種用來提供在被保險人因故過世之後所失去的收入保障的人身保險。指定的受益人會收到保險理賠，所以可以得到被保險人死亡後在財務方面不受到影響的保障。人壽保險的目的是提供被保險人的家庭在財務上的保障，所以在購買壽險保單之前，被保險人應考慮他或她的財務狀況以及他或她想要為他或她的家屬或遺屬所維持的生活水準。

單元暖身小練習 Warm-up conversation and practice

針對以下每個空格，請選一個最適合的字填入。這是協助你對於本主題進行初步的暖身，以利對於後續的介紹可以更有效率的吸收。

(a) dependents	(b) premiums	(c) insured	(d) insurer
(e) funeral	(f) Protection	(g) beneficiary	(h) suicide
(i) term	(j) prudent		

Vito wants to know what a life insurance is.
維托想知道什麼是人壽保險。

Insurance agent: Good morning, Mr. He, may I help you?
（早安，賀先生，我可以幫您嗎？）

Vito: Yes, I would like to know what a life insurance is.

（是的。我想知道人壽保險是什麼。）

Insurance agent: Certainly. Life insurance offers you the protection against the loss of income if the ....1.... would pass away. The designated ....2.... receives the insurance proceeds and is thereby protected from the financial impact as a result of the passing of the insured.

（當然可以。人壽保險為您提供因被保險人去世而導致收入損失的保護。指定的受益人可以得到保險理賠，並藉此不會因為被保險人死亡而在財務上受到影響的保障。）

Vito: What should I consider before buying a life insurance policy?

（在我購買壽險保單之前，我應該考慮什麼？）

Insurance agent: The purpose of life insurance is to provide financial security for your family after you die. So, before buying a life insurance policy, you should consider your current financial situation and the standard of living you want to maintain for your ....3.... or survivors. For example, who will be responsible for your ....4.... costs and final medical bills? Would your family have to relocate? Will there be sufficient funds for future or ongoing expenses, such as child care, mortgage payments, and education? It is ....5.... to update your life insurance policies annually or when you have a major life event like marriage, divorce, the birth or adoption of a child, or purchase of a major asset

such as a house or business.
（人壽保險的目標是在您死了之後，為您的家庭提供財務保障的措施。所以，在購買壽險保單之前，您應該考慮您的財務狀況和您想為您的扶養人或遺屬保持的生活水準。例如，誰負責您的喪葬費用和最後的醫療費用？您的家人是否會因此需要搬遷？是否會有足夠的資金以備將來或現在正在持續發生的費用，如托兒費用、房貸付款和教育費用？謹慎的做法是每年或當您遇到重大生活事件就像結婚、離婚、生育或收養子女；或在購買主要資產時，如房屋或生意時，更新你的壽險保單。）

Vito: I see. How many types of life insurance are there?
（我明白了。那麼壽險有幾種類型呢？）

Insurance agent: Life insurance generally falls into two major types: ⑴ ....6.... policies which are formulated to provide a lump-sum payment, in the occurrence of certain events. The generic form of a protection policy is ....7.... insurance. ⑵ Investment policies, and their purpose is to enhance the growth of capital by regular or single....8.... . The common forms of this type of insurance include whole life, universal life, and variable life policies.
（人壽保險一般分為兩大類：（1）風險保障型人壽保險，而其目的是為了在某些事件發生時，提供一次性的付款。一般常見的保障型保單是定期壽險。（2）投資理財型人壽保險，而其主要目的是通過定期或單次保費的投入來促進資本的增長。這類型的保險比較常見的形式包含終身壽險，萬能壽險，和變額壽險。）

Vito: Are there any exclusions that I should pay attention to in the policy?

（在保單裡，是否有任何除外責任的情況我應該注意的？）

Insurance agent: The common exclusions which are often seen in the insurance policy to limit the liability of the ....9.... are claims related to....10...., fraud, war, riot, and civil commotion.

（一般在保單裡常見的用來限制保險人責任的除外責任有關於自殺、詐欺、戰爭、暴亂，以及民間騷動的索賠內容。）

Vito: Thank you. Please give me some life insurance pamphlets for me to carefully choose the kind of policy that is most suitable for me.

（謝謝您。請您給我一些壽險小冊子讓我仔細選擇，看哪一種壽險是最適合我的。）

答案 ANSWERS:

1.c 2.g 3.a 4.e 5.j 6.f 7.i 8.b 9.d 10.h

認識壽險

人壽保險是一種用來提供在被保險人因故過世之後所失去的收入保障的人身保險。指定的受益人會收到保險理賠，所以可以得到被保險人死亡後在財務方面不受到影響的保障。人壽保險的目的是提供被保險人的家庭在財務上的保障，所以在購買壽險保單之前，被保險人應考慮他或她的財務狀況以及他或她想要為他或她的家屬或遺屬所維持的生活水準。

保險的歷史

在古老的羅馬時期，有一個叫做「Collegia Tenuiornm」（互助協會）的宗教組織，而加入組織的會員們須繳交定額的人會費，死亡時，會員的遺族可以領到一筆葬儀費用。

中世紀歐洲時出現了一個名為「基雨特」（Guild）的組織。它是一種由同業者基於相互扶助觀念所組成的團體，他們對於會員的死亡、火災、疾病、竊盜等災害，共同出資救濟。

之後，英國的「友愛社」、德國的「救濟金庫」、法國的「相互救濟會」等組織，對保險的發展，特別是人壽保險的發展都具有相當的影響力。

現今人壽保險制度的建立，要從「生命表」運用於計算人壽保險的保費開始。所謂生命表，就是利用大數法則統計出來的死亡率表 (mortality table)。在1762年時，英國倫敦的「衡平保險社」（ Equitable Assurance Society）首先根據生命表，按年齡及身體健康狀況計算合理的保險費。由於計算過程十分科學化，逐漸改變了一般人對人壽保險的看法，自此人壽保險也受到大眾的接受而開始快速發展。經歷二百多年的發展，目前人壽保險已成為自由經濟國家重要的社會保障經濟制度之一。

人壽保險交易中存在四種法律意義上的人：保險人、被保險人、投保人和受益人。

保險人通常是一家保險公司，而投保人和被保險人經常是同一個人。例如，阿牛購買了人壽保險，他是投保人和被保險人；但如果阿牛的妻子小花經阿牛同意給阿牛購買了人壽保險，小花是投保人，阿牛則是被保險人。保險人和投保人構成人壽保險合同的當事人，被保險人是保險合同的關係人。

另外一個重要的關係人是受益人。受益人是因被保險人的死亡而獲取保險金的人。受益人不是保險合同的當事人，對自己是否受益無法自行決定，而是被投保人選定，投保人若要變更或者指定受益人需要經被保險人同意，而受益人則必須接受這個改變。

人壽保險合同與其他類型的保險合同一樣，是一個指定承擔風險的期限和條件的法律合同。在除外責任中約定了包括自殺條款在內的一些限制條款。自殺條款規定，如果被保險人投保後於一定時間內（通常是一年或兩年）自殺，保險人不承擔給付責任。多數人壽保險合同有一個觀察期（通常是兩年），如果被保險人在這個期間之內去世，保險人有法定權利決定是給付保險金還是退還保險費。

當被保險人去世或者達到保險合同規定的年齡時，保險人給付保險金。人們購買人壽保險的主要原因是防止受益人因為被保險人死亡導致陷入金融困境。保險金所得可以支付葬禮和其它死亡費用，並且可以通過投資收益替代逝者的薪水。購買人壽保險的另外一個原因是，人壽保險可以進行家庭財產規劃。防止退休後的生活受到因退休導致的收入減少而造成的影響。

保險人的定價政策與預定給付保險金數額、管理費用和預定利潤有關。預定保險金給付數額通過保險統計參照生命表（Life table）確定。保險統計使用的數學方法有機率論和數理統計。生命表是一種顯示平均餘命（平均剩餘壽命）的表格。通常，生命表僅考慮被保險人的年齡和性別。

保險公司從投保人或者被保險人那裡收取保險費，使用該資金在一定時間段的本利和來確定保險金給付數額。所以，人壽保險的費率對被保險人的年齡很敏感，因為保險人認為年齡較老的人所繳納的保險費用於投資的時間太短。

因為有害習慣可能有對保險人的經營成果起到消極作用，所以保險人會在政策允許範圍內，最大限度對被保險人展開健康情況調查。保險人會在承保前儘量詳細地詢問並記錄被保險人的生活方式和健康狀況。在特定的條件下，例如保險金額很高時或者懷疑隱匿告知事項時，保險人將作進一步調查。很多情況下，保險人從被保險人的醫師那裡獲得被允許獲得的信息。

法律並沒有強制要求人壽保險要提供保險給所有的人。保險公司自行確定哪些人可以承保，哪些人因為他們自己的健康狀況和生活方式而拒保。但是如果非健康的生活方式導致的風險可以被估測，保險公司可能會同意加保費承保。

當被保險人死亡，受益人向保險人必須提交死亡證明和索賠表格，來提出索賠申請。如果被保險人的死亡可疑，保險人可能對被保險人死亡的事件是否符合保險合同的規定開展調查。

保險金的給付有時候是一次性給付，也可按照合約約定分期給付，以保障受益人在未來（通常是老年退休之後）較長一段期間的生活。

人壽保險的類型

人壽保險可以被劃分成風險保障型人壽保險和投資理財型人壽保險。

(1) 風險保障型人壽保險

風險保障型人壽保險偏重於保障人的生存或者死亡的風險。風險保障型人壽保險又可以分為定期死亡壽險、終身死亡壽險、兩全保險、年金保險。

(1.1) 定期死亡壽險

定期死亡壽險提供特定期間死亡保障。保險期間經常為1年、5年、10年、20年或者保障被保險人到指定年齡時止。該保險不積累現金價值，所以定期死亡壽險一般被認為是無任何投資功能的保險。

購買定期死亡壽險要考慮三個關鍵的因素：保險金額、保險費和期間的長短。保險市場上出售的定期死亡保險有許多種，均是這些三個參量的許多不同的組合。定期死亡壽險價格一般低廉，適合收入較低或者短期內承擔危險工作的人士們購買。

定期壽險屬純粹人壽保險，並無儲蓄、投資成分、紅利，只會在投保人去世時提供理賠，合約設有定期時限，例如10年或20年。期滿而未有索償的話，合約便會自動終止。

(1.2) 終身死亡壽險

終身死亡壽險提供被保險人終身的死亡保障，保險期間一般到被保險人年滿100周歲時止。無論被保險人在100周歲前何時死亡，受益人將獲得一筆保險金給付。如果被保險人活到100歲時，保險公司會給付被保險人一筆保險金。由於被保險人何時死亡，保險人均要支付保險金，所以終身死亡壽險有儲蓄性質，其價格在保險中是較高的。該保險有現金價值，有些保險公司的險種提供保險單貸款服務。終身壽險計算保險費時，皆假設所有被保險人在100歲以前死亡，並且給付所保之保險金額，故終身死亡壽險亦有「100歲的養老險」、「100歲的定期壽險」之稱。

(1.3) 兩全保險

兩全保險也稱「生死合險」或「儲蓄保險」，無論被保險人在保險期間死亡，還是被保險人到保險期滿時還活著，保險公司均給付保險金。該保險是人壽保險中價格最貴的。兩全保險可以提供老年退休基金，可以為遺屬提供生活費用，特殊情況下，可以作為投資工具、半強迫性儲蓄工具，或者可以作為個人借貸中的抵押品。

(1.4) 年金保險

年金保險在約定的期間或被保險人的生存期間，保險人按照一定周期給付一定數額的保險金。年金保險的主要目的是為了保證年金領取者的收入。純粹的年金保險一般不保障被保險人的死亡風險，僅為被保險人因長壽所致收入損失提供保障。

⑵ 投資理財型人壽保險

投資理財型人壽保險產品側重於投資理財，被保險人也可獲取傳統壽險所具有的功能。該類型保險可分為分紅保險、投資連結保險和萬能人壽保險。

(2.1) 分紅保險

分紅保險保單持有人在獲取保險保障之外，可以獲取保險公司的分紅，即與保險公司共享經營成果。該保險是抵禦通貨膨脹和利率變動的主力險種。

分紅保險的紅利主要來源於「三差」：利差、死差和費差。

利差是保險公司實際投資收益率和預定投資收益率的差額導致的收益或者虧損； 死差是預定死亡率和實際死亡率的差額導致的收益或者虧損；費差是保險公司預定費用率和實際費用率的差額導致的收益或者虧損。一般來說，在規範的保險市場，保險公司之間死差和費差差異不大，紅利主要來源於利差收益。

(2.2) 投資連結保險

投資連結保險保單持有人在獲取保險保障之外，至少在一個投資帳戶擁有

一定資產價值。投資連結保險的保險費在保險公司扣除死亡風險保險費後，剩餘部分直接劃轉客戶的投資帳戶，保險公司根據客戶事先選擇的投資方式和投資渠道進行投資，投資收益直接影響客戶的養老金數額。

(2.3) 萬能人壽保險

萬能人壽保險具有彈性，成本透明，可投資的特徵。保險期間，保險費可隨著保單持有人的需求和經濟狀況變化，投保人甚至可以暫時緩交、停交保險費，從而改變保險金額。萬能人壽保險將保險單現金價值與投資收益相聯繫，保險公司按照當期給付的數額、當期的費用、當時保險單現金價值等變量確定投資收益的分配，並且向所有保單持有人書面報告。

一般常見壽險名詞解釋

保險保單 **Insurance Policy**	保險保單是保險人與被保險人之間的合約，其中規定了有關保險人所需要提供的保障以及被保險人必須支付的保費費用的條款。	Insurance policy is a contract between the insurer and the insured, and it states the terms related to the protection provided by the insurer and the required premium paid by the insured.
保險憑證 **Certificate of Insurance**	保險憑證是由保險公司所發出用來確認保險細節，如保險生效日，保險的種類和適用的賠償的金額等內容的文件。	Certificate of insurance is a document issued by an insurance company to verify the details of insurance coverage, such as the effective date of the policy, the type of insurance coverage, and the dollar amount of applicable liability, etc.

保險索賠 **Insurance claim**	保險索賠是由被保險人或者他/她的法定代表人向保險公司正式要求其根據保單的條款支付保險理賠金額。它通常是由保險公司審查其有效性，一旦索賠批准之後，再支付保險額給被保險人或代表被保險人的請求方。	Insurance claim is a formal request from the insured or his/her legal representative to an insurance company for a payment based on the terms of the insurance policy. It is usually reviewed by the insurance company for its validity and then paid out to the insured or requesting party on behalf of the insured once it is approved.
可轉換定期壽險 **Convertible term insurance**	可轉換定期壽險是一種允許投保人從定期壽險轉換為終身壽險或萬能壽險而無需再做健康檢查的壽險。	Convertible term insurance is a type of life insurance that allows the policyholder to change a term policy into a whole or universal policy without doing the health check again.
承保單 （附條文收據） **Cover note (conditional receipt)**	承保單是由保險公司發出的臨時文件用來提供保險，直到最終的保單發出為止。它和保險憑證和保險保單都不同。它的內容包含了被保險人的名字、保險人、保險種類，以及被保險的內容。	Cover note is a temporary document issued by an insurance company to provide insurance coverage until a final insurance policy is issued. It is different from a certificate of insurance or an insurance policy document, and it states the name of the insured, the insurer, the coverage, and the contents that are covered by the insurance.

批單或附加條件 **Endorsement or Rider**	批單或附加條件是保險保單的附件，它通常用來修訂或增補保單所規定的條款。而它通常會導致保險費的增加，因為它為被保險人提供了額外的好處。	Endorsement or rider is an attachment to an insurance policy to amend or add provisions to the policy. It usually causes the increase of insurance premium as it gives additional benefit to the insured.
保險核保人 **Insurance underwriter**	保險核保人是一個評估保護人或資產不受損失的保險風險，並設定保單保費的專業人員。	An insurance underwriter is a professional who evaluates the insurance risks to protect a person or asset from losses and set premiums for insurance policies.
退保手續費 **Surrender charge**	退保手續費是壽險投保人在取消他或她的壽險保單時所應該支付的費用。	Surrender charge is what a life insurance policyholder shall pay upon cancellation of his or her life insurance policy.
現金提取條款 **withdrawal provision**	某些保險有允許投保人從他們的保險單裡借錢的現金提取條款 。這些貸款可以隨時償還。但是，如果被保險人沒有在死亡之前償還的話，貸款的餘額和所有應計的利息都將在被保險人死亡後從保險額裡扣除。	Certain insurance policies have withdrawal provisions that allow policyholders to borrow money from the cash values of their policies. The loans may be repaid at anytime. However, if it is not repaid by the time the insured dies then the loan balance and all accrued interests will be deducted from the policy proceeds at death.

常用業務例句 Common business terms

1. mortality 死亡

Vito: What is a **mortality** table?

（什麼是死亡率表？）

Insurance agent: A mortality table counts the rate of deaths occurring in a particular population during a certain time interval, or survival rate from birth to a given age. Statistics in the mortality table shows the probability of a person dies before their next birthday, based on their age. Death rate data help determine the prices to be paid by people who want to purchase life insurance.

（死亡率統計在一個特定的時間段裡一個特定的人口族群的死亡率或者從出生到特定年齡的存活比率。死亡率表中的統計數據顯示，根據他們的年齡，一個人在他的下一個生日之前的死亡機率。死亡率數據有助於決定最近想要購買人壽保險的人所必須支付的價格。）

2. Incontestability 不可爭議

provision 條款

void 廢止

false statement 誤報

Vito: What is **incontestability provision**?

（什麼是不可爭議條款？）

Insurance agent: Incontestability provision is a common provision in life insurance policies that prevents the insurance company from **voiding** coverage due to a **false statement** by

the insured after a certain amount of time has passed.
（不可爭議條款是人壽保險保單上常見之條款，說明在某段時間後，保險公司不得以受保人誤報等原因為理由而廢除保險合約。）

3. Contestable 可爭辯期
rescind 撤銷
omission 遺漏

Vito : What does the **Contestable** period mean in an insurance policy?
（保單裡的可爭辯期指的是什麼意思？）

Insurance agent: Contestable Period is a certain period of time during which the insurance company can **rescind** a policy if it was approved with a false statement or **omission** of information, or deny a claim if it was excluded by the policy.
（可爭辯期是指在某一段時間內，保險公司可以撤銷因提供誤報或信息遺漏而獲得的保單，或者拒絕因此被撤銷的保單的索賠。）

4. contingent 可能發生的
alternate 替代
deceased 死亡
Secondary 附帶的

Vito: What does a **contingent** beneficiary mean?
（次要受益人代表的是什麼？）

Insurance agent: A contingent beneficiary is an **alternate** beneficiary

listed on an insurance policy who will receive the benefit if the primary beneficiary is **deceased**. This is sometimes referred to as a **secondary** beneficiary.
（次要受益人是在保險單所列出在主要受益人死亡時取代主要受益人收到保險收益的替代受益人。有時也稱為附帶受益人。）

 單元短文 Unit reading

The common reasons why insurance company does not approve you for insurance coverage
保險公司不願意批准你的保險申請的幾個比較常見的原因

The most common ones that you are not approved for an insurance application are the following:

1) Overweight or Obesity: This is a common reason for getting yourself declined for an insurance, because it indicates that you are not healthy enough to be considered a good candidate to be the insured. Even if you do get approved for an insurance with an overweight condition, most likely the premium will be higher than average.

2) Low Income: Certain life insurance companies do not insure people with low income as that they represent policies with reduced premiums. This is a consideration for the insurance company's profitability.

3) Alcohol or drug addiction: People with any kinds of addictions appear to be more susceptible to liver problem and other problems.

Underwriting insurance for this group of people could be interpreted as more insurance claims and lower profit for the insurance company.

4) Health related problems, such as high cholesterol, lipids and triglycerides, liver problems, blood or protein in urine, AIDS or HIV, high Glucose or Blood Sugarm or Hepatitis B or C, etc.: Having health related problems means a higher risk for serious health conditions, so insurance company is not willing to provide insurance coverage to people with some medical conditions.

5) Hazardous Occupations: Some occupations may be so dangerous that the life insurance companies may be reluctant to approve policies if you are working in one of such hazardous occupations. Some of the most hazardous jobs include loggers, fishers, airline pilots, roofers, iron and steel workers, recyclable material collectors, electrical power-line installers, drivers, farmers, construction laborers, etc.

6) Hazardous Extra-Curricular Activities: There are also extracurricular activities that are considered hazardous, and may have a higher risk of premature death. Some of the more hazardous activities include skydiving, scuba diving, flying, base jumping and etc.

7) Bad Driving Record: A bad driving record can indicate that you live a dangerous lifestyle and hence more risks for the insurance company to insure you.

8) Family History of Cancer: Even though there have been more remedies for cancers in recent years, life insurance companies continue to see cancer as a high risk condition.

9) Previous Declines on Life Insurance Applications. If you have been declined an insurance application before, you would have a higher chance not to be approved again.

In order to successfully get yourself approved for life insurance, you need to find out exactly what is in the way, so you can improve and make yourself eligible for life insurance approval in the future.

最常見的幾個保險公司不批准你的保險申請的原因如下：

1）超重或肥胖症：這是一個讓自己的保險申請被拒絕常見的原因，因為它代表你不健康，無法被認為是一個適合的被保險人人選。即使你在超重的狀態下被批准保險申請，你的保費很可能會高於平均費用。

2）低收入：某一些壽險公司不提供保險給低收入人群，因為他們代表低保費的保單。這是保險公司對其自身盈利能力的考慮。

3）酒精或藥物成癮：有任何一種癮的人顯得更容易患肝臟方面的問題和有其他的問題。如果提供保險給這一群人可以被視為有更多的保險索賠案件和保險公司有較低的利潤。

4）健康方面的問題，如高膽固醇，高血脂和高三酸甘油酯，肝臟問題，尿血或尿蛋白，愛滋病，高血糖，B型肝炎或C型肝炎等：有健康方面的問題的代表有更高的風險發生嚴重的健康狀況，因此保險公司不是很願意提供保險給一些健康方面有狀況的人。

5）危險職業：有些職業可能危險到讓壽險公司可能不願意批准你的保險，如果你從事的是這樣危險的職業之一。一些最危險的工作包括伐木工，漁夫，飛行員，屋頂修理工人，鋼鐵工人，回收材料收集人員，電源線的安裝人員，司機，農夫，建築工人，等。

6）高危險性的休閒活動：有休閒活動被認為是危險的活動，而且可能有更高的死亡風險. 這些高危險性的活動包括跳傘，潛水，飛行，跳傘，等。

7）不良駕駛記錄：不良駕駛記錄可以代表危險的生活方式，因此保險公司要承擔更多的風險來為你提供保險。

8）家族癌症病史：即使近年來有越來越多的癌症治療方法，壽險公司仍然認為癌症是高風險的病症。

9）曾經被拒絕過人壽保險的申請。如果保險公司以前已經拒絕過你的保險申請，您將有較高的機會下回也不會被批准。

為了成功地讓自己被批准壽險的申請，你需要找出到底阻礙是什麼，這樣才可以改善讓自己在未來有資格獲得壽險的批准。

常用片語 Common phrases

• fall into 分成
Life insurance generally **falls into** two major categories
（壽險通常分成兩大類。）

• be written into 寫入
Please make sure every item you discussed with the insurance agent **is written into** the insurance policy.
（請確保您和保險仲介討論的所有項目都要寫入保單內。）

重點字彙 Important words to know

名詞 Nouns		動詞 Verbs	
人壽保險	life insurance	保障	safeguard
被保險人	the insured	搬遷	relocate
受益人	beneficiary	促進	facilitate
保單持有人	policy owner/holder	廢止	void
核保人	underwriter	撤銷	rescind

核保	underwriting		
扶養人	dependant／dependent		
遺屬	survivor		
保費	premium		
批單	endorsement		
條款	provision		
死亡	mortality		
誤報	false statement		
遺漏	omission		
可能發生的／備用的	contingent		

財產保險 Property Insurance

什麼是財產保險

財產保險為財產提供大部分的風險保障，例如火災，盜竊和某些天然災害。它也包含某些特定的保險，如火災險、洪水險、地震險、住房保險或鍋爐保險等。財產保險主要以兩種方式來投保：除外責任保險和指定風險保險。除外責任保險指的是除了保單裡列出的除外責任項目之外，所有的風險都在投保範圍內。一般常見的除外責任項目有地震、水災、恐怖行動和戰爭等。最常見的指定風險有火險、竊盜險、雷電險和爆炸險等。

單元暖身小練習 Warm-up conversation and practice

針對以下每個空格，請選一個最適合的字填入。這是協助你對於本主題進行初步的暖身，以利對於後續的介紹可以更有效率的吸收。

(a) causes (b) Peril (c) covers (d) terrorism

(e) against (f) eligible (g) contents (h) qualify

(i) locations (j) disasters

Alberto wants to know the basics about property insurance.

Alberto想知道有關產物保險的基本信息。

Insurance agent: Good morning, Mr. Allegro, may I help you?

（早安，Allegro 先生，我可以幫您嗎？）

Alberto: Yes, I would like to know about business property

insurance.
（是的，我想要了解有關商業產物保險的信息。）

Insurance agent: Certainly. Property insurance insures your business ....1.... loss or damage to your business premises and to its....2..... It will also insure against loss or damage to property under your control. If your business rents or leases a location or travels to other physical....3...., then the property owner will require your business to carry property insurance, according to the terms of the lease or contract.
（當然可以。產物保險為您的公司以及公司場所的物件提供損失或損害的保險。它也可以對您掌控下的物件提供損失或損害的保險。如果您的公司租用或租賃場地或移動到其他的場所，那麼你的公司將被屋主要求透過租賃或合約的條款來進行產物保險。）

Alberto: I see. Typically, how many kinds of loss does a property insurance policy cover?
（了解。通常情況下，產物保險會涵蓋幾種類型的損失？）

Insurance agent: The more types of loss the policy....4...., the higher the premium will be. Property insurance falls into two types: (1) Broad Form – This type of policy lists a number of different types of ....5.... and covers against loss from all listed ....6....in the policy. (2) Single or Specific ....7....– This type of

policy insures against loss only from the identified peril. Fire policy is a typical example of this type of insurance. However, other single perils can also be insured against, for example,....8.....
保單涵蓋的損失類型越多，保費就越高。產物保險一般有兩種形式：（1）廣泛的形式 - 這種類型的保單辨認出一些不同類型的災害，而且在保單裡涵蓋了所有已辨認出所造成災害的原因。（2）單一或特定的風險 - 這種保單只涵蓋已經識別的風險所造成的損失。防火保險就是一個典型的例子。然而，還有其他單一風險可以投保，例如恐怖主義的活動。

Alberto: Can any business ....9.... for the broad form property insurance policy?
（任何公司都有資格申請廣泛形式的產物保險嗎？）

Insurance agent: For small businesses, a broad form property insurance policy is part of the packaged policy called "business owners' policy" and it will be the best coverage for the premium. However, certain businesses, either because the nature of their business implies specific risks or unusually high risk, may not be ....10.... for such a package. In that case, certain specific peril policies may need to be re-priced and re-examined.
（對於小企業來說，廣泛形式的產物保險已經包含在所謂的"企業老闆的保單"套餐裡面，而且那是最划算的保險。然而，某些公司因為其行業有特定的風險或不尋常的高風險而可能沒有資格享有這樣的保險。在這種情況下，某些特定風險的保單可能需要另外定價和接受審核。）

Alberto: I see. Thank you for your explanation.（明白了。謝謝您的解釋。）

答案 ANSWERS:

1.e 2.g 3.i 4.c 5.j 6.a 7.b 8.d 9.h 10.f

認識產險

財產保險為財產提供大部分的風險保障，例如火災、盜竊和某些天然災害。它也包含某些特定的保險，如火災險、洪水險、地震險、住房保險或鍋爐保險等。

我國保險法的分類：財產保險，包括火災保險（fire）、海上保險（marine）、陸空保險（land and air）、責任保險（liability）、保證保險（bonding）及經主管機關核准之其他保險。

保險依客戶的種類來分有：

（1）個人保險（Personal）：住宅火災保險 、汽車保險及個人責任及健康、傷害保險等。

（2）商業保險（Commercial）：商店或中小型企業之相關財產保險

（3）工業保險（Industrial）：大型企業之相關財產保險（如製造業或服務業）。

依財產保險之特性來分：（與人身保險比較）

（1）經營範圍不同

－ 財產保險：包含火災保險、海上保險、汽車保險、工程保險、責任保險、其他新種保險及傷害險。

－ 人身保險：包含人壽保險、健康保險、傷害保險及年金保險

（2）經營技術不同

－ 財產保險：危險事故之發生較不規則，並缺乏穩定性，在保險之採用極為重要。

－ 人身保險：危險機率計算較為精密，危險事故發生亦較規則與穩定，除保額累積較大時以外，再保險之重要性較小。

財產保險的特性（與人身保險比較）

（1）承保的標的不同

－ 財產保險：以財產或責任為保險標的。

－人身保險：以人的生命或身體為保險標的。

（2）合約的期間之不同

－財產保險：通常為一年、一年以內之短期合約。

－人身保險：大都為長期性質。

（3）賠償方式之不同

－ 財產保險：屬損失賠償保險，以不定值或定值保單為理賠基礎。

－ 人身保險：為定額給付保險，因人身無價故均按照預定之金額給付。

（4）資金運用－（流動性與安全性）

－ 財產保險：現金準備比率需在可運用資金的40%～50%間，而其貸放款項之比率僅在10%以下。金融機能較弱。

－ 人身保險：現金準備比率通常在可運用資金的10%以下，而其貸款比率可高達40%。

（5）代位求償原則：財產保險適用，人身保險不適用。

（6）保費之延緩繳付

－ 財產保險：火險及住宅地震險允許要保人一個月的保費延緩繳付期，住宅地震險於被保險人貸款期間內，更給予其自動續保之效力。

－ 人身保險：第一期保費不得延欠，且保費未繳前，合約不生效力

（7）特別準備金提存之需求不同

－ 財產保險：重視巨災準備之提存

－ 人身保險：重視利差損準備之提存

財產保險的保險標的

有形財產：指占有一部分空間而有實體存在之財產而言。

－ 不動產：土地及其定著物；但土地通常不包括在內；定著物指固定於土地，而未構成土地之一部分之物，如房屋及其他類型建築物。

－ 動產：指不動產以外之物，如貨物、汽車、飛機、傢俱、衣物等。

無形財產：指無實體存在之財產而言，包括：

－ 收益（利潤、租金收入）。

－ 費用（額外生活費用、額外租金支出、額外運輸費用）。

－ 責任（指各種依法應負的損害賠償責任）。

－ 權利（專利權、商標權、商譽、秘方、特許權等）。

財產保險之保險金額

財產保險之保險金額

保險金額 (amount or sum insured)：指的是保險人在保險期間內所負的最高賠償責任金額；亦即要保人所投保之金額．如投保房屋住宅火險三百萬元。

財產保險之保險價額

保險價額(insurable value)：指的是保險標的（物）的價值，亦為保險利益的金錢價值；保險標的物的買價並不一定與保險價額一致；保險價額只適用於財產保險，人身保險則無。

不定值保險

實際現金價值(actual cash value)：指的是標的物重置成本減去折舊後的價值。

重置成本(replacement cost)：指的是重新置換同一類型保險標的物所需之實際成本。

一般常見產險名詞解釋

業務項目 Business Item		
不可抗力 **Act Of God**	不可抗力是一個法律術語，它指的是人類無法控制的事件，例如突發性的自然災害像洪水或地震。	An act of God is a legal term and it refers to the events beyond human control, such as sudden natural disasters like a flood or an earthquake.
精算師 **Actuary**	精算師通常是保險公司聘請來為它們衡量人身或財產的風險和不確定性的專業人士。	An actuary is a professional who is usually hired by insurance companies to measure risk and uncertainty for them.
委付條款 **Abandonment clause**	委付條款是財產保險合約裡的一個條款。在某些情況下，它允許業主拋棄丟失的或損壞的財產，而仍然能夠向保險公司要求理賠全額。	An abandonment clause is a clause in a property insurance contract. Under certain circumstances, it permits the property owner to abandon lost or damaged property and still claim a full settlement amount.

強制保險 **Compulsory Insurance**	強制保險是一種在法律上有要求所有的個人或企業都要購買的保險。強制保險對於從事某些高風險活動，如駕駛汽車或開公司聘請員工的的個人和企業是有強制性的。	Compulsory insurance is the type of insurance all individuals or businesses are legally required to buy. Compulsory insurance is mandatory for individuals and businesses that engage in certain risky activities, such as driving an car or running a business with employees.
第三方責任保險 **Third-Party Liability Insurance**	第三者責任險是保險的一種，它是買來保障第三方的行為造成損害的保險。它一般是由被保險人（第一方）向保險公司（第二方）投保，來保障第一方免受另一方（第三方）的行為所造成的損害的保險。	Third-party liability insurance is a type of insurance policy purchased for protection against the actions of a third party. It is purchased by the insured (the 1st party) from an insurance company (the 2nd party) for protection against damage from the actions of another party (a third party).
殘值 **Salvage Value or Residual value**	殘值是資產已經在完全折舊後的剩餘價值。	Salvage value or residual value is the remaining value of an asset after it has been fully depreciated.

自付額/免賠額 **Deductible**	免賠額是在保單裡所規定的一筆必須由被保險人先支付的費用金額，等被保險人支付了之後，保險公司才會開始給付被保險人來賠償其剩餘的損失。	Deductible is the amount of expenses, in an insurance policy, that must be paid by the insured before an insurer will pay to compensate the insured's remaining loss.
責任保險 **Liability Insurance**	責任保險是一種用來保護被保險人因訴訟和索賠所需負擔的風險的保險。當被保險人被起訴的原因是在保險的覆蓋範圍之內時，保險就是有效的。	Liability insurance is a type of insurance to protect the insured from the risks of liabilities imposed by lawsuits and claims. It protects the insured in the event he or she is sued for claims that are within the coverage of the insurance policy.
火災險 **Fire Insurance**	火災險是一種特殊的保險，它的主要目的是用來支付更換、重建或修復的費用，而其承保範圍超出了一般的財產保險。	Fire insurance is a specialized form of insurance beyond property insurance, and is meant to cover the cost to replace, reconstruct or repair beyond what is covered by the property insurance policy.
理賠師 **Loss adjuster or Claim adjuster**	理賠師透過採訪被保險人、證人、警察、審查醫院記錄，並檢查財產損失情況等，來調查保險理賠案件以及決定保險公司所應該承擔的賠償責任。	Loss adjuster or claims adjusters investigate insurance claims by interviewing the insured, witnesses, the police, reviewing hospital records, and inspecting property damage to determine the insurance company's liability.

代位求償 **subrogation**	代位求償指的是保險人向第三方對被保險人所造成的損失要求賠償的合法權利。這樣是收回支付給被保險人的損失索賠金額的方法。	Subrogation refers to a legal right of an insurer to pursue a third party that caused an loss to the insured. This is done as a means to recover the amount of the claim paid to the insured for the loss.

常用業務例句 Common business terms

1. endorsements 批註書
exclusions 不保項目
take away 減少，撤除
such-and-such 這樣的和那樣的
hurricanes 颶風

Alberto: What is the difference between the **endorsements** and the **exclusions** in an insurance policy?
（保險單裡的批單和不保項目之間的區別是什麼？）

Insurance agent: Endorsements are used to add more coverage or more business locations to be covered. Endorsements generally mean big benefits for your business. They can be added, simply by a phone call, to a policy very easily if you have a good insurance agent. However, exclusions **take away** coverage. Your insurance agent or insurer will tell you that property policies are "always" written with the "**such-and-such**" exclusion. Exclusions are the business insurance purchaser's worst enemies. The well known example is the American **hurricanes** in 2004-2005. Many insurers claimed that the "wind" exclusion in their policies ruled out much of the damage from covered risks.

（批單增加保險範圍或被保險的場所。批單對您公司而言有很大的好處，而且如果你有一個很好的保險經紀，一般可以很容易的通過電話就可以添加在保單裡。然而，不保項目會減少保險範圍。你的保險經紀或保險公司會告訴你，產險保單「永遠」會寫有「這樣的和那樣的」不保項目。不保項目是商業保險購買者的最大敵人。眾所皆知的例子是美國在2004 - 2005年的颶風。許多保險公司聲稱在其保單的「風」所造成的災害屬於不保項目，所以當時很多的災害都被排除在保險的風險範圍之外。）

2. utmost good faith 最高誠信
discloses 披露

Alberto: What is **utmost good faith**?

（什麼是最高誠信？）

Insurance agent: Utmost good faith is a legal term to describe the requirement that all parties entering into an insurance contract must behave in good faith by making a full declaration of all material facts in the contract. For example, if you are applying for life insurance, you are required to **disclose** any previous health problems you may have had. Likewise, the insurance agent must disclose the critical information you need to know about the contract and its terms.

（最高誠信是用來描述要求訂立保險合約的雙方都必須表現得誠並且完整的披露合約中所有重要事實的一個法律術語。例如，在申請人壽保險時，你必須披露你以前可能有的任何健康問題。同樣的，保險經紀人必須要披露你需要知道的有關合約及其條款的重要信息。）

3. actual cash value 實際現金價值
replacement value 重置成本
depreciation 折舊
reimbursed 獲得賠償

Alberto: What is the difference between **actual cash value** and **replacement value**?

（實際現金價值和重置成本的差別是什麼？）

Insurance agent: Property insurance can pay damages or loss based on two different ways: (1) Actual Cash Value - your loss or damage is valued at the value of the property loss (actual replacement value minus **depreciation**). (2) Replacement Value - you are **reimbursed** the actual amount needed to replace the property when it is lost. Replacement value coverage typically carries higher premiums.

（財產保險根據這兩種不同的方式支付損害或損失的賠償：（1）實際現金價值- 你的損失將以受損的財產來計算價值（重置成本減去折舊）。（2）重置成本－你將得到需要更換損失的設備的實際金額的賠償。重置成本的保險的保費通常較高。）

4. schedules 保險項目清單
modified 修改

Alberto: Aside from adding endorsements and exclusions, how can a property insurance policy be modified?

（除了加入批註書和不保項目之外，如何能修改財產保險內容？）

Insurance agent: Property insurance policies can be **modified** by changing the **schedules** as well. Schedules are lists of locations and property covered by the policies. These must be updated regularly and at any time a location or equipment changes or is bought. Good insurance agents will contact you on a regular basis to discuss the updating of scheduled locations and equipment. If a location or a piece of equipment is not on the schedule, there is a possibility that a claim against that specific location or equipment would be denied.

（財產保險還可以通過改變保險項目清單來進行修改。保險項目清單是受保的地點和財產的清單。它必須定期更新和在受保的地點或主要受保的設備有變更或購置後進行更新。好的保險經紀會定期與您聯繫來討論需要更新的地點和設備。如果某個地點或設備沒有列在清單上，則被保險人在向保險公司要求理賠時有可能會被拒絕。）

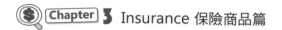

單元短文 Unit reading

Reminders for homeowners who are buying insurance
對想要買保險的購屋者的提醒

Insurance for homeowners can be very expensive, especially for those who live in high-risk areas such as areas next to major waterway or other high claims areas will likely to pay more.

Here are some tips to get the right coverage for your home while minimizing the cost:

1. Install Burglar Prevention System and Smoke Alarms: Installing a house alarm or a smoke alarm can possibly reduce the annual insurance premiums by about 5% to 10%, and they can also help lower the probability of intrusion by burglars and reduce damage caused by fire.

2. Increase insurance Deductible: The higher the insurance deductibles are, the lower the premiums will likely be, as insurance companies calculate the risks they are exposed to comparing different levels of deductibles.

3. Consider Buying Different Policies from the Same Insurer for Potential Discounts: Insurance companies usually offer a discount of 10% or more to customers who buy different kind of insurance policies under the same roof. It might be in the customers' best interest to compare and save on the premiums.

4. Plan In Advance for Modifications to Existing Homes : Construction in different materials might result in different levels of insurance premiums, as some materials are more flammable than others. Choose the less flammable to possible get a discount on the insurance premiums.

5. Pay off the Mortgage: Insurance companies tend to reduce premiums for homeowners who pay off their mortgages. Therefore, it would be sensible to find out the discounts available in this aspect.

6. Review and Compare Policies: It is necessary to review and update insurance needs periodically to find the best deal in town and also revise any changes as needed. Major events could also lead to savings on the premiums.

房屋保險有可能會非常昂貴。那些生活在高風險地區，例如靠近主要水道，或其它索賠較高的地區將會付出最多的保險費。

這裡有六種方式來確保你在儘量減少成本的情況下也能得到適當的房屋保險：

1）裝置防盜系統和煙霧報警器：裝置警鈴或煙霧報警器有可能使每年的保險保費降低大約5%到10%，同時還可以降低竊賊侵入的概率和減少火災可能造成的損害。

2）提高保險自付額／免賠額：免賠額越高，年度的保費就有可能越低，因為保險公司會依據不同的免賠額來計算他們所要承擔的風險。

3）考慮向同一個保險公司買多保單來獲得折扣：保險公司通常會提供10%或以上的折扣給向他們買多種不同保單的客戶。所以，多比較不同公司的保費再作決定對客戶來說有能夠節省保費的好處。

4）提前計劃家裡的改建工程：用不同的建築材料來加建有可能影響到保費的計算，因為某些材料會比較易燃。選擇不易燃的材料有可能能夠獲得保費上的折扣。

5）還清房屋貸款：保險公司傾向於為已經付清貸款或沒有貸款的客戶降低保費。因此，去了解這類折扣的詳情是明智的抉擇。

6）審查和比較保單：定期的檢查和比較保單來找到最划算的選擇以及作修改更新是必須的。某些重要事件的發生也可能是降低保費的因素。

常用片語 Common phrases

- take away 減少，撤銷
  The insurance company can **take away** your right to claim for compensation due to misstatement of age.
  （保險公司可以因 年齡錯報而撤銷你要求賠償的權利。）

- be adjacent to 相鄰的
  He is sure he got the best insurance coverage when compared with the people living **adjacent to** his house.
  （他確信和與他相鄰的人們相比較，他得到了最好的保險涵蓋範圍。）

重點字彙 Important words to know

名詞 Nouns		動詞 Verbs	
財產保險	property insurance	索賠	claim
恐怖份子活動	terrorism	披露	disclose
符合資格	eligible	補償	reimburse
災難	disaster	修改	modify
保險價額	insurable value		
保險金額	sum insured		
實際現金價值	actual cash value		
重置成本	replacement cost		
不保項目	exclusions		
項目清單	schedules		
批註書	endorsement		
定值保單	valued policy		
不定值保單	unvalued policy		
足額保險	full insurance		
不足額保險	underinsurance		
超額保險	overinsurance		

Unit 3 再保險 Re-Insurance

什麼是再保險

再保險是保險公司（原保險公司 original insurer 或分出公司 ceding company）向其他的保險公司（再保險公司 reinsurer 或 分入公司 ceded company）所購買的保險，用來分擔並減低其承保客戶的保險所承擔的風險。該原保險公司與再保險公司訂立保險協議，在協議中詳細註明再保險公司將分擔分出公司所支付的理賠的部分和條件，而再保險公司會得到由原保險公司所付的分保費，而此分保費是分出公司承包保險向客戶收取的保險費用的一部分。再保險公司可以是一個專業的再保險公司，或只是另一家保險公司。

單元暖身小練習 Warm-up conversation and practice

針對以下每個空格，請選一個最適合的字填入。這是協助你對於本主題進行初步的暖身，以利對於後續的介紹可以更有效率的吸收。

(a) reinsurer (b) original (c) in exchange for (d) take on
(e) absorb (f) transferring (g) ceding (h) garnered
(i) surplus (j) agreement

Elise wants to know what reinsurance is.
Elise想知道再保險是什麼。

Insurance agent: Good afternoon, Miss Liu, may I help you?
（午安，劉小姐，我可以幫您嗎？）

Elise: Yes, I was wondering if you could tell me what reinsurance is.
（是的，我想知道，是否您能告訴我什麼是再保險。）

Insurance agent: Absolutely. Reinsurance is the action of insurers ....1.... part of their risk portfolios to other insurance companies by some forms of ....2.... in order to reduce the probability of paying a large obligation resulting from an insurance claim. The purpose of reinsurance is for insurance companies to have an option to reduce risks associated with the policies they have underwritten by spreading risks across alternative companies. Reinsurance is also known as "insurance for insurers" or "stop-loss insurance". As a whole, the reinsurance company receives part of a larger potential obligation....3.... some of the money the ....4.... insurer received to accept the obligation. And the party that diversifies its insurance portfolio is known as the ....5.... party. The party that accepts part of the potential obligation in exchange for some of the insurance premium is known as the....6.....
（當然可以。再保險是保險公司為了減少因保險索賠而支付大量保險額的可能性，而通過某種形式的協議，將風險的一部分轉移給其他保險公司的做法。再保險的目的是為了讓保險公司有可以分散承保保險帶來的風險給其他的公司, 來降低風險的選擇。再保險也被稱為「保險公司的保險」或「停損保險」。總體而言，再保險公司接收較大保險的部分責任來換取一些原保險人所收到的保費。而分散保險組合的一方被稱為分出方。接受潛在保險責任來換取取保費一部分的一方被稱為再保險人。）

Elise: I see. Aside from reducing the risk to pay a large amount of claim, does reinsurance offer other benefits?
（我明白了。除了減少索賠時要支付了大量保險額的風險之外，再保險還有什麼其他的好處？）

Insurance agent: In addition to spreading risk, with reinsurance, an insurance company can....7.... clients whose coverage would otherwise be too great burden for a single insurance company to take on alone. When reinsurance happens, the premium paid by the insured is usually shared by all of the insurance companies involved. Therefore, reinsurance can also help a company by providing: (1) Risk Transfer - Companies can share risks with other companies. (2) Arbitrage - Additional profits can be ....8....by purchasing insurance elsewhere for less than the premium the company receives from policyholders. (3) Capital Management - Companies can avoid having to ....9.... large losses by sharing risk; this frees up additional capital. (4) Solvency Margins - The purchase of ....10....relief insurance allows companies to serve new clients and avoid the need to raise additional capital. ⑸ Expertise - The expertise of another insurer can help a company get a proper rating and premium.

（除了分散風險之外，藉由再保險，保險公司能夠擔負原本無法單獨承保的相對保險項目比較大的客戶。當再保險發生時，被保險人支付的保費通常由所有參與的保險公司共同分享。所以，再保險也可以通過提供以下來幫助公司：（1）風險轉移 - 公司可以與其他公司分享風險。（2）套利 - 可以透過在其他地方購買保費比向投保人收取的費用更低的保險來獲取額外的利潤。（3）資本管理公司 - 公司可以通過分散風險而避免吸收大量的損失。這將釋放更多的資金可作他用。（4）償付能力保證金 - 購買多餘的救災保險使企業能夠服務新的客戶和避免需要籌集額外的資金（5）專業知識 - 有其他保險公司的專業知識可以幫助公司獲得適當的評價和保費。）

Elise: I got it. That is a very detailed explanation of reinsurance. Thank you so much.

（我知道了。那真是對於再保險很詳細的說明。非常感謝。）

答案 ANSWERS:

1.f 2.j 3.c 4.b 5.g 6.a 7.d 8.h 9.e 10.i

認識再保險

再保險（reinsurance），是保險公司通過簽訂分保合約，將其所承保的部分風險和責任轉移給其他保險公司的行為。

在再保險業務中，分出保險的公司稱為原保險公司（Original insurer）或分出公司（Ceding company），接受所分出的保險的公司稱為再保險公司（Reinsurer），或分保接受公司或分入公司（Ceded company）。

再保險公司接受分出公司所分出的風險責任而收取的保費叫做分保費或再保險費；由於分出公司在招攬業務過程中支出了一定的費用，由分入公司支付給分出公司的費用佣金報酬稱為分保佣金（Reinsurance commission）或分保手續費。

如果分保接受公司又將其接受的再保險再分給其他保險人，這種業務活動稱為轉分保（Retrocession）或再再保險，雙方分別稱為轉分保分出人和轉分保接受人。

自留額（retained amount）與分保額（ceded amount）

對於每一危險單位的保險責任，分保雙方通過合約按照一定的計算基礎對其進行分配。分出公司根據償付能力所確定留下來自行承擔的責任限額稱為自留額或自負責任額；經過分保由接受公司所承擔的責任限額稱為分保額，或分保責任額或接受額。

自留額與分保額可以以保險額為基礎計算，也可以以賠償款項為基礎計算。計算基礎不同，決定了再保險的方式不同。自留額與分保額可以用百分率或者用絕對數字表示。

根據分保雙方承受能力的大小，自留額與分保額均有一定的控制，如果保險責任超過自留額與分保額的控制線，則超過部分應由分出公司自行負責或另行安排分保。為了確保保險企業的財務穩定性及其償付能力，許多國家通過立法將再保險的自留額列為國家管理保險業的重要內容。

分保業務形式

再保險有以下幾種不同分保情況：

⑴ 再保險的雙方都是經營直接保險業務的保險公司（直接保險公司），一方將自己直接承攬的保險業務的一部分分給另一方。參與分保的雙方都是直接公司，前者是分出公司，後者是分入公司。

⑵ 雙方都是直接保險公司，二者之間互相分出分入業務。這種分保活動稱為相互分保，雙方互為分出、分入公司。

⑶ 參與分保活動的雙方，一方是直接保險公司，另一方是專門經營再保險業務的再保險公司，前者把自己業務的一部分分給後者，後者則分入這部分業務。在這種情況下，直接保險公司是分出公司，再保險公司是分入公司。

⑷ 參與分保業務的雙方，一方是直接保險公司，另一方是再保險公司。再保險公司將自己分入的保險業務的一部分，再分給直接保險公司，直接保險公司則分入這部分業務。在這裡，再保險公司為分出公司，而直接保險公司則為分入公司。

⑸ 參與分保業務的雙方都是再保險公司，一方將自己分入的一部分保險業務再分給另一方，另一方則分入這部分業務。前者為分出公司，後者為分入公司。

⑹ 是兩個再保險公司之間相互分保，即相互轉分保。

再保險分類

按責任限制分類，再保險可分為比例再保險和非比例再保險。

⑴ 比例再保險

比例再保險是原保險人與再保險人，即分出人與分入人之間訂立再保險合約，按照保險金額，約定比例，分擔責任。對於約定比例內的保險業務，分出人有義務及時分出，分入人則有義務接受，雙方都無選擇權。

在比例再保險中，又可分為成數再保險、溢額再保險以及成數和溢額混合再保險。

(1.1) 成數再保險是原保險人在雙方約定的業務範圍內，將每一筆保險業務按固定的再保險比例，分為自留額和再保險額，其保險金額、保險費、賠付保險金的分攤都按同一比例計算，自動生效，不必逐筆通知，辦理手續。

(1.2) 溢額再保險是由原保險人先確定自己承保的保險限額，即自留額，當保險業務超出其自留額而產生溢額時，就將這個溢額根據再保險合約分給再保險人，再保險人根據雙方約定的比例，計算每一筆分入業務的保險金額、保險費以及分攤的賠付保險金數額。

⑵ 非比例再保險

在非比例再保險中，原保險人與再保險人協商議定一個由原保險人賠付保險金的額度，在此額度以內的由原保險人自行賠付，超過該額度的，就須按協議的約定由再保險人承擔其部分或全部賠付責任。非比例再保險主要有超額賠款再保險和超過賠付率再保險兩種。

按照安排方式分類，再保險可分為臨時再保險（Facultative Reinsurance）、合約再保險（Treaty Reinsurance）、預約再保險（Facultative Obligatory）。

關係區別

再保險與原保險的關係

再保險的基礎是原保險，再保險的產生，正是基於原保險人經營中分散風險的需要。因此，原保險和再保險是相輔相成的，它們都是對風險的承擔與分散。再保險是保險的進一步延續，也是保險業務的組成部分。

再保險與原保險的區別

1) 主體不同

2) 保險標的不同

3) 合約性質不同

再保險具有兩個重要特點：

(1) 再保險是保險人之間的一種業務經營活動。

(2) 再保險合約是獨立合約。

 一般常見再保險名詞解釋

分出公司 **ceding company**	分出公司是透過向另一家保險公司購買再保險，來把它保單組合裡的部分或全部風險轉給再保險的保險公司。	A ceding company is an insurance company that purchases reinsurance from another insurance company in order to pass part or all of its risks from its insurance policy portfolio to a reinsurance company.
分保接受公司（分入公司） **reinsurer (ceded company)**	分保接受公司是透過從分出公司接收部分或全部風險而取得來自分出公司從原有保險客戶收到的一部分保費的再保險公司。	Reinsurer or ceded company is a reinsurance company that accepts part or all risks from a ceding company by receiving part of the insurance premium the ceding company received from its original insurance clients.
自留額 **retention or retained amount**	自留額是分出公司在轉移部分風險或債務給再保險公司之後所留下由自己承擔的風險或負債的金額。	Retention or retained amount is the amount of risk or liability (arising from an insurance policy) that is retained by a ceding company after reinsuring the remaining amount of the risk or liability.

分保額 **ceding amount**	分保額是由分出公司轉移給再保險公司的那一部分風險或債務。	Ceding amount is the part of of risk or liability that the ceding company passes to a reinsurer.
再保險費（分保費） **reinsurance premium**	再保險費是由再保險公司收取的保費收入用來接收分出公司所轉讓的部分保險風險或債務。	The sum of premiums received by a reinsurance company to accept part of risk from the ceding company.

常用業務例句 Common business terms

1. facultative reinsurance 臨時再保險

case-by-case 按個別情況

uncertainty 不確定性

unreliability 不可靠性

Elise: I was told that there are many types of reinsurance. What is **facultative reinsurance**?

（我聽說有許多類型的再保險。什麼是臨時再保險？）

Insurance agent: Facultative reinsurance is a type of reinsurance coverage which the reinsurer evaluates the risk on a **case-by-case** basis. Facultative reinsurance is negotiated individually for each insurance contract that is to be reinsured.

（臨時再保險是再保險人按個別情況來評估案件的特定風險的再保險。臨時再保險的每個再保險合約是個別單獨談判完成的。）

Elise : What are the advantages and disadvantages of facultative reinsurance?

（臨時再保險有什麼利弊？）

Insurance agent: The advantages of facultative reinsurance are flexibility (the ability to arrange reinsurance to fit any particular scenario.), stability (stability in the operations of the insurer as large losses can be passed to the reinsurer.) and more business (increases the insurer's capacity to take on larger amounts of insurance business.) . And the disadvantages are uncertainty (the ceding insurer cannot plan in advance as it does not know whether the reinsurer will accept the risk for sure.), delays for the insurer (because the policy will not be issued unless and until the reinsurance is obtained, it leads to delay.), and **unreliability** (bad market conditions and poor loss outcomes can weaken the reinsurance market, making it difficult for the insurer to get reinsurance.)

（臨時再保險的優點是靈活性（安排再保險合約來適應任何特定情況的能力）、穩定性（保險公司有營運的穩定性，因為大型的損失可以轉移給再保險人）和有更多的業務（增加了保險公司承擔較大的保險業務量的能力）。而缺點是不確定性（分出保險公司不能提前計劃，因為它不知道再保險人是否會接受風險。），耽擱保險人的時間（因為保險手續在找到再保險公司之前不會完成，所以它會造成時間的延遲），和不可靠性（不良的市場條件和惡劣的損失結果會削弱再保險市場，讓保險公司很難獲得再保險。））

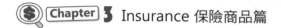

2. treaty reinsurance 合約再保險

standing 長期的

cede 讓出

is bound to 勢必要

negotiations 談判

terms 條款

Elise : What is **treaty reinsurance**?

（什麼是合約再保險？）

Insurance agent: Treaty reinsurance (or Automatic Treaty) is a **standing** contract between insurers and reinsurers. By contract, the ceding company is obligated to **cede** and the reinsurer **is bound to** assume a specified part of risk insured by the ceding company. Once the **negotiations** of the contract are over, the reinsurer must automatically accept all business included within the **terms** of the reinsurance contract with the ceding company.

（再保險（或自動條約）是保險公司和再保險公司之間的長期合約。分出公司依合約有義務讓出而再保險人勢必要承擔分出公司所承保的特定部分的風險。一旦他們之間的合約談判結束，再保險公司必須自動接受包含在與分出公司的再保險合約條款中的所有業務。）

Elise: What are the advantages and disadvantages of treaty reinsurance?

（合約再保險有哪些利弊？）

Insurance agent: The advantages of treaty reinsurance are the fact that it is economical (The insurer does not have to shop for a reinsurer before underwriting the policy.) and fast (There is no delay or uncertainty involved.). And the disadvantages are the fact that it is expensive (Administrative expenses can be quite high.) and complex (It is complicated and requires more record keeping.).

（合約再保險的優點是經濟的（保險人在核保保單之前不需要再物色一家再保險公司。）和快速的（不會延遲或涉及不確定性）。而缺點是昂貴的（管理費用可以是相當高的。）和錯綜複雜（它是複雜的而且需要較多的記錄保存。）。）

3. proportional reinsurance 比例再保險

Pro-Rata 按比例

predetermined 預定的

Elise: What is **proportional reinsurance**?

（什麼是比例再保險？）

Insurance agent: Proportional reinsurance (or **Pro-Rata** Reinsurance) involves one or more reinsurers taking a **predetermined** percent share of each policy that an insurer takes on. Premiums and losses are shared based on an agreed upon percentage between reinsurer and ceding company.

（比例再保險（或者按比例再保險）涉及一個或多個再保險人在每次保險公司承保新的保單時承擔預定百分比的份額。保費和損失的風險是依再保險人與分出公司之間達成一致的比例共同分享的。）

4. Non-Proportional Reinsurance 非比例再保險
Excess Of Loss Reinsurance 超過損失再保險

Elise: What is **Non-Proportional Reinsurance**?
（什麼是非比例再保險？）

Insurance agent: With non-proportional reinsurance, the reinsurer does not share similar ratios of the premiums earned and losses with the ceding company. The reinsurer's participation in the loss depends on the size of the loss. Excess of loss is an example of non-proportional reinsurance. For **Excess Of Loss Reinsurance**, losses exceeding the insurer's retention limit are taken over the reinsurer up to a predetermined limit.
（對於非比例再保險而言，再保險公司與分出公司不依損失的類似比例來分配保費。再保險公司參與承擔損失的多少取決於損失的大小。溢額再保險是非比例再保險的例子。對於溢額再保險，損失將由保險人支付到預定的自留額限額為止, 超出自留額的部分將由再保險人承擔。）

5. Retrocession 轉分保
retrocedent 轉分保分出方
retrocessionaire 轉分保接受方

Elise: What is **Retrocession**?
（什麼是轉分保？）

Insurance agent: Retrocession is the reinsurance bought by reinsurers to protect reinsurer's financial stability - to cover their own risk exposure or to increase their capacity. The ceding reinsurer is referred to as retrocedent and the reinsurer that assumes the risk in **retrocession** is called the **retrocessionaire**.

（轉分保是通過讓再保險人購買再保險，來保障再保險公司的金融穩定性 - 來承擔他們自己的風險或提高自己的能力。再保險的分出方稱為轉分保分出方而承擔轉分保風險的再保險公司被稱為轉分保接受方。）

單元短文 Unit reading

Technology Trends: Reinsurance

科技趨勢：再保險

The reinsurance industry has many challenges. After years of weak market conditions followed by sudden and sharp difficult periods, extreme losses from man-made and natural disasters and open-ended liabilities, such as air crash and terrorism are putting serious pressure on reinsurers.

These difficulties challenge reinsurers to adapt and come up with innovative solutions. Reinsurers control their risk through complicated risk analysis, through careful pricing and setting of terms and conditions, and through capital management – including retrocessions when needed.

To realize these solutions, reinsurers are investing in technology, including BI and data analytics, work flow and core systems replacement, and the use of sophisticated specialized components, such as modeling tools.

再保險行業有多重的挑戰。多年的市場形勢疲軟之後接著突然急劇而困難的期間，來自人為和自然災害和開放式的責任造成的巨大損失，如空中失事和恐怖主義活動，都給予再保險公司嚴重的壓力。

這些困難挑戰著再保險公司去適應並拿出創新性的解決方案。再保險公司通過複雜的風險分析，通過謹慎的定價和條款和條件的設定，並通過資產管理 - 包括在需要的時候進行轉分保，來控制自己的風險。

為了落實這些解決方案，再保險公司投資於多個科技領域，包括商業智能和數據分析，工作流程和核心系統更換，並使用精密的專門組件如模塊工具。

常用片語 Common phrases

• spread across 分散到	Reinsurance helps an insurance company reduce its risks by **spreading** risks **across** alternative companies. （再保險幫助保險公司通過分散風險到其他公司來降低自身的風險。）
• take on 承擔	Reinsurance increases the insurer's capacity to **take on** greater amounts of insurance business. （再保險提高了保險公司能夠承擔較大的保險業務量的能力。）
• in exchange for 來換取	The party that accepts part of the potential obligation **in exchange for** a portion of the insurance premium is known as the reinsurer. （接受潛在保險責任來換取保費一部分的一方被稱為再保險人。）

重點字彙 Important words to know

名詞 Nouns		動詞 Verbs	
再保險	reinsurance	儲存	garner
組合	portfolio	分散	diversify
責任	obligation	吸收	absorb
出讓方	ceding party	讓出	cede
再保險人	reinsurer	承擔	assume
套利	arbitrage		
資產管理	capital management		
償付準備金	solvency margins		
專業知識	expertise		
讓出	cession		

金融小百科 3
基本各項數值表達（比率、小數、分數）
Financial Tips (3) - The Basic Expressions of Values - Ratios, Decimals, Fractions

比率（Ratios）

比率是一個數字相對於另一個數字的關係，藉著除以另一個數字來表示。

例如：

15 個人和 5個人的關係可以用比率表示。我們可以說15個人是5個人的三倍。15 people are three times more than 5 people.

當我們說15個人是5個人的三倍時，三倍（three times more than）就是比率的名稱。

我們也可以用冒號來表示兩個數字的比率：

例如：

15:5

我們可以說 The ratio is fifteen to five.

我們也可以用以下方式表達較小的數字是較大的數字的多少比率。

讓較小的數字用基數表示（1，2，3 ...等），而較大的數字用序數表示（1st, 2nd, 3rd....等）。

例如：

What ratio has 2 to 3?（2 是 3 的什麼比率？）

2 is two thirds of 3.（2 是 3 的 2／3）

What ratio has 4 to 5?（4 是 5 的什麼比率？）

4 is four fifths of 5.（4 是 5 的 4／5）

由此可見：

1 is one fifth of 5.（1 是 5 的 1／5）

2 is two fifths of 5.（2 是 5 的 2／5）

3 is three fifths of 5.（3 是 5 的 3／5）

百分數（Percentages）

百分數也是比率。

例如：

6個人是12個人的一半。

six people are half of 12 people.

我們也可以說 6個人是12個人的50%。

six people are 50% of 12 people.

百分數由“percent”表示。

百分數的讀法：

100%: one hundred percent

0.5%: point five percent

0.46%: point four six percent

20%: twenty percent

16.09%: sixteen point zero nine percent

0.5%: (zero) point five percent（zero可省略）

95.99%: ninety-five point nine nine percent

50 bps（基本點）: fifty basis points（就等於0.5%）

分母（denominator）和分子（numerator）

如果我們要表達1990 年特拉華州的性別比率，我們可以說：

The sex ratio of Delaware in 1990 was: 343,200 females to 322,968 males or 1.06.（特拉華州在1990年的性別比率為：女性 343,200人比男性322968人

或者 1.06。)

當我們決定好哪個數字是分母，哪個數字是分子時，我們可以用：

males to females, .94（男性比女性，0.94）

或者females to males, 1.06（女性比男性，1.06）來表示女性相對於男性的比率是1.06:1。我們也可以說：There are 106 females for every 100 males.（相對於每106個女性有100個男性。）來表示同樣的意思。

在表示人口密度時（Population Density － the number of people per square mile， 每平方英里的人數），我們可以說：In 1990 in Delaware, the population density was: 666,168 persons / 1955 sq. miles = 341 persons per square mile.（美國特拉華州在1990年的人口密度為：666,168人/1955平方英里=每平方英里341人。）

In New Castle County, the population density was: 441,946/426 = 1,037 persons per square mile.（新城堡縣的人口密度為：441,946/426=每平方英里1037人。）

扶養比率（Dependency Ratio - the number of people under age 15 plus the number of people 65 and over divided by the number of people between 15 to 64， 15歲以下的人口數加65歲及以上的人口數再除以15人至64歲之間的人口數）是一個假設年齡界定經濟貢獻的用來測量依賴扶養關係的粗略數據。

In 1994 in Delaware, the dependency ratio was estimated as: (152,869+ 90,329)/462,396 = .53（美國特拉華州在1994年的撫養比率估計為：（152,869+90329）/462396=0.53）

也就是說，For every 100 workers there are 53 dependents, or（每100名工人有53名需要接受扶養的家屬）或者For every dependent, there are 1.9 workers.（每一名接受扶養的家屬有1.9名工人。）

比例（Proportions）

比例是一個特殊的比率，其中分母為總數，而分子是總數的一個子部分。

例如：

While the ratio of females to males in Delaware is 1.06, females represent .515 proportion of the total.（女性對男性在美國特拉華州的比例為1.06，所以女性佔總數的0.515的比例。）

百分比是根據100人為基礎的一種比例形式。如果要計算百分比，我們只要把比例乘以100。

例如：

Females are 51.5% of the total.

（女性佔總數的51.5%。）

小數（Decimals）

小數點左邊的數通常按基數詞讀，若為三位以上的數，也可按編碼式讀法讀出，即將數位單個讀出；小數點右邊的數通常按編碼式讀法單個讀出。 小數的讀法：小數點讀作“point”，小數後各位數要分別讀，小數點前的數若為“0”可略去不讀。

例如：

6.86: six **point** eight six

14.15: fourteen point one five

345.456: three four five **point** four five six 或 three hundred and forty－five **point** four five six

3,485.3451: three thousand four hundred and eighty-five **point** three-four-five-one

2.468: two **point** four six eight

1.5: one **point** five

0.157: (zero) **point** one five seven

0.23: (zero) **point** two three

2.05: two **point** O（字母) five

6.003: six **point** O O (字母) three

78.12 : seventy-eight **point** one two

小數的四捨五入（round off）

四捨五入到小數點第二位的說法是：round off to the 2nd decimal place

小數點後四捨五入的說法：round off after the decimal

四捨五入到小數點第N位：round off after the Nth place

round off 是四捨五入

round down 和 truncate 則是完全的捨去；round up 是完全進位。

分數（Fractions）

分數詞是由基數詞的序數詞合成的，分子用基數詞表示，分母用序數詞表示，除了分子是“1”的情況外， 序數詞都要用複數形式。

例如：

1/2: one half 或 one **over** two

1/3: one-third

1/4: one-fourth 或 one quarter

2/3: two-third**s**

7/12: seven-twelfths

3/4: three quarters

1/5: one-fifth

2/5: two-fifths

3/5: three-fifths

3/7: three-sevenths

7/8: seven-eighths

1/10: one-tenth 或 a tenth

1/100: one-hundredth 或 one per cent

1/1000: one-thousandth

1/10000: one ten-thousandth

1/100000: one hundred-thousandth

1/1000000: one millionth

比較複雜的分數讀法如下：

20/87: twenty over eighty-seven

33/90: thirty-three over ninety

22/9: twenty-two over nine

a/b: a over b 或 a divided by b

43/97: forty-three over ninety-seven

159/234: one hundred and fifty-nine over two hundred and thirty-four

整數與分數之間須用and連接：

例如：

2 1/2: two **and** a half 或 two **and** one half

4 1/2: four **and** a half

4 2/3: four **and** two-thirds

9 2/5: nine **and** two fifths

5 2/3：five **and** two-thirds

分數用作前置定語時，分母要用單數形式。

例如：

a one-third mile 1/3英里

a three-quarter majority 3/4的多數

20%
10%
40%

4 Chapter

Accounting & Taxation

會計財稅篇

財務報表 Financial Statements

什麼是財務報表

財務報表是公司、個人或其他單位所有金融活動的正式記錄。相關的財務信息用結構化，讓人易懂的方式編列而成。它通常包括資產負債表、損益表、股東權益表和現金流量表，而且通常附有管理分析意見和財務報表的註解。它的主要目的是協助股東或潛在的投資者了解公司的財務狀況。

單元暖身小練習 Warm-up Conversation and Practice

針對以下每個空格，請選一個最適合的字填入。這是協助你對於本主題進行初步的暖身，以利對於後續的介紹可以更有效率的吸收。

(a) standard (b) cash flow (c) adhere to (d) continuity
(e) entity (f) jurisdiction (g) outline (h) preparation
(i) across (j) accuracy

Tracy wants to know what financial statements are .
崔西想知道財務報表是什麼。

Accountant: Good afternoon, Miss Nishimura, may I help you?
（午安，西村小姐，我可以幫助您嗎？）

Tracy: Yes, I would like to know what financial statements are.
（是的，我想知道財務報表是什麼。）

Accountant: Of course. Financial statements are official records that

....1.... the financial activities of a business, a person or on entity. They are meant to show the financial information of the ....2.... as clearly and concisely as possible for both the entity itself and their for readers. Financial statements of a business usually include: income statements, balance sheet, statements of....3....and statements of change in equity, as well as management analysis and footnotes to the financial statements.

（當然。財務報表是描述公司、個人或單位財務活動的正式記錄。它是為了單位本身和其讀者而儘可能清晰而簡潔地呈現一個單位的財務信息。公司的財務報表通常包括：損益表、資產負債表、現金流量表和所有者權益變動表，以及管理分析意見和財務報表的註解。）

Tracy: Are there any accounting principles for the financial statements? Who checks them for....4....?

（是否有針對財務報表的任何會計原則？誰會檢查他們的準確性？）

Accountant: It is a ....5....practice for businesses to provide financial statements that ....6....generally accepted accounting principles (GAAP), to maintain ....7....of information and presentation ....8....international borders. In addition, financial statements are often audited by government agencies, accounting firms, etc. to ensure accuracy.

（標準的做法是讓公司提供遵守一般公認會計原則的財務報表，才能保持跨國界的信息和呈現的連續性。除此之外，財務報表往往是由政府機構、會計師事務所……等來確保其準確性。）

Tracy: What are generally accepted accounting principles?
（什麼是一般公認的會計原則？）

Accountant: Generally accepted accounting principles (GAAP) are the standard guidelines for financial accounting used in any given....9.... They include the standards, conventions, and rules that accountants follow in recording and summarizing and in the ....10.....of financial statements.
（一般公認會計原則（GAAP）是用於任何司法管轄區所使用的財務會計準則。它們包括會計師在記錄、總結和編制財務報表所遵循的標準、慣例和規則。）

Tracy: I see. Thank you so much for the information.
（我明白了。多謝您提供的信息。）

答案 ANSWERS:

1.g 2.e 3.b 4.j 5.a 6.c 7.d 8.i 9.f 10.h

認識財務報表

財務報表通常可以反映一個公司在過去的某個財政時間段的財務表現狀況以及期末狀況，所以它能幫助投資者和股東了解公司的經營狀況，而進一步幫助經濟決策。財務報表是以一般公認會計原則下有選擇性地報告財務狀況。

財務報表通常包含：

⑴ 利潤表（Income Statement）或損益表（Profit and Loss Statement）：它反映公司收入、支出及盈利（或虧損）的表現。

⑵ 資產負債表（Balance Sheet）：它反映公司所擁有的資產、負債及資

本的期末狀況。

⑶ 現金流量表（Statement of Cash Flow）：它反映公司現金流量的狀況，其中分為經營活動、投資活動及融資活動三部分。

⑷ 股東權益變動表（Statement of Stockholders Equity）：它反映股東權益和盈餘分配的狀況。

附在財務報表上的相關報告

財務報表上一般會附上會計師的管理分析意見和其對財務報表的註解。在會計師的管理分析意見中，如果附有會計師事務所的審計報告，它可信性將會更高。所以在股東大會上，財政報告一般要附有會計師報告。至於財務報表的註解，它主要是說明會計政策和資產折舊的方式等。

財務報表的基本架構：

⑴ 利潤表（Income Statement）或損益表（Profit and Loss Account）

是反映公司在一定會計期間的經營成果的報表。

⑵ 資產負債表（balance sheet）

資產負債表是指反映公司在某一特定日期的財務狀況的報表。資產負債表主要反映資產、負債和所有者權益三方面的內容，並滿足「資產 = 負債+所有者權益」平衡式。資產分為流動資產和非流動資產兩大類。負債分為流動負債和非流動負債兩大類。所有者權益分為實收資本、資本公積、盈餘公積和未分配利潤幾大類。

⑶ 現金流量表（Statement of Cash Flow）

是反映公司在一定會計期間現金和現金等價物流入和流出的報表，其目的在於提示償債能力和變現能力。

⑷ 股東權益變動表（Statement of Stockholders Equity）

反映本期公司股東權益總量的增減變動情況以及結構變動的情況，特別是要反映直接記入所有者權益的利得和損失。

財務報表附註（Notes to financial statements）

是為了便於財務報表使用者理解財務報表的內容而對財務報表的編製基礎、編製依據、編製原則和方法及主要項目等所作的解釋。其主要內容有：主要會計政策；會計政策的變更情況、變更原因及其對財務狀況和經營成果的影響；非經營項目的說明；財務報表中有關重要項目的明細資料；其他有助於理解和分析報表需要說明的事項。

報表說明

財務報表主要是反映公司一定期間的經營成果和財務狀況變動，對財務報表可以從六個方面來看，以發現問題或作出判斷。

⑴ 看利潤表

比較相鄰兩年收入的增長是否在合理的範圍內。如果利潤表上現年比上年增加幾百個百分點，這就是不可信的，問題非常明顯。那些增長點在50%－100%之間的公司，都要特別關注。

⑵ 看公司的壞帳準備

有些公司的產品銷售出去，但款項收不回來，但它在帳面上卻不計提或提取不足，這樣的收入和利潤就是不實的。

⑶ 看長期投資是否正常

有些公司在主營業務之外會有一些其他投資，看這種投資是否與其主營業務相關聯，如果不相關聯，那麼，這種投資的風險就很大。

⑷ 看其他應收款是否清晰

有些公司的資產負債表上，其他應收款很不清楚，許多陳年舊帳放在裡面，有很多是收不回來的。

⑸ 看是否有關聯交易

尤其注意年中大股東向上市公司借錢，到年底再利用銀行借款還錢，從而在年底報表上無法體現大股東借款的做法。

⑹ 看現金流量表是否能正常地反映資金的流向

注意現金注入和流出的原因和事項。

財務報表的種類

財務報表可以按照不同的標準進行分類。

⑴ 按服務對象，可以分為對外報表和內部報表。

⑵ 按報表所提供會計信息的重要性，可以分為主表和附表。

⑶ 按編製和報送的時間分類，可分為中期財務報表和年度財務報表。廣義的中期財務報表包括月份、季度、半年期財務報表。

⑷ 按編報單位不同，分為基層財務報表和匯總財務報表。基層財務報表由獨立核算的基層單位編製的財務報表，是用以反映該基層單位財務狀況和經營成果的報表。匯總報表是指上級和主管部門將本身的財務報表與其所屬單位報送的基層報表匯總編製而成的財務報表。

⑸ 按編報的會計主體不同，分為個別報表和合併報表。

⑹ 按照企業資金運動形態的不同，可以分為靜態報表和動態報表。靜態報表是指某一時點的報表，例如：資產負債表動態報表是指某一時期的報表，例如：利潤表和現金流量表, 所有者權益。

報表的作用

財務報表是財務報告的主要組成部分，它所提供的會計信息具有重要作用，主要體現在以下幾個方面：

⑴ 全面系統地顯示公司一定時期的財務狀況、經營成果和現金流量，有利於經營管理人員了解公司各單位各項任務指標的完成情況，評價管理人員的經營業績，以便及時發現問題，調整經營方向，制定措施改善經營管理水平，提高經濟效益，為經濟預測和決策提供依據。

⑵ 有利於國家經濟管理部門了解國民經濟的運行狀況。

⑶ 有利於投資者、債權人和其他有關各方掌握公司的財務狀況、經營成果和現金流量情況，進而分析公司的盈利能力、償債能力、投資收益、發展前景等，為他們投資、貸款和貿易提供決策依據。

⑷ 有利於滿足財政、稅務、工商、審計等部門監督公司經營管理。

一般公認會計原則（Generally Accepted Accounting Principles，GAAP）

指因應會計事項所制定的全球性原則，會計個體之資產、負債、資本、費用、收入等任何一環都必須遵守。一般而論，全世界所有會計事務上的認定、分析、紀錄、分類和財務報表製作均需這些原則。因此可說會計原則為一種跨國語言。也就是如此，使用會計原則處理事務的會計師與醫師或護士一般在異國處理事務上，並毋須絕對上的語言溝通。此原則尤為資本主義世界所公認，但並不代表只有一個準則能被接受，例如存貨計價法就有先進先出法、後進先出法、平均法等（Moving Average）等，這些方法（部分）都是被GAAP名列接受的會計帳務處理方法，各公司個體可依照實際其行業的環境，選定會計政策來記帳。

國際財務報告準則（International Financial Reporting Standards，縮寫IFRS）

是指國際會計準則理事會（IASB）編寫發布的一套致力於使世界各國公司能夠相互理解和比較財務信息的財務會計準則和解釋公告。國際會計準則理事會的前身為國際會計準則委員會，主要是由日本、法國、德國與美國等會計團體發起。

國際財務報告準則是一系列以原則性為基礎的準則，它只規定了廣泛的規則而不是約束到具體的業務處理。到2002年為止，大量的國際會計準則提供了多種可選的處理方法；國際會計準則委員會的改進方案是儘量找到並減少同一業務的可選處理方案。準則還為通用財務報告中重要的交易和財務事件設定識別、計量、報告和披露標準。也可能為特定的產業設置特定的規則。

一般常見財務報表名詞解釋

資產 **Assets**	資產指的是可以透過擁有或控制以產生正面經濟價值的經濟資源，可以是有形或是無形的。	Assets refer to tangible or intangible economic resource that can be owned or controlled to generate positive economic value.
負債 **Liabilities**	負債是一個公司的債務或義務，表示債權人對公司資產的權利。	Liabilities are debts or obligations of a business, and they indicate the creditor's claim on the business assets.
股東權益 **Shareholder's equity**	股東權益代表由公司的全體股東擁有的公司股權。它通常是公司的資產和負債之間的差額。	Shareholders' equity represents a company's equity owned by all shareholders of a company. It is usually the difference between a company's assets and liabilities.
淨利 **Net income**	在會計裡，淨利等於在特定會計期間內的公司收入減去銷售商品的成本、費用和稅後得到的金額。	In accounting, net income is a company's income minus cost of goods sold, expenses and taxes for a specific accounting period.
費用 **Expense**	在會計裡，費用是現金或資產從公司流出到另一家公司。現金的流出通常是用來支付公司所交易的產品或服務。	In accounting, expense is an outflow of cash or assets from a company to another company. This outflow of cash is generally paid out to trade for products or services.

現金流 **Cash flow**	在會計裡，現金流是流入或流出公司的金錢。它通常是在一個特定的時間段作測量的。	In accounting, cash flow is the movement of money into or out of a company, and it is usually measured during a specific period of time.
先進先出法 **FIFO**	當使用FIFO（先入先出）的庫存記錄方法時，最久的庫存會優先記錄為已經售出了，但它並不代表記錄已經售出的最古老庫存實際真的已經售出了。	When FIFO（first-in, first-out）is used, it means the oldest inventory is recorded as sold first but it does not mean that the exact oldest inventory has been sold.
後進先出法 **LIFO**	當使用LIFO（後進先出）的庫存記錄方法時，最後購買或生產的庫存會記錄為是最先出售的庫存。	When LIFO（last-in, first-out）is used, it means the most recently bought or produced inventory is recorded as sold first.

常用業務例句 Common business terms

1. global standardization 全球標準化
converge 匯集
conform to 符合
statutory 法定的
jurisdictions 管轄區

Tracy: I know what GAAP is, but what is IFRS ? Who uses it?

（我知道什麼是一般公認會計原則，但什麼是國際財務報告準則？誰在使用它？）

Accountant: Due to **global standardization**, many countries tend to **converge** on the International Financial Reporting Standards (IFRS) that was created and maintained by the International Accounting Standards Board. In certain countries, local accounting principles are used for regular companies, but listed companies must conform to IFRS, so **statutory** reporting is comparable internationally, across **jurisdictions**. All listed and grouped EU companies have been required to use IFRS since 2005, Canada in 2009, and Taiwan in 2013.

（由於全球標準化的結果，許多國家已經趨向使用由國際會計準則理事會（IFRS）建立並維持的國際財務報告準則。某些國家本地的公司會用當地的會計準則，但上市公司或大型公司必須符合國際財務報告準則，所以法定報告是具有國際跨區可比性的。自2005年以來所有上市分公司和歐盟大公司都被要求使用國際財務報告準則，加拿大在2009年跟進，台灣在2013年跟進。）

2. accompanied by 伴隨著
assets 資產
liability/liabilities 負債
equity 權益
cash flow 現金流量

Tracy: What does a financial statement typically include?
（財務報表一般包括哪些內容？）

Accountant: A financial statement typically include basic financial statements, **accompanied by** a management analysis and notes to financial statements. And the basic financial statements include: 1) balance sheet - reports on a company's **assets**, **liabilities**, and ownership **equity** at a given point in time. 2) income statement, reports on a company's income, expenses, and profits over a period of time. 3) statement of **cash flows** reports on a company's cash flow activities, spcifically its operating, investing and financing activities.
（財務報表通常包括基本的財務報表，伴隨管理分析與財務報告附註。而基本的財務報表包括：1）資產負債表 - 是在特定時間點對公司的資產、負債和所有者權益的報告。2）利潤表，是一個公司在一段時間內的收入、費用和利潤的報告。3）現金流量報表報告公司的現金流活動，特別是對其營運活動、投資活動和籌資活動的報告。）

3. entity/entities 單位
collective bargaining agreements 集體談判協議
viability 可行性

Tracy: What is the purpose of a business **entity's** financial statements?
（商業單位的財務報表的目的是什麼？）

Accountant: Financial statements may be used by users for different purposes: 1) They help owners and managers to make business decisions that could affect its continued operations. These statements are also used as part of management's annual report to the stockholders. 2) Employees also need these statements when making **collective bargaining agreements** with the management, in the case of labor unions or for individuals in discussing their compensation, promotion and rankings. 3) Potential investors make use of financial statements to assess the **viability** of investing in a business. 4) Financial institutions use them to decide whether to grant a company with fresh working capital or extend debt securities to finance expansion and other significant expenditures.
（財務報表可以因使用者不同而有不同的目的：1）它們幫助業主和管理者來作出影響其持續經營的重要業務決策。這些報告也被用來作為管理層對股東的年度報告的一部分。 2）員工也需要這些報表來和管理作集體談判協議，不論是以工會身分，或者是一個人員工身分討論他們的薪資、升遷和表現的排名。 3）準投資者利用財務報表來評估投資一個公司的可行性。 4）金融機構（銀行和其他貸款公司）用它們來決定是否批准新的營運資金給公司或延長債券來融資擴建和重要的支出。）

4. consolidated 合併的
subsidiary/subsidiaries 子公司

Tracy: What is a **consolidated** financial statement?
（什麼是合併會計報表？）

Accountant: Consolidated financial statements are financial statements of a group in which the assets, liabilities, equity, income, expenses and cash flows of the parent (company) and its **subsidiaries** are integrated as a single economic entity.
（合併財務報表是一個集團的財務報表，其中母公司的及其子公司的資產、負債、股東權益、收入和費用（公司）現金都整合在一個經濟單位的財務報表裡。）

 單元短文 Unit reading

Electronic financial statements
更換為電子財務報表

The paper version of financial statements has been created for hundreds of years. The growth of the Web has promoted more and more financial statements created in an electronic form, which is exchangeable over the Web. Common forms of electronic financial statements are PDF and HTML formats. These types of electronic financial statements have their drawbacks in that it still takes a human to read the information in order to reuse the information contained in a financial statement.

More recently a market driven global standard, XBRL (Extensible Business Reporting Language), which enables the creation of financial statements in a structured and computer readable format, and has become a more popular format for creating financial statements. Many regulators around the world such as the U.S. Securities and Exchange Commission have mandated XBRL for the submission of financial information.

紙版的財務報表自創建以來已經有數百年了。透過網絡的發展我們可以看到越來越多可通過網絡交換的電子版財務報表。常見的電子財務報表形式是PDF和HTML。這些類型的電子財務報表的缺點在於，它仍然需要有人去讀信息，才能夠重新使用包含在財務報表的信息。

最近一個市場驅動的全球標準：XBRL（可擴展商業報告語言），因其可以用來創建結構性的和計算機可讀的格式的財務報表，已經成為作為製作財務報表更受歡迎的格式。世界各地的許多監管機構如美國證券交易委員會已經規定以XBRL提交財務信息。

常用片語 Common phrases

- adhere to 遵循

  Accountants are required to **adhere to** the generally accepted accounting principles when they prepare financial statements.
  （會計人員編制財務報表的時候，必須遵循一般公認的會計原則。）

- dispose of 處理掉

  The farmers are trying to **dispose of** the grain surplus.
  （農民們正試圖處理掉過剩的穀物。）

重點字彙 Important words to know

名詞 Nouns		動詞 Verbs	
財務報表	financial statement	概述	outline
資產負債表	balance sheet	審計	audit
損益表	income statement	產生	incur
現金流量表	statement of cash flow	匯集	converge
所有者權益變動表	statement of change in equity	遵守	conform
一般公認會計原則	generally accepted accounting principles (GAAP)		
管轄範圍	jurisdiction		

連續性	continuity		
折舊	depreciation		
庫存	inventory		
應計	accrual		
法定的	statutory		
可行性	viability		

所得稅－個人所得稅／營利事業所得稅
Income Tax - Individual income tax/Corporate income tax

什麼是所得稅

所得稅是一種個人和公司依法必須支付給政府的稅，而稅的多少會根據收入的種類、收入的金額和納稅人的特性而有改變。所得稅是稅率乘以應納稅所得額的乘積。稅率一般隨著納稅所得額的增加而增加。稅率也因收入的種類而有所不同，例如薪資、資本利得、利息和股息等。也會有各種扣除額讓符合條件的納稅人來運用並減免他們應付的稅。

單元暖身小練習 Warm-up conversation and practice

針對以下每個空格，請選一個最適合的字填入。這是協助你對於本主題進行初步的暖身，以利對於後續的介紹可以更有效率的吸收。

(a) determine (b) progressive (c) jurisdiction (d) debt
(e) impose (f) given (g) eligible (h) depreciation
(i) repealed (j) profit

Miki wants to know what income tax is.
米奇想知道所得稅是什麼。

Accountant: Good afternoon, Miss Miyano, may I help you?
（午安，宮野小姐，我可以幫助您嗎？）

Miki: Yes, I would like to know what income tax is.
（是的，我想知道所得稅是什麼。）

Accountant: By all means. Income tax is a tax that governments impose on income earned by all individual and companies within their....1..... By law, companies and individuals must file an income tax return every year to ....2....whether they owe taxes or are ....3.... for a tax refund.

（當然。所得稅是政府在其管轄範圍內對於所有個人和公司所徵收的一種稅。根據法律規定，公司和個人每年都必須提交所得稅申報表，以決定它們是否欠任何稅或有資格獲得退稅。）

Miki: Why do governments need to ....4....income tax on their people?

（為什麼政府需要對人民徵收所得稅？）

Accountant: Well, income tax is a major source of income that the government uses to support its operations and serve the public. For example, the first income tax in America was imposed during the War in 1812. Its original purpose was to fund the repayment of a $100 million ....5.... incurred through war-related expenses. After the war, the tax was....6...., but income tax became permanent during the early 20th century.

（嗯，所得稅是政府用來資助其政府運作和為公眾服務的主要資金來源。例如，美國第一次徵收所得稅是在1812年戰爭時。原來的目的是用來資助因戰爭期間所產生相關費用而造成100萬美元債務的還款。戰爭結束後，稅收廢除了，但在20世紀初時所得稅成為永久的。）

Miki: What kinds of tax rates do most governments use?

（大多數政府使用什麼樣的稅率？）

Accountant: Most countries adopt ....7....income tax rates, so people with higher income will pay a higher tax rate compared to people with lower earnings.
（大多數國家採用累進所得稅率，其中高收入者比低收入者支付更高的稅率。）

Miki: So, according to what you just said, individual income tax is a tax paid by people from the money they earn, right?
（因此，根據您剛才所說的，個人所得稅是針對人們所賺來的錢而徵稅的，對嗎？）

Accountant: Definitely.
（那是絕對的。）

Miki: What about corporate income tax?
（那麼企業所得稅呢？）

Accountant: Corporate income tax is a tax placed on the ....8....of a firm, with different rates used for different levels of profits. Corporate taxes are taxes against profits earned by businesses during a ....9....taxable period; they are generally applied to companies' operating earnings, after expenses and ....10....have been deducted from revenues.
（企業所得稅是對企業的盈利徵稅，不同的盈利用不同的稅率。企業的稅收是在特定的納稅期間針對企業所賺取盈利的稅收；通常適用在營業收入已經扣除開支和折舊之後。）

Miki: I see. I appreciate your explanation.
（我明白了。感謝您的解釋。）

答案 ANSWERS:

1.c 2.a 3.g 4.e 5.d 6.i 7.b 8.j 9.f 10.h

認識所得稅－ 個人所得稅／營利事業所得稅

綜合所得稅

指的是每人一年當中各項所得的綜合總計。而所得稅分為綜合所得稅及營利事業所得稅。依我國綜合所得稅的規定，個人的綜合所得稅，就是用個人的綜合所得總額，減除免稅額、寬減額及扣除額後的綜合所得淨額，以累進稅率來計算的。

非居住者課稅方式

如果有個人在我國境內無住所，而且於一課稅年度內在我國境內居留合計不滿183天者，就是非居住者。非居住者的所得屬於扣繳範圍之所得，是以就源扣繳方式履行納稅義務，就源扣繳不能列報前述免稅額及扣除額。非居住者如有非屬扣繳範圍之所得，則應依規定稅率申報納稅。

依我國稅法規定，個人綜合所得總額包括下列九類所得，應合併計算繳納綜合所得稅：1）營利所得；2）執行業務所得；3）薪資所得；4）利息所得；5）租金和權利金所得；6）自力耕作、漁撈、畜牧、森林花木、採掘礦石所得；7）財產交易所得；8）競技，競賽及機會中獎金或給與；9）其他所得。

免稅額

納稅義務人按規定減除其本人，配偶及合規定扶養親屬之免稅額；納稅義務人本人、配偶及受扶養直系尊親屬年滿70歲者，免稅額增加50%。2014及2015年度每人免稅額分別為新臺幣85,000元；納稅義務人、配偶及受其扶養直系尊親屬年滿70歲者，免稅額為127,500元。

標準扣除額

2014年納稅義務人單身者扣除79,000元；夫妻合併申報者扣除158,000元。2015年納稅義務人單身者扣除90,000元；夫妻合併申報者扣除180,000元。

營利事業

指的是公營、私營或公私合營，以營利為目的，具備營業牌號或場所的獨資，合夥，公司及其他組織方式之工，商，農，林，漁，牧，礦，冶等營利事業，凡在我國境內經營之營利事業依法須課徵營利事業所得稅。

營利事業所得稅課稅範圍

總機構在我國境內的營利事業（含外商在臺子公司），應就我國境內外全部營利事業所得，合併課徵營利事業所得稅。但其來自我國境外之所得，已依所得來源國稅法規定繳納之所得稅，得由納稅義務人提出所得來源國稅務機關發給之同一年度納稅憑證，並取得所在地我國使領館或其他經我國政府認許機構之簽證後，自其全部營利事業所得結算應納稅額中扣抵。

總機構在我國境外的在臺營利事業（例如：外商在臺分公司），而有我國來源所得者，應就其在我國境內之營利事業所得，依所得稅法規定課徵營利事業所得稅。

一般常見所得稅－個人所得稅／營利事業所得稅名詞解釋

所得稅申報 **Income tax return**	所得稅申報指的是由個人或公司填寫所得稅表格並呈交所得稅試算結果給相關稅務機關的行為。	Income tax return refers to the actions by individuals or companies to fill out income tax form and file income taxes with the relevant tax authority.
應納稅所得額 **Taxable income**	應納稅所得額一般包括所有收入的總和，然後減除費用和適用的扣除額。它是計算所得稅的基礎。	Taxable income generally includes the sum of all sources of income and is deducted by expenses and applicable deductions. It is the base upon which the income tax is calculated.

扣除額 **Tax deductions**	扣除額是應納稅所得額的減項，通常是為了增加收入而產生的費用。	Tax deduction is a reduction of taxable income, usually as a result of expenses incurred to generate more income.
免稅額 **Tax exemption amount**	免稅額通常是指因法定的例外而免除特定項目的稅收，而不同於扣除額。	Tax exemption generally refers to a statutory exception to remove taxation of a particular item rather than a deduction.
退稅 **Tax refund**	退稅的產生是因為所計算出的應繳納稅額小於實際已經繳納的稅額。	A tax refund or tax rebate incurs when the tax payable is less than the taxes already paid.
稅務年度 **Tax year**	個人和公司申報和繳納所得稅的會計年度通常被稱為納稅人的納稅年度。	The fiscal year for individuals and companies to report and pay income taxes is often known as the taxpayer's tax year.
稅率 **Tax rate**	稅率指的是企業或個人徵稅的百分比。	The tax rate refers to the percentage at which a business or person is taxed.
應繳納之所得稅 **Income tax payable**	應繳納之所得稅是按淨收入和適用的稅率所計算的納稅額。	Income tax payable is the tax that is calculated on net income according to the applicable tax rate.

邊際稅率 **Tax bracket**	邊際稅率指的是在累進稅率裡，每個層級的稅率依照應繳納所得額的增加而增加。這一層一層的不同稅率就是邊際稅率。其所反映的是收入越高，稅率就越高。	Tax brackets are the tiers at which tax rates change in a progressive tax system. Basically, they are the cutoff values for taxable income — income pasts a certain value will be taxed at a higher rate.

常用業務例句 Common business terms

1. product 乘積
times 乘

Miki: How is income tax calculated?

（所得稅是如何計算出來的？）

Accountant: Income tax is the **product** of tax rate **times** taxable income. The tax rate may increase as taxable income increases. Tax rates may vary according to the type of in come orcharacteristics of the taxpayer.

（所得稅是稅率乘以應納稅所得額的乘積。稅率有可能會因應納稅所得額的增加而增加。稅率可能會依所得的類型和納稅人的特性而有所不同。）

2. capital gains 資本利得

Miki: Are different types of income taxed by the same rate?

（不同類型的收入會有相同的稅率？）

Accountant: Different tax rates apply to different types of income. For example, **capital gains** may be taxed at different rates

from salary income.

（不同的稅率適用於不同類型的收入。資本利得有可能和薪資收入使用不同的稅率。）

3. taxable 應納稅
deductions 扣除額

Miki: What is taxable income?

（應納稅所得額是什麼？）

Accountant: **Taxable** income is basically the total income less income-producing expenses and other **deductions**. Generally, net gain from sale of property is also included in income. Income of a corporation's shareholders should include distributions of profits from the corporation.

（應納稅所得額一般是總收入減去賺取收入的費用及其他扣除額。一般情況下，出售房地產的淨收益也會包括在收入裡面。公司股東的收入通常包括公司的利潤分配。）

4. taxpayers 納稅人
subject to 受到
penalties 處罰
jail 入獄
revocation 撤銷

Miki: What happens to taxpayers not paying taxes on time?
（納稅人不按時繳稅會發生什麼情況呢？）

Accountant: **Taxpayers** not paying tax owed on time are generally **subject to** significant **penalties**, which may include **jail** for individuals or **revocation** of an entity's legal existence.
（納稅人未準時繳納所欠稅款，一般會受到重大的處罰，其中可能包括納稅人個人入獄或單位的合法存在權被撤銷。）

單元短文 Unit reading

How differently is wage income taxed around the globe?
世界各地對工資的課稅在程度上有什麼區別？

Wage income is taxed differently around the world.

The OECD recently released a report comparing the tax on wages in the world's developed countries. One of the main tools the OECD used in the report is the "tax wedge". This is a combination of personal income taxes and social security taxes, less any benefits received by the taxpayer. OECD sampled the average tax wedge of a various types of family in 34 OECD countries.

It was closely examined how tax wedges have changed for an average full-time worker between the time before the Great Recession and the present. The country with the highest average tax burden — Belgium, at 55.6% of income — and the lowest — Chile, at just 7.0% — both showed no change between 2007 and 2014.

Other countries; however, showed larger shifts. The tax wedge in Hungary dropped 5.5 percentage, from 54.5% in 2007 to 49.0% in 2014. Ireland's tax increased by 6.0 points, from 22.2% to 28.2%.

The OECD observes that changes in tax wedges in recent years have less to do with changes in actual statutory tax rates, and instead with shifting income distributions: Countries with increasing wages will also see rising tax burdens, as workers move away from government support and into higher income-tax brackets.

世界各地對工資所得的課稅程度上有很大的區別。

經濟合作暨發展組織（Organization for Economic Cooperation and Development）最近發表針對已開發國家工資課稅負擔所作比較報告。其中經合組織在報告裡使用的主要工具之一是「稅賦楔子」。這是由工資和社會保障稅，減去納稅人所收到的福利的數字組合。 OECD計算了在34個經合組織國家裡的各種類型的家庭的平均稅賦楔子。

他們仔細檢視普通的全職工人的稅賦楔子從大蕭條到現在這段時間是如何改變的。最高平均稅負的國家 －比利時，佔收入的55.6% -- 還有平均稅負最低的國家 - 智利，僅為7.0% - 兩者在2007年至2014年間都沒有變化。

但其他一些國家，我們看到了較大的變化。稅賦楔子在匈牙利下降了5.5個百分點，從2007年的54.5%降到2014年的49.0%。愛爾蘭的稅收負擔增加了6.0點，從22.2%增加到28.2%。

經合組織指出，近年來稅賦楔子的改變與實際的法定稅率的改變比較沒關係，反而是與收入分配轉移比較有關係：工資上漲的國家我們也看到它們的稅負上升，因為工人從失業接受政府的資助轉變成為支付高所得稅的族群。

常用片語 Common phrases

- subject to 受到
  The prices of air tickets are **subject to** last minute changes.（機票價格受最後一刻改變的影響。）
- impose on 把……加予；給……帶來麻煩
  I don't want to **impose on** you.（我不想麻煩您。）

重點字彙 Important words to know

名詞 Nouns／形容詞 Adjectives		動詞 Verbs	
個人所得稅	individual income tax	提交	file (income tax)
企業所得稅	corporate income tax	徵收	impose
應納稅所得額	taxable income	廢除	repeal
稅率	tax rate		
扣除	deduction		
（稅賦）減免	(tax) credit		
應交所得稅	income tax payable		
累進的	progressive		
徵收	levy		
邊際稅率	tax bracket		
稅務機關	tax authority		
資本利得	capital gains		
處罰	penalty		
撤銷	revocation		

營業稅／扣繳稅 Sales tax/ Withholding tax

什麼是 營業稅／扣繳稅

營業稅是消費者在購買商品或服務時支付的一種稅。通常情況下，銷售商品或服務的公司會依法在銷售點先向消費者收取銷售稅，之後再按照規定定期轉付給政府。除了經批准免用發票的店家之外，大多數公司都必須依法在銷售時開具發票，以證明其所代收的營業稅。

扣繳稅一般指的是薪資所得在發放時由雇主預先扣除相應比例的金額再轉付給政府的預繳所得稅，而預繳的金額一般參照特定的薪資所得扣繳表來決定。已經扣繳的稅額可以在申報綜合所得稅時再與該年度實際必須繳交的稅額做比較，來決定是否要補繳或者能夠得到超繳的退稅。對於非居民的薪資、利息和股利收入的所得稅也會採取由雇主、銀行或發放股利的公司扣繳的方式，但一般是用固定的比例來扣繳，而且沒有退稅的選擇。

單元暖身小練習 Warm-up conversation and practice

針對以下每個空格，請選一個最適合的字填入。這是協助你對於本主題進行初步的暖身，以利對於後續的介紹可以更有效率的吸收。

(a) non-resident (b) percentage (c) retail (d) excise
(e) passed on to (f) delinquent (g) deducted (h) combat
(i) register (j) conventional

Mary wants to know what sales tax and withholding tax are .
瑪麗想知道營業稅和扣繳稅是什麼。

Accountant: Good afternoon, Miss Chen, may I help you?
（午安，陳小姐，我可以幫助您嗎？）

Mary: Yes, I would like to know what sales tax and withholding tax are.
（是的，我想知道營業稅和扣繳稅是什麼。）

Accountant: Of course. Sales tax is a tax that the consumers pay when they purchase ...1....goods and services. The tax is first collected by the retailer and ....2....the tax authority, and by law, the retailer has to issue an invoice to prove the collection of sales tax. It is based on a ....3....of the goods and services and set by the tax authority.
（當然。營業稅是購買零售商品和服務時所付的稅。它是由零售商先收取再轉付給稅務機關的，而且零售商依法必須開具發票來作為課稅的憑證。它是根據商品和勞務的銷售價格以及由稅務機關訂定的百分比來計算的。）

Mary: What about withholding tax?
（那麼扣繳稅呢？）

Accountant: As for withholding tax, it can be income tax the employers withhold from their employees' wages and pay directly to the government or a tax on interest and dividends from securities owned by a....4.... . The amount withheld is a credit against the income taxes the employee must pay during the year. Tax is ....5....not only from dividends, but from other source of income paid to non-residents of a country.

（至於扣繳稅，它可以是雇主從員工的工資裡預先扣除來直接繳給政府的所得稅，或者是從非居民擁有的證券利息和股利所徵收的稅。扣繳的金額可以作為員工必須在當年支付的所得稅的扣除額。稅的扣除不只是針對股利收入，同時也是針對一個國家的非居民所賺取的其他來源的收入。）

Mary: What are the general types of sales taxes?
（營業稅一般有哪些類型？）

Accountant: The most common type of sales tax we see every day is what the cash ....6....receipt shows. And this is the ....7....retail sales tax that is payable on the sale of a good to its final end user, and is charged every time that item is sold at retail. There are also manufacturers' sales tax (a tax on sales by manufacturers and producers), wholesale sales tax (a tax on sales of wholesale products), ...8.....taxes (tax on gasoline or alcohol), use tax (tax on automobiles and boats), securities turnover excise tax (a tax on the trade of securities), value added taxes (in some jurisdictions, value added tax is charged on all sales), etc.
（最常見的營業稅就是我們每天在收銀單據上所看到的。這種常規的零售營業稅是在銷售貨物給最終使用者時徵收的，並且每一次同一件貨物於零售再次銷售都要再徵收。除此之外，也有針對製造商的營業稅（製造商和生產商的營業稅）、批發營業稅（對批發銷售產品的稅）、特許權稅（汽油或酒類的稅）、使用稅（汽車和船隻的稅）、證券營業消費稅（證券交易稅）、增值稅（在某些管轄區，所有的銷售都要被課稅）……等。

Mary: Why would governments withhold tax?
（政府為什麼要預先扣稅呢？）

Accountant: Governments employ withholding tax as a means to ....9....tax evasion, and sometimes impose additional withholding tax requirements if the taxpayer has been ....10....in filing tax returns, or in industries where tax evasion is perceived to be common.
（政府利用扣繳稅作為打擊逃稅的手段，有時如果納稅人經常延誤提交報稅表，或者所在的行業被認為經常逃稅，有時政府會施加額外的扣繳稅要求。）

Mary: I understand now. Thank you for the information.
（現在我知道了。感謝您的信息。）

Accountant: You are welcome!
（不用客氣！）

答案 ANSWERS:

1.c 2.e 3.b 4.a 5.g 6.i 7.j 8.d 9.h 10.f

認識營業稅和扣繳稅

營業稅

營業稅是對營業人在銷售貨物或提供服務給消費者時，向消費者所收取的消費稅，稅率一般為5%。不論獨資、合夥組織、有限公司等營利事業，除享受免稅條件及免開發票者外，均應按營業人（營利事業）開立銷售發票時限表，開立統一發票，並於每單月15日前向政府申報及繳納營業稅。營業稅稅率，最低不得少於百分之五，最高不得超過百分之十；其徵收率，由行政院定之。

進項稅和銷項稅

營業稅也是公司行號對進出貨時，所產生進項稅額及銷項稅額。進項稅額，指營業人購買貨物或服務時，依規定支付之營業稅額。每二個月必需依所收集到的發票及單據，統計出所謂的進項稅額總數。每二個月開立銷貨之發票，計算出銷項稅額總數。

課稅範圍

在中華民國境內銷售貨物或勞務及進口貨物，均應依營業稅法規定課徵營業稅。

在中華民國境內銷售貨物包括：

⑴ 以自己產製、進口、購買供銷售之貨物轉供自用，或無償移轉他人者。

⑵ 註銷營業時之存貨，或以貨物抵債、分配股東或出資人者。

⑶ 代購貨物。

⑷ 委託代銷。

⑸ 受託代銷。

在中華民國境內銷售服務包括：

⑴ 銷售之服務是在中華民國境內提供或使用。

⑵ 國際運輸事業自中華民國境內載客、貨出境者。

⑶ 外國保險業自中華民國境內保險業承保再保險者。

進口貨物：

貨物自國外進入中華民國境內者。但下列情況不包在內：

⑴ 進入政府核定的免稅出口區內的外銷事業。

⑵ 科學工業園區內的園區事業。

⑶ 海關管理的保稅工廠或保稅倉庫者。

營業人營業稅納稅方式

我國營業稅稅額計算及納稅方式分為二大類：

⑴ 一般稅額計算的營業人，計算方式採當期銷項稅額扣減進項稅額後之的餘額為當期應納或溢付營業稅額，納稅方式為營業人自動報繳；

⑵ 特種稅額計算的營業人，包含金融業、特種飲食業及查定計算營業稅額

的營業人，除查定計算營業稅額之營業人是由稽徵機關按查定稅額計算填發繳款書通知繳納外，其他為自動報繳。

一般常見營業稅和扣繳稅名詞解釋

扣繳義務人 **Tax withholder**	扣繳義務人指的是向員工或投資人先預扣扣繳稅再轉付給到稅務機關的那一方。它通常是雇主或銀行。	Tax withholder refers to the party that collects tax from employees or investors to pass on to the tax authority. it is usually the employers or banks.
估稅人員 **Assessor**	估稅人員是評估資產的價值而用來作為課稅參考的政府官員。	Tax assessor is a government official who determines the value of assets for taxation purposes.
逃稅人 **Tax dodger**	逃稅人是實行避稅或逃稅做法的人。	Tax dodger is the person who practices tax avoidance or tax evasion.
退稅 **Drawback**	出口退稅是退回給那些把商品先進口然後再出口的進口商和出口商所付的商品稅。	Drawback is the kind of tax refund that is returned to importers and exporters who paid tax on goods imported into their home country, and then exported those goods after they arrived.

常用業務例句 Common business terms

1. ancient 古代的
depicted 描繪
Egyptian tombs 埃及古墓

Mary: Do you know of any early example of sales tax in ancient history?
（您知道古代歷史上有任何早期的營業稅的例子嗎？）

Accountant: Yes, I happen to know there was a tax levied on the sale of goods **depicted** on the walls of **ancient Egyptian tombs**, which was dated as far back as 2000 BC. These paintings describe the collection of tax for certain commodities, such as cooking oil.
（有的，我碰巧知道早在公元前2000年時埃及古墓的牆壁上有描繪對所銷售的商品徵稅。這些畫作描述對特定商品徵收稅，例如食用油。）

Mary: Really? That is so interesting!
（真的嗎？那真有趣！）

2. value-added taxes (VATs) 增值稅
Scandinavia 斯堪的納維亞
Norway 挪威
Denmark 丹麥
Sweden 瑞典
Hungary 匈牙利
groceries 雜貨

Mary: Which countries have high sales tax or **value-added taxes (VATs)**?

（哪些國家是因為有高銷售稅或增值稅而聞名？）

Accountant: In Western Europe, some countries in **Scandinavia** have some of the world's highest valued-added taxes. **Norway**, **Denmark** and **Sweden** have VATs at 25%, **Hungary** has the highest at 27%, even though some specific items are subject to reduced rates such as **groceries**, art, books and newspapers.

（在西歐，特別是在斯堪的納維亞地區的某些國家有世界上最高的附加值稅。挪威、丹麥和瑞典的增值稅為25%，匈牙利最高為27%，儘管某些特定的品項，例如，雜貨、藝術、圖書和報紙可以適用降低的稅率。）

3. multiple 多重的

consisting of 包含；由……組成

Metropolitan Pier and Exposition Authority 大都會碼頭和博覽會管理局

Mary: Are there any places where there are **multiple** levels of sales taxes?（有哪些地方收多層次的銷售稅？）

Accountant: Yes. In some regions of the United States, there are multiple levels of government, and each imposes a sales tax. For example, sales tax in Chicago (Cook County), IL is 10.25%—**consisting of** 6.25% state, 1.25% city, 1.75% county and 1% regional transportation authority. Chicago also has the **Metropolitan Pier and Exposition Authority** tax on food and beverage of 1% (which means eating out is taxed at 11.25%). For Baton Rouge, Louisiana, the tax is 9%, consisting of 4% state and 5% local rate.

（有的。在美國的某些地區，有多層次政府，而每個層次都徵收銷售稅。例如，伊利諾州的芝加哥營業稅（庫克縣）是10.25%，其中包含州政府6.25%、市政府1.25%、縣政府1.75%和區域交通管理局1%。芝加哥也有大都會碼頭和博覽會管理局對食物和飲料課1%的稅（這表示總稅率為11.25%）。對於路易斯安那州巴吞魯日而言，稅是9%，包含州政府4%和當地政府5%。）

4. conventional 傳統的
adopted 採用
retain 保留

Mary: Between sales tax and value added tax, which one is more widely used in the world?
（銷售稅和增值稅之間，何者較為世界廣泛使用？）

Accountant: The conventional sales taxes are gradually being replaced by more broadly-based value added taxes. Value added taxes account for an approximately 20 percent of worldwide tax revenue and **adopted** by more than 140 countries. The United States is now one of the few countries to **retain** conventional sales taxes.
（傳統的銷售稅已漸漸被更加廣泛的增值稅所取代。增值稅估計已佔全球稅收的20%，而且已有140多個國家採用。美國是目前少數幾個保留傳統銷售稅的國家之一。）

單元短文 Unit reading

Amazon has begun declaring sales in major European markets and will start paying tax in those markets
亞馬遜已經開始申報在歐洲主要市場的銷售並將開始在這些市場納稅

Amazon, the online giant retailer has jast started declaring sales in major European markets instead of Luxembourg, and it will pay taxes on the sales in the respective nations.

Starting from May 2015, Amazon is reporting all retail sales in the UK, Germany, Spain and Italy. Previously, these retail sales were reported in Luxembourg. Amazon is also working on opening a branch for France.

Amazon's tax deals in Luxembourg had received howls of criticism that the giant was trying to evade taxes, and EU has initiated a probe into this matter.

網路零售巨頭亞馬遜表示它已經開始在歐洲主要市場而不是盧森堡申報銷售，而且將在個別的國家開始繳稅。

自2015年5月起，亞馬遜開始在英國、德國、西班牙和意大利等國家申報零售記錄。這些零售銷售額之前都是在盧森堡紀錄的。亞馬遜也正在準備在法國開設分公司。

盧森堡給亞馬遜的稅收優惠備受批評，主要是批評逃避稅收，同時歐盟開始對此進行調查。

常用片語 Common phrases

- pass on to
  轉給
  By law, employers are required to withhold tax from employees' wages and **pass** it **on to** the tax authority.
  （根據法律規定，雇主必須從僱員的工資代扣稅並且轉給稅務機關。）

- at the point of sale
  在銷售點
  Sales tax incurs **at the point of sale** on retail goods and services.
  （營業稅在零售商品和服務的銷售點產生。）

重點字彙 Important words to know

名詞 Nouns／形容詞 Adjectives		動詞 Verbs	
營業稅	sales tax	打擊	combat
預扣稅／扣繳稅	withholding tax	預扣	withhold
股利	dividend	描繪	depict
傳統的	conventional	採用	adopt
特許權	excise	保留	retain
古代的	ancient	包括/由...組成	consist of
增值稅	value-added tax		
雜貨	groceries		
多重	multiple		
拖欠	delinquent		
逃漏稅	tax evasion		

金融小百科 4 基本各項數值表達（數量換算與表達方式）Financial Tips(4)-The Basic Expressions of Values

公制（Metric system）

公制一個國際化的十進位量度系統，1799年時法國是第一個開始使用公制的國家。源自公制的國際單位制已成為國際大多數國家的主要量度系統。美國是工業化國家中唯一未將國際單位制設定為官方量度系統的國家，不過從1866年起也已開始使用國際單位制。英國政府已承諾要將許多量測單位改為公制系統，但一般常用的單位仍是英制單位。

公制的單位有一系統以十進位為準的詞頭（Prefix），當單位在實際使用上太大或太小時，可以用詞頭調整單位的大小，調整方式是將原單位乘或除以10、100或其他10的倍數。

例如：

詞頭kilo（千）是一單位的一千倍，而詞頭 milli（毫）則是一單位的千分之一。因此公斤（kilogram）及公里（kilometer）分別是一克和一米的一千倍，而毫克（milligram）及釐米（millimeter）則是一克和一米的千分之一。

上述關係可以用下式表示：

1 mg (milligram)= 0.001 g (gram)

1 km (kilometer) = 1000 m (meters)

當詞頭用在用長度的平方或立方表示的面積或體積單位時，平方及立方的運算不只針對單位，也同時針對詞頭：

1 mm2（平方公釐 square millimeter）= (1 mm)2 = (0.001 m)2 = 0.000

001 m2

1 km2（平方公里 square kilometer）= (1 km)2 = (1000 m)2 = 1,000,000 m2

1 mm3（立方公釐 cubic millimeter）= (1 mm)3 = (0.001 m)3 =0.000 000 001 m3

1 km3（立方公里 cubic kilometer）= (1 km)3 = (1000 m)3 = 1,000,000,000 m3

詞頭也用在非國際標準制的體積單位：

例如：

1 ml (millimeter) = 0.001 l (liter)

1 kl (kiloliter) = 1000 l (liter)

大於1的詞頭一般我們會用由希臘文衍生的的詞頭，而小於1的詞頭則會用由拉丁文衍生的詞頭。例如，常見的kilo-及mega-都是由希臘文衍生的，而centi-及milli-是由拉丁文衍生的。不過後來的國際標準制在表示小於1的詞頭時，已不使用拉丁文衍生的詞頭，例如nano-及micro-都是由希臘文所衍生。

國際單位制

國際單位制（SI，來自法語：Système International d'Unités），源自公制，又稱萬國公制，是世界上最普遍採用的標準度量衡單位系統。國際單位制最早於法國大革命時期的1799年被法國作為度量衡單位。國際單位制是在公制基礎上發展起來的單位制，於1960年第十一屆國際度量衡大會通過，推薦各國採用，其國際縮寫為SI。

單位名稱	單位符號	單位英文名稱	物理名稱
公尺	m	meter	長度 length
公斤	kg	kilogram	質量 mass
秒	s	second	時間 time

安培	a	ampere	電流 electrical current
克耳文	k	kelvin	溫度 temperature
莫耳	mol	mole	質量 amount of substance
燭光	cd	candela	發光強度 luminous intensity

國際單位制基本單位（Basic unit of SI system）

國際單位制應用於世界各地。除美國、緬甸及賴比瑞亞未主要採用國際單位制外，其它國家均以國際單位制作為主要的度量衡系統。這其中包括絕大多數前英制國家，例如英國、加拿大、澳大利亞等大英國協國家，它們均在20世紀後半葉進行了向國際單位制的轉換。

在航空管制方面，國際上仍使用英制為主（例如飛行高度以英尺為單位）。

中華民國臺灣（ROC Taiwan）

雖然經濟部已公告使用國際單位制，但一部份非國際單位制的單位仍是民眾常用的，例如台斤、台尺、坪和英吋。經濟部於1930年1月1日實施了《中華民國度量衡法》，統一了傳統度量衡地域與行業標準混亂的局面，規定公製單位與市制單位均可使用。

而台灣用來測量面積的單位是坪；因為台灣是唯一用坪的國家， 所以一般英文用發音 Ping 或 Taiwanese Ping來代表坪。坪和公制的面積換算如下：

1 坪（Ping） = 3.3058 平方公尺（square meters）

1 平方公尺（square meter）= 0.3025坪（Ping）

而一台斤（catty)＝0.6 公斤 (kilogram)＝ 600 公克 (grams)

英制單位（Imperial units）

英制單位是源自英國的度量衡單位制。英國自1965年起立例轉換成國際單位制（International System of Units，SI），並於1995年完成了單位制的轉換（但陸路交通仍以英哩作為單位）。但國際上許多個別領域，仍沿用英制；例如電視機、電腦顯示器、手機螢幕大小以英吋表示；航空管制上，如飛行高度、跑道長度等，多以英呎為單位。

其量度單位為了與公制或中國傳統單位區別，多在單位前加一「英」字，或冠以口字旁稱之，如：英里（英哩）、英尺（英呎）、英寸（英吋），或簡稱哩、呎、吋。

英制單位與其他單位制的關係（Imperial units vs. other unit systems）

大多數英制單位與現在應用於美國的美制單位（又稱美式英制單位）的名稱相同，但是具體的定義不同。在英國，一些英制仍舊保留（如路標的英哩），但使用國際單位制用於食品銷售等已日趨普遍。古老英制的參考紀錄在如今能夠得以保留，以下是美式英制及其差別。

英制長度單位（Imperial length units）

1959年後，美式英制的中的英吋（inch）和英制中的英吋在科學應用和商業用途中統一為25.4公釐，但美式保留了有稍微不同的測量中使用的測量英吋。

1英吋（inch）= 2.54公分（cm）

1英呎（foot）= 12英吋 (inches) = 30.48公分（cm）

1碼（yard）= 3英呎 (inches) = 91.44公分（cm）

1英尋（fathom）= 6英呎 (inches)= 182.88公分（cm）

1鏈（chain）= 22碼 (yards) = 2011.68公分（cm）

1浪（furlong）= 10鏈 (chain) =220碼 (yards) = 0.201168公里（km）= 20116.8公分（cm）

1英哩（mile）= 80鏈 (chain) = 1760碼 (yards) = 5280英呎 (feet) =

1.609344公里（km）

以上的換算的中間單位如：鏈（chain）和浪（furlong）在英國使用較多。

英制體積單位（Imperial volume units）

如今的英式加侖（gallon，4.55升）和英式蒲式耳（bushel，36.4升）分別比美式加侖（3.79升）和美式蒲式耳（35.2升）大20%和3%。1英式加侖定義為華氏62度下10磅重的水的體積，1英式蒲式耳為8英式加侖。

英式加侖分為160液量盎司（fluid ounces），美式則為128液量盎司（fluid ounces）。

1 液量盎司（fluid ounces）= 28.4 毫升（milliliters）

1 及耳（gill）= 5 液量盎司（fluid ounces）= 142 毫升（milliliters）

1 品脫（pint）= 4 及耳（gill）= 568 毫升（milliliters）

1 夸脫（quart）= 2 品脫（pint）= 1.14 升（liters）

1 加侖（gallon）= 4 夸脫（quart）= 4.55 升（liters）

1 配克（peck）= 2 加侖（gallon）= 9.09 升（liters）

1 坎寧（kenning）= 2 配克（peck）= 18.2 升（liters）

1 蒲式耳（bushel）= 8 加侖（gallon）= 36.4 升（liters）

1 夸特（quarter）= 8 蒲式耳（bushel）= 2.91 百公升（liters）

英式和美式體積單位的換算（Conversion between Imperial and US volume units)

1 美式液量盎司（US fluid ounces）= 1.041 英式液量盎司（Imperial fluid ounces）= 29.6 毫升（milliliters）

1 英式液量盎司（Imperial fluid ounces）= 0.961 美式液量盎司（US fluid ounces）= 28.4 毫升（milliliters）

1 美式加侖（US gallon）= 0.833 英式加侖（Imperial gallon）= 3.79 升（liters）

1 英式加侖（Imperial gallon）= 1.201 美式加侖（US gallon）= 4.55 升（liters）

英制重量單位（Imperial weight units）

1 格令（grain）= 64.8 毫克（milligrams）

1 打蘭（drachm）= 1/16 盎司（ounce）= 1.77 克（grams）

1 盎司（ounce）= 1/16 磅（pound）= 28.3 克（grams）

1 磅（pound）= 7000 格令（grain）= 454 克（grams）

1 英石（stone）= 14 磅（pounds）= 6.35 公斤（kilograms）

1 夸特（quarter）= 2 英石（stones）= 28 磅（pounds）= 12.7 公斤（kilograms）

1 英擔（hundredweight）= 4 夸特（quarts）= 112 磅（pounds）= 50.8 公斤（kilograms）

1 英噸（ton）= 20 英擔（hundredweight）= 2240 磅（pounds）= 1016 公斤（kilograms）

英噸（長噸 long ton）是2240磅，較美噸（短噸short ton）是2000磅（907公斤）更接近於國際單位制的公噸。

英制單位使用情況

現在還正式採用英制單位的國家十分少，如賴比瑞亞和緬甸。美國使用的乃是美式英制單位，跟傳統的英制單位有異。美式車輛的儀錶板上，會同時出現英哩（mph, miles per hour）和公里（km/h, kilometer/hour）兩種時速單位，在跨境行駛時，於美國採用英制，並在加拿大、墨西哥採用公制；另外在美國職棒中，投手的投球時速是採用英制單位，而國際棒總、日本職棒、韓國職棒、中華職棒的投手投球速度則採用公制單位。

美制單位（United States customary units）

美式英制單位，是目前在美國被普遍使用的一種計量單位，可被視為英制單位的一種。由於美國曾是大英帝國殖民地，因此美國使用的大多數非公制單位都和現在英國的英制單位在名稱上相同。然而，英國的制度在1824年被翻修，一些單位的定義被改變，而當時已獨立的美國則未跟隨，所以兩個系統之間存在分歧，比如加侖現在在英美兩國的定義是不同的。

美制長度單位（US length units）—英寸inch (in), 英尺foot (ft), 碼yard (yd), 和 英里（mile）.

1英尺（foot ）= 12英寸（inches）

1碼（yard ）= 3英尺（ feet）= 36英寸（inches）

1英里（mile）= 1760碼（yards）= 5280 英尺（feet）

美制體積單位（US volume units）—美國液量盎司 US fluid ounces (fl oz), 美國杯 US cup (cp), 美國品脫 US pint (pt), 美國夸脫 US quart (qt), 和 美國加侖 US gallon (gal).

1美國杯（US cup) = 8美國液量盎司（US fluid ounces）

1美國品脫（US pint)= 2美國杯（US cups）= 16美國液量盎司（US fluid ounces）

1美國夸脫（US quart）= 2美國品脫（US pints）

1美國加侖（US gallon）= 4美國夸脫（US quarts）= 8美國品脫（US pints）

美制重量單位（US weight units）— 重量（weight）和質量（mass）用盎司 ounces (oz) , 磅pounds (lb)和英石 stone (st) 衡量。

1磅（pound）= 16盎司（ounces）

1英石（stone）=14磅（pounds）

美制單位與公制單位的換算（Conversion between US and metric units）

由公制到美制（conversion from metric units to US units）

1米（meter）= 1.09（碼）= 39.37英寸（inches）

1升（liter）= 33.3 液量盎司（US fluid ounces）= 1.76 美國品脫（US pints）= 0.26 美國加侖(US gallon）

1公斤（kilogram）= 35.32 盎司（ounces）=2.2磅（pounds）

由美制到公制（conversion from US units to metric units）

長度（length）

1英寸（inch）= 2.54厘米（centimeters）

1英尺（foot）= 30.48厘米（centimeters）

1碼（yard）= 0.914米（meters）

1英里（mile）=1.61公里（kilometers）

體積（volume）

1液量盎司（US fluid ounces）= 29.6毫升（milliliters）

1品脱（pint）= 473.1毫升（milliliters）

1加侖（gallon）= 3.79升（liters）

1杯（cup）=16盎司（ounces）

重量（weight）

1盎司（ounce）= 28.35克（grams）

1磅（pound）= 0.45千克（kilograms）

20%
10%
40%

5 Chapter

Financial knowledge 金融常識篇

主要政府金融機構及監理機構
Major Government Financial Organization and Supervisory Organizations

什麼是主要政府金融機構及監理機構

中央銀行是大部分國家主要的政府金融機構及監理機構。它是政府批准的銀行，而且負有穩定宏觀經濟表現的具體職責。通常，中央銀行是由中央政府賦予其責任來控制貨幣供給以促進經濟穩定為目的。它對金融體系也有一定程度的監管權力，同時也操作支票結算系統，或為中央政府提供一般的銀行服務。它的目標是實現貨幣穩定、降低通貨膨脹率和充分就業等。

單元暖身小練習 Warm-up conversation and practice

針對以下每個空格，請選一個最適合的字填入。這是協助你對於本主題進行初步的暖身，以利對於後續的介紹可以更有效率的吸收。

(a) achieve　(b) supervise　(c) failure　(d) monetary
(e) formerly　(f) stability　(g) integrity　(h) oversee
(i) sound　(j) enforces

Emily wants to know what a central bank is .
艾米莉想知道什麼是中央銀行。

Emily: Professor Milton, could you tell me what a central bank is?
（米爾頓教授，你能告訴我什麼是中央銀行嗎？）

Professor Milton: A central bank is usually a government sanctioned bank, and is authorized by the central government to control the money supply for the purpose of promoting economic....1..... It may have other duties, such as certain degree of regulatory power over the financial system, operating the check-clearing system, performing general banking services for the central government, issuing currency, overseeing commercial banks, and managing exchange reserves. It is supposed to ....2....certain goals such as currency stability, low inflation and full employment by overseeing ....3....policy. Most industrialized countries have central banks. The Bank of England, the Bank of Japan, the German Bundesbank, and the United States Federal Reserve are all central banks. While their organizational structures and powers may be different, each bank is responsible for controlling its country's money supply.

（中央銀行通常是政府認可的銀行，並且由中央政府賦予其責任來控制貨幣供給，以促進經濟穩定為目的。它可能也有其他的職責，例如對金融體系有一定程度的監管權力，操作支票結算系統，為中央政府提供一般的銀行服務、發行貨幣、監督商業銀行和管理外匯存底。它的具體目標是透過監督貨幣政策來完成穩定貨幣、降低通貨膨脹和充分就業。大多數的工業化國家都有自己的中央銀行。英國央行、日本央行、德國央行和美國聯邦儲備銀行都是中央銀行。雖然他們的組織結構和權力有所不同，每家銀行都負責控制國家的貨幣供應量。）

Emily: Aside from the Federal Reserve, which other organizations ....4....and regulate the financial system in the USA?
（在美國，除了美國聯邦儲備銀行之外，哪一個機構負責監督和規範金融系統？）

Professor Milton: In the USA, Federal Deposit Insurance Corporation (FDIC), Financial Industry Regulatory Authority (FINRA) , Securities and Exchange Commission (SEC), and many other relevant government organizations help ....5....the financial system.
（在美國有美國聯邦存款保險公司、美國金融業監管局、美國證券交易委員會，以及其他許多相關政府機構協助監督金融系統。）

Emily: What is FDIC?
（什麼是美國聯邦存款保險公司呢？）

Professor Milton: The Federal Deposit Insurance Corporation is the U.S. corporation insuring deposits in the U.S. against bank....6..... The FDIC was created in 1933 to maintain public confidence and encourage stability in the financial system through the promotion of ....7....banking practices.
（美國聯邦存款保險公司是對在美國的存款提供針對銀行倒閉保險的美國企業。聯邦存款保險公司於1933年創建，通過提升健全的銀行運作來安定民眾的信心和促進穩定的金融系統。）

Emily: What about FINRA?

（那麼美國金融業監管局是什麼？）

Professor Milton: FINRA,....8....the National Association of Securities Dealers (NASD), is the largest self-regulatory organization (SRO) in the securities industry in the United States. An SRO is a membership-based organization that creates and ....9....rules for members based on the federal securities laws. SROs, which are supervised by the SEC, are the forefront in regulating the broker.

（美國金融業監管局的前身是美國證券商協會。它是美國國內證券行業最大的自律監管機構。自律監管機構是一個根據美國聯邦證券法，以創建並執行成員規則的成員組織。自律監管機構是由美國證券交易委員會所監督，而且是規範證券商的第一線。）

Emily: What is SEC responsible for?

（美國證券交易委員會負責什麼呢？）

Professor Milton: The main responsibilty of the SEC is to protect investors and ensure the ....10....of the securities markets.

（美國證券交易委員會的主要任務是保護投資者並且維護證券市場的完整性。）

Emily: I got it. Thank you, Professor!

（我明白了。謝謝您，教授！）

答案 ANSWERS:

1.f 2.a 3.d 4.h 5.b 6.c 7.i 8.e 9.j 10.g

認識主要政府金融機構及監理機構

中華民國中央銀行（Central Bank of the Republic of China (Taiwan)）是中華民國政府的金融機構。中央銀行（簡稱央行）是中華民國的國家銀行，直屬於行政院，具有部會級地位；其肩負穩定國家金融發展、維持物價平穩、維護國幣（新臺幣）幣值等重要任務。

中央銀行組織架構

中央銀行設有監事會及理事會，下設總裁及副總裁負責營運，再下設所屬部門及單位。

－ 監事會（設監事5至7人，由行政院報請總統派任。行政院主計長為當然監事，監事會置主席一人，由監事互推之。監事任期為三年，可續任）

－理事會（設理事11至15人，由行政院報請總統派任，其中5至7人為常務理事，組織常務理事會。本行總裁為當然主席、財政部長及經濟部長為當然理事與常任理事，並為常務理事。理事任期為五年，可續任）

－總裁（特任，任期五年，可續任）

－副總裁（兩人，職務比照簡任第十四職等，任期五年，可續任）

央行附屬機關有中央印製廠和中央造幣廠；駐外單位有駐紐約代表辦事處和駐倫敦代表辦事處。內部及業務單位有：業務局、發行局、外匯局、國庫局、金融業務檢查處、經濟研究處、秘書處、會計處、資訊處、人事室、政風室和法務室。

金融監督管理委員會

金融監督管理委員會（簡稱金管會）是中華民國監督與管理金融事務與規劃金融政策的部會，成立於2004年7月，目標包含維持金融穩定、落實金融改革、協助產業發展、加強消費者與投資人保護與金融教育。

一般常見主要政府金融機構及監理機構名詞解釋

金融系統 **Financial system**	金融系統指的是促成貸款人和借款人之間錢的流轉的系統。	Financial system is the system allows the transfer of money between savers and borrowers.
金融監理 **Financial regulation**	金融監管是強制要求金融機構遵循一定的規定、限制和準則以保持金融系統的完整性的監管制度。	Financial regulation is a system of supervision to enforce financial institutions to follow certain requirements, restrictions and guidelines, in order to maintain the integrity of the financial system.
監理套利 **Regulatory arbitrage**	監理套利指的是企業利用監管系統的漏洞來規避不利於它們的監管規定的做法。	A practice when firms utilize loopholes in regulatory systems to avoid unfavorable regulation.
道德風險 **Moral hazard**	發生道德風險指的是以消息比較不靈通的一方的角度來看，會認為消息比較靈通的一方比較會有表現不適當的傾向。	Moral hazard refers to when the party with more information has the tendency to behave inappropriately from the perspective of the party with less information.
金融監理一元化 **Integrated supervisory authority**	金融監理一元化指的是有一個統一的機構負責監督一個國家的證券業、銀行業和保險業。	Integrated supervisory authority refers to a single unified institution in charge of overseeing a country's securities, banking and insurance sectors.

金融監理架構 **Financial supervisory structure**	金融監理架構指的是一個國家用來監控其金融系統的機構的數量。	Financial supervisory structure refers to the number of regulators a country uses to monitor its financial system.

常用業務例句 Common business terms

1. fairness 公平性
virtually 實質上，幾乎
stockbrokers 股票經紀
brokerage firms 經紀公司

Emily: What is the different between FINRA and SEC?
（請問美國金融業監管局和美國證券交易委員會有什麼不同？）

Professor: The SEC is responsible for ensuring **fairness** for individual investors, and FINRA'S responsiblity is to supervise **virtually** all U.S. **stockbrokers** and **brokerage firms**.
（美國證券交易委員會負責為個人投資者確保公平性，而美國金融業監管局負責監督幾乎美國所有的股票經紀及經紀公司。）

2. institution 機構

Emily: What amount of deposits does FDIC insure?
（美國聯邦存款保險公司保險多少金額的存款？）

Professor: The FDIC insures deposits of up to US$250,000 per **institution** as long as the bank is a member firm. Therefore, before opening an account with a bank, be sure to check that it is FDIC insured.

（美國聯邦存款保險公司對於每個美國金融機構存款的保額高達250,000美金，只要該銀行是它的成員即可。因此，銀行開立帳戶之前時，一定要確認它是否有投保美國聯邦存款保險公司。）

3. money supply 貨幣供給量
profit-seeking 營利事業

Emily: What are the functions of the Bank of the United States?
（美國銀行的功能是什麼？）

Professor: The Bank of the United States had both public and private functions. Its most significant public function was to control the **money supply** by regulating the quantity of notes that the state banks could issue, and by transferring reserves to different parts of the country. It is also a privately owned, **profit-seeking** institution. It competes with other banks for deposits and loan customers.
（美國銀行有公營和私營的功能。其最重要的公營功能是透過調節國家銀行的鈔票發行量，以及透過轉移儲備金到國家的不同地區來控制貨幣供應量。它也是一個私營的營利事業機構。它與其他的銀行競爭存款和貸款的客戶。）

4. steer 引導

Emily: What are the main tasks of the Federal Reserve?
（美國聯邦儲備銀行的主要任務是什麼？）

Professor: The main tasks of the Federal Reserve are to supervise and regulate banks, implement monetary policy by buying and selling U.S. Treasury bonds and steer interest rates.

（美國聯邦儲備銀行的主要任務是監督和監管銀行，透過買入和賣出美國國債來執行貨幣政策，和引導利率。）

 單元短文 Unit reading

What exactly does SEC do?
美國證券交易委員會到底負責做什麼？

The Securities & Exchange Commission (SEC) was created as a regulatory organization not long after the stock market crash in 1929. Its mission was to bring back investor confidence in a financial sector that was scandalous for deceitful activities, easy credit and risky investments. SEC's four divisions are Corporate Finance, Market Regulation, Investment Management and Enforcement.

Division of Corporate Finance

This division ensures the documents that filed by the companies with the SEC provide prudent and truthful disclosure of financial and material information, so the information, transparency is increased and the investors can make informed desisions.

Division of Market Regulation

This division regulates the participants in the securities industry by establishing the rules of the investment industry.

Division of Investment Management

This division supervises the investment management industry by ensuring that all rules affecting investment companies and their advisors are followed.

Division of Enforcement

This division works closely with the other three divisions, and investigates possible violations of securities laws and provides recommendations when further action is needed.

證券交易委員會（SEC），作為一個監管機構於1929年股市崩盤不久之後成立了。它的目的是恢復投資者對一個以詐騙活動、寬鬆的信貸和危險的投資等惡名昭彰的金融業的信心和信念。美國證券交易委員會分為四個主要部門。包括企業金融部、市場監管部、投資管理部和執法部。

企業金融部

該部門負責監督確保公司提交給證券交易委員會文件都能夠提供的審慎和真實財務披露和重大信息，因此提升信息透明度，而讓投資者能作出明智的決定。

市場監管部

該監管部透過建立規範證券投資行業的規則來規範證券行業的參與者。

投資管理部

該部門透過確保影響投資公司及其顧問的所有規則都被遵循著而來監督投資管理行業。

執法部

這個部門與其他三個部門密切合作來調查可能違反證券法的事件，並在需要採取進一步行動時提供建議。

常用片語 Common phrases

• is divided into 分為	The SEC **is divided into** four main divisions. （美國證券交易委員會分為四個主要部門。）
• range from...to 範圍從……到……都有	The participants **range from** the largest corporations **to** small firms. （參與者的範圍從最大的公司到小型企業都有。）

重點字彙 Important words to know

名詞 Nouns		動詞 Verbs	
金融系統	financial system	制裁	sanction
金融機構	financial organization	引導	steer
金融監管/監督	financial regulation/ supervision	監督	oversee
批准的	sanction	調節	regulate
貨幣政策	monetary policy	監督	supervise
貨幣供給	money supply	強制執行	enforce
執法	enforcement	利用	capitalize
完整性	integrity	規避	circumvent
漏洞	loophole	監控	monitor
監管套利	regulatory arbitrage	恢復	restore
道德風險	moral hazard		

金融市場 Financial Market

什麼是金融市場

金融市場是人們以反映市場供需的價格來交易金融證券、商品和其他有價資產的場所。證券通常包括股票和債券等，而商品包括貴金屬和農產品等。傳統的金融市場可以是一個實際的地點，如股票交易市場；但現代化的金融市場指的可能是現在大部分的交易所進行的電子交易系統。

單元暖身小練習 Warm-up conversation and practice

針對以下每個空格，請選一個最適合的字填入。這是協助你對於本主題進行初步的暖身，以利對於後續的介紹可以更有效率的吸收。

(a) marketplace (b) converse (c) norms (d) Broadly
(e) intrinsic (f) determining (g) downturns (h) transparency
(i) criteria (j) nearly

Vicki wants to know what a financial market is .
維奇想知道什麼是金融市場。

Vicki: Professor Milton, could you tell me what a financial market is?
米爾頓教授，您能告訴我金融市場是什麼嗎？

Professor Milton: ....1....speaking, a financial market is a place ....2....where buyers and sellers trade their assets such as equities, bonds, commodities, currencies and derivatives. Financial markets are generally known for having transparent pricing, basic rules for trading, costs and fees and the market forces ....3....the prices of securities. Certain financial markets only let participants that meet certain....4....trade, and it can be based on the amount of money they invest, their geographical location, their knowledge of the market or their profession.

（從廣義上來說，金融市場是買方和賣方交易他們的資產，例如股票、債券、商品、貨幣和衍生產品的市場。金融市場通常具有透明的定價、基本交易規定、交易成本和費用以及由市場機制決定證券交易的價格。某些金融市場只讓符合一定標準的參與者交易，其有可能根據參與者投資的錢的金額、投資者的地理位置、他們對市場的知識或他們的職業。）

Vicki: Could you give me some examples of the financial market?

（您能給我一些金融市場的例子嗎？）

Professor Milton: Financial markets can be found in ....5....every country in the world. Some are very small, with only a few participants, while others – like the New York Stock Exchange (NYSE) and the forex markets – trade trillions of dollars daily.

（金融市場幾乎可以在世界上每一個國家找到。有些是非常小的，只有少數的參與者，而其他的

－如紐約證券交易所（NYSE）和外匯市場－每天有上萬億美金的交易量。）

Vicki: What makes a financial market efficient?
（是什麼讓一個金融市場有效率的？）

Professor Milton: Most financial markets have heavy trading periods and high demand for securities; in these periods, prices may rise beyond historical....6..... The ....7....is also true – ....8....may push prices to fall past levels of ....9....value, based on low demand, high tax rates, low domestic production or high employment rates. Information ....10.....is important to boost the confidence of participants and therefore uphold an efficient financial marketplace.
（大多分的金融市場會有經歷高交易量和證券高需求的時期；在這些期間，價格可能上漲到高於歷史水平。反過來也是如此—經濟衰退時可能是因為低需求、高稅率、低生產量或高失業率而導致價格下跌到低於內在的價值。信息透明化對於增加參與者的信心，以及維持一個有效率的金融市場是重要的。）

Vicki: I see. I know what a financial market is now. Thank you.
我明白了。現在我知道什麼是金融市場了。謝謝。

答案 ANSWERS:
1.d 2.a 3.f 4.i 5.j 6.c 7.b 8.g 9.e 10.h

認識金融市場

金融市場指的是資金融通、貨幣借貸和買賣有價證券的活動和場所。金融市場不一定要在固定的場所中，透過電子交易系統等方式完成的交易，也可以被認為是金融市場的一部分。金融市場又稱為資金市場（financial market），包括貨幣市場（money market）和資本市場（capital market），是資金融通市場。

資金融通，融資（financing）

所謂資金融通，指的是資金供需雙方運用各種金融工具調節資金盈餘的活動，是所有金融交易活動的總稱。在金融市場上交易的是各種金融工具，如股票、債券、儲蓄存單等。

貨幣市場（money market）和資本市場（capital market）

貨幣市場是融通短期資金的市場，資本市場是融通長期資金的市場。

金融市場的形成條件

⑴ 商品經濟高度發達，市場上存在著龐大的資金需求與供給。

⑵ 擁有完善和健全的金融機構體系。

⑶ 金融交易的工具豐富，交易形式多樣化。

⑷ 有健全的金融立法。

⑸ 政府能對金融市場進行合理有效的管理。

金融市場的形態

金融市場的形態有兩種：一種是有形市場，即交易者集中在有固定地點和交易設施的場所內進行交易的市場，證券交易所就是典型的有形市場；另一種是無形市場，即交易者分散在不同地點或採用電訊手段進行交易的市場，如場外交易市場和全球外匯市場就屬於無形市場。

金融市場的功能

金融市場對於一國的經濟發展具有多方面的功能：

⑴ 融通資金的媒介器。透過金融市場使資金供給者和需求者自主地進行資金融資通，把多渠道的小額貨幣資金聚集成大額資金來源。

⑵ 調節資金供需。中央銀行可以通過公開市場活動，調劑貨幣供應量，有利於國家控制信貸規模，並有利於由資金供需關係決定市場利率，促進利率作用的發揮。

⑶ 潤滑經濟發展的。金融市場有利於促進地區間的資金運作，有利於開展資金融通方面的競爭，提高資金使用效益。

金融市場的基本要素

一個完備的金融市場，應包括三個基本要素：

⑴ 資金供給者和資金需求者。包括政府、金融機構、企業事業單位、居民、外商等等，既能向金融市場提供資金，也能從金融市場籌措資金。這是金融市場得以形成和發展的一項基本因素。

⑵ 信用工具：這是借貸資本在金融市場上交易的標的。如各種債券、股票、票據、可轉讓存單、借款合同、抵押契約等，是金融市場上實現投資、融資活動必須依賴的標的。

⑶ 信用中介。這是指一些充當資金供需雙方的中介人，聯繫、媒介和代客買賣作用的機構，如銀行、投資公司、證券交易所、證券商和經紀人等。

一般常見金融市場名詞解釋

融資 Financing	融資是指資金在資金供給者與資金需求者之間的流動，這種流動是雙邊的過程，包括資金的融入，也包括資金的融出。	Financing refers to the capital flows between suppliers and demanders of capital. The capital flow is bilateral, including both inflows and outflows of funds.
貨幣市場 Money market	貨幣市場是金融市場的一部分，其中到期日在一年或一年以內的短期資產進行借貸和買賣的地方。	Money market is part of the financial markets, where the borrowing, lending, buying and selling of short-term assets with maturities of one year or less take place.
資本市場 Capital market	資本市場是金融市場的一部分，其中長期債務或股票擔保證券進行買賣的地方。	Capital market is part of the financial market, where the buying and selling of long-term debt or equity-backed securities take place.
金融工具 Financial instrument	金融工具是任何可以交易的資產。它們可以是現金，所有權的證明，或者是接受或交付現金或其他金融工具的權利。	Financial instruments are any kinds of assets that can be traded. They can be cash, evidence of an ownership, or a right to receive or deliver cash or another financial instrument.
衍生性工具 Derivative	衍生性工具指的是價值源於相關標的資產的合約。該標的資產可以是股市指數或者利率。	Derivative is a contract that derives its value from an underlying asset. This underlying asset can be an index or interest rate.

倫敦銀行同業拆放利率 **London Interbank Offered Rate** **（ICE LIBOR）**	倫敦銀行同業拆放利率是倫敦的主要銀行向其他銀行借款時估計要付的平均借款利率。	The London Interbank Offered Rate is the average borrowing interest rate estimated by leading banks in London when they borrow from other banks.

常用業務例句 Common business terms

1. aggregate 總和

facilitate 促進

merger 合併

spinoff 分割

Vicki: What does “market” mean?

（「市場」是什麼意思？）

Professor: Economically, the market refers to the **aggregate** of potential buyers and sellers of a certain good or service and the transactions between them. It could also be exchanges, that **facilitate** the trading of securities, for example, a stock exchange or commodity exchange. It may also be a physical location (like the NYSE) or an electronic system (like NASDAQ). Although most trading of stocks takes place on an exchange still, corporate actions (**merger**, **spinoff**) are outside an exchange, while any two companies or people, may agree to sell stock from the one to the other without using an exchange.

（在經濟學中，市場是指特定的商品或服務的潛在買家和賣家以及他們之間的交易的總和。它也可能是方便證券進行交易的交易所，例如證券交易所或商品交易所。它可能是實際的場所（如紐約證券交易所）或電子系統（如納斯達克）。雖然大部分的股票交易是在交易所進行的，某些公司行為（合併，分割）則是在交易所外進行的，同時有時是兩個公司或個人，可能會同意由一方賣股票給另一方，而不使用交易所。）

2. raise finance 融資
redistribution 重新分配

Vicki: How many types of financial markets are there?
（金融市場有哪些類型？）

Professor: Financial markets often refer to the place that are used to **raise finance**: there is the Capital markets for long term finance, and there is also the Money markets for short term finance. There are also stock markets where stocks are traded; bond markets where bonds are traded; commodity markets where commodities are traded; derivatives markets where derivatives are traded; futures markets where futures are traded; insurance markets where redistribution of risks happens; foreign exchange markets where foreign exchange is traded, etc.
（金融市場常常被用來指那些進行融資活動的市場：資本市場是進行長期融資的地方；貨幣市場則是進行短期融資的地方。還有股票進行交易的股票市場；債券進行交易的債券市場；商品進行交易的商品市場；衍生工具進行交易的衍生工具市場；期貨進行交易的期貨市場；風險進行再分配的保險市場；外匯進行交易的外匯市場等。）

3. primary 一級
secondary二級
initial public offerings 首次公開發行

Vicki: Are there different types of capital markets?
（是否有不同類型的資本市場？）

Professor: The capital markets may be categorized into **primary** markets and **secondary** markets. Newly issued securities are traded in primary markets, such as **initial public offerings**. Secondary markets allow investors to buy and sell existing securities. The transactions in primary markets exist between issuers and investors, while secondary market transactions exist among investors.
（資本市場可以分類為一級市場和二級市場。新發行的證券交易在一級市場進行，例如首次公開發行的股票。二級市場讓投資者買賣已經存在的證券。一級市場的交易是在發行人和投資者之間進行，而二級市場的交易則是在投資者之間進行。）

4. liquidity 流動性
vital 關鍵的
crucial 至關重要的
get rid of 脫手，擺脫

Vicki: Why is **liquidity** a **vital** factor in secondary financial markets?
（為什麼流動性在二級金融市場是一個關鍵的因素？）

Professor: Liquidity is a **crucial** factor for securities that are traded in secondary markets. Liquidity refers to the ease with which a security can be sold without any loss of value. Securities with an active secondary market mean that there are many buyers

and sellers at a given point in time. Investors benefit from liquid securities because they can sell their assets whenever they want; an illiquid security may force the seller to **get rid of** their asset at a large discount.

（在二級市場上交易的證券流動性是一個關鍵的因素。流動性是指證券可以沒有任何價值的損失而售出的難易程度。在二級市場活躍的證券表示在特定的時間點有很多的買家和賣家。投資者受益於流動性高的證券，因為他們可以隨時在他們想要時賣出自己的資產；而流動性差的證券可能會迫使賣方賤賣他們的資產。）

單元短文 Unit reading

LIBOR's Role in Financial Markets
倫敦銀行同業拆放利率在融資市場所扮演的角色

The International Exchange London Interbank Offered Rate (ICE LIBOR), is a set of daily average borrowing rates at which banks pay to borrow money from one another. It is usually just called the LIBOR, and these rates are widely used as a base interest rates by financial institutions around the globe. The LIBOR rates influence almost all players in the financial world from student loans holders, mortgage holders, and small business owners to large corporations and the world's largest banks.

LIBOR offers daily average interest rates in five currencies (the U.S. dollar, euro, British pound, Japanese yen, and Swiss franc) and for seven lending periods (ranging from overnight to 12 months). As a whole, there are 35 different daily LIBOR rates. LIBOR is managed by the International Exchange Benchmark Administration（IBA）. The Administration calculates the LIBOR rates every day by surveying participating banks.

Although LIBOR stands for London Interbank Offered Rate, its significance spreads far beyond the City of London to fact, the LIBOR rate is one of the most globally significant numbers in finance. Banks, financial institutions, and credit agencies all over the world use LIBOR as a reference to set their own interest rates. According to the UK Treasury, the value of financial contracts tied to LIBOR is around $300 trillion,and this does not even include consumer loans or adjustable rate home mortgages yet.

ICE LIBOR 代表國際交易倫敦銀行同業拆放利率，是一組銀行向彼此借錢的每日平均利率。通常只是叫LIBOR，這些基準利率在世界各地的金融機構廣泛地作為基準利率。因此，這個利率幾乎影響了世界金融市場的所有的參與者，從學生貸款人、抵押貸款持有人和小企業老闆，到大公司以及世界上最大的銀行。

LIBOR為五種貨幣（美元、歐元、英鎊、日元和瑞士法郎）和7個貸款週期（從隔夜至12個月）提供每日平均利率。總共有35種不同的每日LIBOR利率。 LIBOR是由國際交易基準管理局（IBA）管轄的。當局每天透過調查參與的銀行而計算LIBOR利率。

雖然LIBOR代表的是倫敦銀行同業拆放利率，但其意義已經擴散到遠遠超出了倫敦市。事實上，LIBOR利率是世界金融中最重要的號碼之一。銀行、金融機構，以及世界各地的信貸機構都參考LIBOR設定自己的利率。根據英國財政部統計，以LIBOR為基準的金融合約的價值已經到達300兆美元，而這還不包括消費性貸款或可調整利率住房抵押貸款。

常用片語 Common phrases

- get rid of 擺脫；去掉

  I finally **got rid of** my last batch of penny stocks at the lowest price I can accept.
  （我終於以我所能接受的最低價格擺脫我的最後一批水餃股。）

- is tied to 與……綁定的

  The performance of the stock markets **is** closely **tied to** the investors' confidence.
  （股市的表現與投資者的信心是緊密的綁在一起的。）

重點字彙 Important words to know

名詞 Nouns		動詞 Verbs	
金融市場	financial market	去掉	rid
透明/透明度	transparent/ transparency	調查	investigate
規範	norms	操縱	manipulate
經濟衰退	downturn	忍受	endure
融資	financing		
倫敦銀行同業拆借利率	LIBOR		
總和	aggregate		
合併	merger		
分割	spin-off		
縮寫	acronym		
基準	benchmark		

經濟指標 Economic Indicator

什麼是經濟指標

經濟指標指的是可以作為依據來分析經濟體的整體表現和預測未來表現的經濟統計數據。經濟指標可以用來研究景氣週期，而最常見的指標是失業率、國內生產毛額（GDP）、消費者物價指數和股市指數。一般來説，經濟指標可以根據其相對於景氣週期的時間點而分為三類：領先指標、落後指標和同時指標。

單元暖身小練習 Warm-up conversation and practice

針對以下每個空格，請選一個最適合的字填入。這是協助你對於本主題進行初步的暖身，以利對於後續的介紹可以更有效率的吸收。

(a) judge (b) common (c) released (d) correlations
(e) schedule (f) verifications (g) data (h) principal
(i) crude (j) signs

Jonathan wants to know what an economic indicator is .
強納森想知道經濟指標是什麼。

Jonathan: Professor Milton, could you tell me what an economic indicator is?
（米爾頓教授，您能告訴我什麼是經濟指標嗎？）

Professor Milton: Certainly. An economic indicator is certain economic....1...., which the investors to use to interpret current or future investment options and ....2....the general health of an economy. Economic indicators can be available in many different forms, but specific data ....3....by government and non-profit organizations are more widely followed.

（當然可以。經濟指標是投資者用來解釋當前或未來的投資機會和判斷一個經濟體的整體健康狀態的經濟數據。經濟指標有各種不同的類型，但是由政府和非營利組織公佈的特定數據是較為廣受遵循的類型。）

Jonathan: What are the ....4....economics indicators?

（哪些是常見的經濟指標？）

Professor Milton: The most common ones are the consumer price index (CPI), gross domestic product (GDP), unemployment figures or the price of ....5....oil, etc.

（最常見的有消費者物價指數、國內生產毛額、失業率或原油價格等。）

Jonathan: Can we use economic indicators to predict the future ?

（我們可以用經濟指標來預測未來嗎？）

Professor Milton: An economic indicator is useful only when it is interpreted properly. From past expriences, we know there are strong ....6....between economic growth (such as GDP) and corporate profit growth. Nevertheless, using the indicators alone to predict whether a company's earnings will increase is nearly impossible. Indicators provide us ....7....along the road, but the rational investors will employ many economic indicators, and discover patterns and ....8....in different sets of data.

（只有正確地解釋經濟指標才會有用。從過往的經驗來看，我們知道經濟增長（國內生產毛額）和企業利潤增長之間有很強的相關性。然而，只用指標就想要預測一個公司的收益是否會增加幾乎是不可能的事。指標一路提供我們一些跡象，但理性的投資者將會運用許多不同的經濟指標，在不同的數據集內發現模式以及核實。）

Jonathan: I see. How often are the indicators usually released?

（我明白了。那麼經濟指標一般是多久發佈一次？）

Professor Milton: Most economic indicators have their own release....9...., and which enables investors to plan on seeing certain data at certain times of the month and year.

（多數經濟指標都有各自的發佈時間表，讓投資者能夠計劃在每月和每年的某些時候看到某些數據。）

Jonathan: Could you give me a couple of examples of organizations that release economic indicators?

（您可以給我幾個發佈經濟指標的組織的例子嗎？）

Professor Milton: Definitely, the leading business cycle research organization in the United States is the National Bureau of Economic Research (private). The Bureau of Labor Statistics is the ....10....fact-finding agency for the U.S. government in the field of labor economics and statistics. Other producers of economic indicators include the United States Census Bureau and United States Bureau of Economic Analysis.

（當然，美國的領先景氣週期研究機構是國家經濟研究統計局（私營）。而勞工統計局是美國政府在勞動經濟學和統計學領域的主要調查機構。其他的經濟指標發布者還有美國人口普查局和美國經濟分析局。）

Jonathan: I see. Thank you for the information, Professor!

（我了解了。謝謝您的信息，教授！）

答案 ANSWERS:

1.g 2.a 3.c 4.b 5.i 6.d 7.j 8.f 9.e 10.h

認識經濟指標

經濟指標是由政府或私人機構處出版的金融及經濟的統計數據。在金融市場，幾乎每一個投資人都會依賴這些數據來作投資的決策。而當眾多投資者都對經濟指標有反應時，那就會對交易及價格變動有很大的影響。

大多數的經濟指標可以依據其在景氣週期的相對時間段而分類為領先指標（leading indicator）、落後指標（lagging indicator）和同時指標（coincident indicator）。

領先指標（leading indicator）

指的是具有領先景氣變動性質之指標，其轉折點會比景氣循環轉折點還要早發生。

落後指標（lagging indicator）

指的是具有落後景氣變動性質之指標，其轉折點會比景氣循環轉折點還要晚發生。

同時指標（coincident indicator）

指的是具有與景氣變動性質同步之指標，其轉折點常和景氣循環轉折點同步發生。

常用業務例句 Common business terms

1. classify 分類

leading indicators 領先指標

lagging indicators 落後指標

coincident indicators 同時指標

Jonathan: How are economic indicators **classified** based on their relation to the business cycle?

（如何根據經濟指標相對於景氣週期的關係來劃分它們的種類？）

Professor: Economic indicators fall into three categories based on to their timing in relation to the business cycle: **leading indicators, lagging** indicators, and **coincident indicators**.

（經濟指標通常可以根據它們對於景氣週期的時間點而分為三類：領先指標、落後指標和同時指標。）

2. as a whole 作為一個整體
predictors 預測因素
decline 下降
slump 不景氣

Jonathan: What are the leading indicators?

（什麼是領先指標呢？）

Professor: Leading indicators are indicators that usually change before the economy **as a whole** changes. Therefore, they can be used as short-term **predictors** of the economy. Stock market indexes are a leading indicator: the stock market usually **begins** to decline before the economy declines and usually begins to rerive before the general economy begins to restore from a **slump**. Other leading indicators include consumer expectations index, building permits, and the money supply.

（領先指標通常在經濟改變之前就變化的指標。因此，它們可以用來作為經濟的短期預測。股市指數是一個領先指標：股市通常在經濟開始下跌前就先下降，也通常在經濟開始從衰退中恢復之前就已經開始復甦。其他的領先指標包括消費者預期指數、營建許可指標，以及貨幣供應量。）

3. lag 落後
upturn 經濟復甦
initiatives 行動

Jonathan: What about the lagging indicators?
（那麼落後指標是怎樣的呢？）

Professor: Lagging indicators are indicators that usually change after the economy does. Usually the **lag** is a few quarters of a year. The unemployment rate is a lagging indicator: employment has the tendency to increase two or three quarters after an **upturn** in the economy. A company's profit is usually a lagging indicator as it reflects a historical performance; similarly, improved customer satisfaction is the result of **initiatives** taken in the past.
（落後指標通常是在經濟變化之後才變化的指標。通常情況下，落後是幾個季度的。失業率是一個落後指標：就業率趨向於經濟復甦後兩個或三個季度才提高。公司的利潤也是落後指標，因為它反映了歷史的表現；同樣的，客戶滿意度的提高也是過往所採取行動的結果。）

4. after the fact 在事後
peaks and troughs 高峰和谷底

Jonathan: What are the coincident indicators?
（什麼又是同時指標呢？）

Professor: Coincident indicators change at around the same time as the economy dose, so they provide information about the current economy. There are many coincident economic indicators, such as Gross Domestic Product, industrial production, personal income and retail sales. A coincident index may be used to identify, after the fact, the dates of peaks and troughs in a business cycle.

（同時指標大約在經濟變化的同時一起變化，所以對當前經濟的狀態提供了信息。有很多同時的經濟指標，例如國內生產毛額、工業生產量、個人所得和零售銷售量。同時指數可以在事後用來辨識景氣週期的高峰和谷底的日期。）

單元短文 Unit reading

Relevant Economic Indicators in the Real Estate Sector
與房地產行業相關的經濟指標

For the real estate sector, there are a few economic indicators that investors can look into before they purchase real related securities. The most common ones are the pending home sales index, housing market index and new home sales numbers.

Pending home sales index

The pending home sales index is released by the National Association of Realtors, and is a leading indicator of real estate activities. A pending home sale is a contract that has been signed, but not yet completed; it usually takes around four to six weeks to close a real estate sale. Real estate investors could use this economic indicator to gauge the demand for real estate.

Housing market index

The National Association of Home Builders (NAHB) produces the housing market index data based on a survey to rate the general economy and housing market or real estate market. This economic indicator is a weighted average of separate indexes, such as present sales of new homes, sales of new homes expected in the next six months, and prospective buyers of new homes. Investors could also use this indicator to gauge the demand for housing.

New home sales numbers

This economic indicator measures the number of newly built homes with committed sales during the month.This economic indicator also provides the demand for real estate. Once a home is sold, it generates revenues for the home builders and the realtors.

By tracking these three indicators, investors could gain specific insights of how they should invest in real estate related securities.

對於房地產行業而言，有幾個經濟指標在投資者購買房地產相關的證券之前可以參考。最常見的有成屋銷售待完成指數、住屋市場指數和新屋銷售數據。

成屋銷售待完成指數

成屋銷售待完成指數是由美國全國房地產經紀人協會所發布的，而它是房地產市場活動的領先指標。成屋銷售待完成是已經簽訂了房屋買賣合約，但合約尚未完成；成屋的銷售一般通常需要大約四至六週來完成。房地產投資者利用這個經濟指標來衡量市場上房地產的需求量。

住房市場指數

住宅建築商協會根據問卷調查來評估整體經濟和住房市場或房地產市場之後而編制住房市場指數的數據。這種經濟指標是幾個指標的加權平均，例如目前新房銷售量、未來六個月的預計新房銷售量，和新房的準買家數。投資者可以用這個指標來衡量市場上對住房活動的需求。

新屋銷售數據

這種經濟指標計量當月已經被預定的新建房屋數量。這種經濟指標提供房地產需求的參考。一旦新屋出售後，它為住房建築商和房地產經紀人都增加了收入。

透過跟隨這三種指標，投資者可以在投資房地產相關的證券之前，對於該如何投資有具體的見解。

常用片語 Common phrases

• after the fact 在事後	We can only know how effective the economic indicators are until **after the fact**. （我們只能在事後才能知道經濟指標是否有效。）
• as a whole 整體來看	**As a whole**, the economic indicators can help us understand the economy better. （整體來看，各項經濟指標可以幫助我們更了解經濟。）

重點字彙 Important words to know

名詞 Nouns		動詞 Verbs	
經濟指標	economic indicator	解釋	interpret
總體經濟	macroeconomic	判斷	judge
全面	overall	測量	gauge
原油	crude oil	發布	release
相關性	correlation	分類	classify
驗證	verification	下降	decline
局	bureau	落後	lag
領先指標	leading indicator		
落後指標	lagging indicator		
同步指標	coincident indicator		
衰退	slump		
復甦	upturn		
經濟衰退	downturn		
行動	initiative		

NOTES

英語學習—職場系列—

定價：NT$349元/HK$109元
規格：320頁/17＊23cm

定價：NT$360元/HK$113元
規格：328頁/17＊23cm

定價：NT$349元/HK$109元
規格：304頁/17＊23cm

定價：NT$360元/HK$113元
規格：320頁/17＊23cm

定價：NT$369元/HK$115元
規格：312頁/17＊23cm/MP3

定價：NT$369元/HK$115元
規格：320頁/17＊23cm

定價：NT$360元/HK$113元
規格：288頁/17＊23cm/MP3

定價：NT$329元/HK$103元
規格：304頁/17＊23cm

定價：NT$369元/HK$115元
規格：328頁/17＊23cm/MP3

英語學習—生活・文法・考用—

定價：NT$369元/K$115元
規格：320頁/17＊23cm/MP3

定價：NT$380元/HK$119元
規格：320頁/17＊23cm/MP3

定價：NT$349元/HK$109元
規格：352頁/17＊23cm

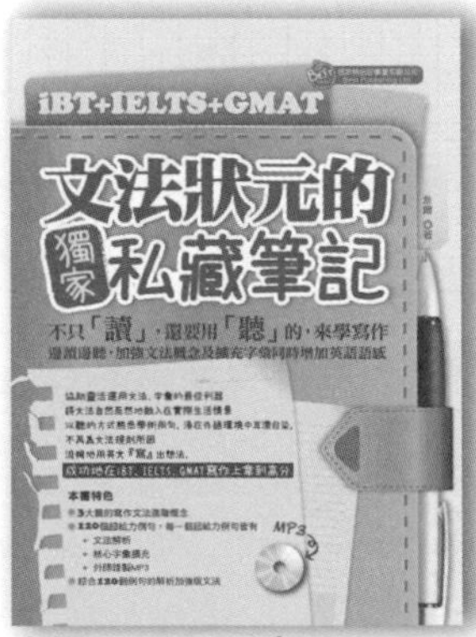

定價：NT$380元/HK$119元
規格：288頁/17＊23cm/MP3

定價：NT$329元/HK$103元
規格：352頁/17＊23cm

定價：NT$349元/HK$109元
規格：304頁/17＊23cm

定價：NT$380元/HK$119元
規格：352頁/17＊23cm

定價：NT$369元/HK$115元
規格：304頁/17＊23cm/MP3

定價：NT$380元/HK$119元
規格：304頁/17＊23cm/MP3

Leader 027

24 天就能學會的基礎財金英文

作　　者　陳和揚
封面構成　高鍾琪
內頁構成　菩薩蠻數位文化有限公司

發 行 人　周瑞德
企劃編輯　徐瑞璞
執行編輯　饒美君
校　　對　陳欣慧、陳韋佑、魏于婷
印　　製　大亞彩色印刷製版股份有限公司
初　　版　2015 年 9 月
定　　價　新台幣 349 元
出　　版　力得文化
電　　話　(02) 2351-2007
傳　　真　(02) 2351-0887
地　　址　100 台北市中正區福州街 1 號 10 樓之 2
E-mail　best.books.service@gmail.com

港澳地區總經銷　泛華發行代理有限公司
地　　址　香港新界將軍澳工業邨駿昌街 7 號 2 樓
電　　話　(852) 2798-2323
傳　　真　(852) 2796-5471

國家圖書館出版品預行編目(CIP)資料

24 天就能學會的基礎財金英文 / 陳和揚著. -- 初版. -- 臺北市 : 力得文化, 2015.09 面 ; 公分. -- (Leader ; 27)
ISBN 978-986-91914-6-3(平裝)

1.英語 2.財務金融 3.讀本

805.18　　104016802